The Mage's Grave

Book One in the Mages of Martir

by Timothy L. Cerepaka

An Annulus Publishing Book

Annulus Publishing, Cherokee, Texas, 2015

Published by Annulus Publishing

Author: Timothy L. Cerepaka

Formatting by Timothy L. Cerepaka

Contact: timothy@timothylcerepaka.com

Cover design by Elaina Lee of For the Muse Design

ISBN-13: 978-0692405024

ISBN-10: 0692405024

Acknowledgments

I would like to thank my uncle, James Wilhite, for helping me get this manuscript into publishable shape. I'd also like to thank the rest of my family for supporting me while I wrote this novel. You guys rock.

Chapter One

Darek Takren, a student at North Academy and a pagomancer-in-training, found himself growing increasingly impatient. He stood on the steps of the Arcanium, the school's main building, along with the hundred and twenty other students who attended the school, as well as with most of the other teachers, too. There were only two people, as far as he could tell, who were not present, and that was the Magical Superior, the headmaster of the school, and Darek's own mother, Jenur Takren, who also happened to be one of the school's teachers.

Around him, the other students chatted and joked with each other. Some of the younger students were using their magic to perform clever little tricks they had learned in class, such as one student (whose name Darek could not recall at the moment) who was using his wand to make a ball of water transform into many different shapes. This student was so talented with his hydromancy that he could even make the water ball look like a miniature replica of the Arcanium itself, an impressive feat for so young a student.

But even while watching what his fellow students were doing to pass the time, Darek kept glancing at the sky and shifting his weight from foot to foot. That was probably because he had been one of the first students out on the front steps to greet their guests, who, according to the Magical Superior's earlier announcement, were supposed to be here any minute now.

That announcement had been an hour ago. At least the weather was nice. Bright sunshine—unusual for North Academy, seeing as it was set in the Great Berg, a massive icy wasteland located hundreds of miles north from the rest of civilization—shone down on them all, warming Darek's skin and giving him a great view of the sky and the gigantic ice Walls in the distance that surrounded the school. A cool breeze blew through, but it was not as cold as it normally was. Meanwhile, the steps beneath Darek's feet were warm, which was normal, seeing as they were made out of heatstone, a type of rock that naturally generated heat at all times. It was what the entire school was made of, in fact, which was the primary way that the students and faculty kept warm during the Great Berg's coldest months.

Purely out of boredom, he looked down at his clothes. He wore the same red-and-black robes that all students wore, as it was the official Academy uniform. The students were supposed to wear these robes at all times, but the Superior had stressed the importance of wearing their robes today in particular in order to give a disciplined, orderly, and effective first impression on their guests.

Straightening out his robes, Darek again looked up at the sky. Still no sign of the guests yet. They were supposed to arrive by airship. According to the gray ghost the guests had sent a while ago, the flying ship would be big and red and impossible to miss.

Darek had never seen an airship before. Having spent a good chunk of his thirty-five-year life in North Academy, he had only ever heard stories from the other students about the rest of the outside world. According to one of the students, who had worked as an airship engineer before making the dangerous trek through the Great Berg to reach the school, the Carnagians had designed and built the first airship, which had led to every other nation in the Northern Isles going on a mad scramble to make their own. Even the aquarians, the peoples of the sea, had joined the scramble, although their airships were different from human airships, as they also doubled as underwater vehicles they called 'submarines.'

The guests who were supposed to arrive on the airship were students from the Undersea Institute, the best and largest aquarian mage school. This was going to be the first time that aquarians had set foot in North Academy in years, which was partly why Darek was so nervous. He had never met an aquarian before, despite having been told all about them by his mother, and so he didn't quite know what to expect from aquarian mages and how they differed from human mages.

Darek's friend and fellow student, a middle-aged man named Jiku Nium, had said that aquarian magic was different from human magic, even though aquarians derived their magic from their connection to the gods just like humans did. According to Jiku, mastery of hydromancy was far more common among the aquarians than it was among humans and the aquarians had come up with

3

different ways to integrate hydromancy with other magical disciplines. Pyromancy was apparently not in great use among them, for obvious reasons. Jiku had also stated that aquarians didn't use talismans to enhance their connection to the gods, which made Darek wonder if aquarian mages were weaker than human mages in terms of sheer magical power.

That had been yesterday, before Darek and Jiku had gone to bed in their shared dorm room, and Darek hadn't seen Jiku at all today. The older man had said that he was going to be there—he had to be, seeing as the Magical Superior had made the welcome of the Institute mages mandatory for everyone but the sickest students—but no matter where Darek looked, he did not see Jiku's silver gray hair that always reminded him of a helmet among the crowd of students awaiting the Institute mages.

As a matter of fact, Darek had not even seen Jiku in their dorm this morning when he got up. He had assumed that Jiku was already at breakfast, but when he had come downstairs to eat with his fellow dorm mates, Jiku had not been there, either, and none of the others had seen him that morning.

Jiku probably got sick, couldn't heal himself, and had to go see Eyurna, Darek thought. *I'm sure he'll be here the minute he's feeling better.*

"Darek!" called out a familiar feminine, musical voice. "There you are."

Darek turned around to see a woman about his height, although much younger-looking than him, walking toward him through the crowd of students, a brilliant smile on her pearly white teeth. She had blonde hair, which actually looked good with her Academy uniform, and slung over her shoulder was her beautiful black guitar, its polished wood surface reflecting the light of the sun that shone down upon it.

"Aorja Kitano," said Darek, returning the smile as Aorja walked past a couple of younger students who were making mini ice statues fight each other. "Where have you been? The Institute mages are supposed to be here any minute. You could have missed them."

Aorja's smile didn't waver as she stopped in front of Darek; if anything, it got wider. "Oh, I just had to run back to the Third Dorm real quick to get my guitar. Thought the Institute mages might be interested in listening to some human music. Mousimancy is the language of the sea, right?"

"I'm not sure that's what that phrase means, but I'm sure the Institute mages will appreciate the thought nonetheless," said Darek. "Have you seen Jiku?"

"Jiku?" said Aorja. "No. I haven't. Why?"

"He's been missing all morning," said Darek, "even though he said he'd been here. I haven't heard from him since last night."

"Maybe he's sick," Aorja offered. "I heard there were a few students in the medical wing as of this morning, but I heard Eyurna was working overtime to get them all healed up so that everyone could be present to greet the Institute mages today."

"That's what I thought, too," said Darek. "It's not good for a man his age to get sick like this."

"He'll probably be fine," said Aorja. "Jiku's a tough old guy and Eyurna is the best panamancer in all of the Northern Isles. If he's sick, I'm sure he'll be fine in no time."

She said that with such confidence that Darek had a hard time doubting her.

So he said, "If you say so, Aorja."

"Of course I do," said Aorja. "Anyway, why don't we sit back and wait for the—"

"Darek, Aorja," said another feminine voice, this one sounding older than Aorja.

Both of them turned to see a middle-aged woman walking toward them, her robes billowing behind her in the wind that had started up. The older woman had short, curly hair that was still quite black, although Darek was starting to notice a handful of gray hairs beginning to appear in a few places. The woman walked far more quickly than most women her age, no doubt due to the fact that she was quite fit due to the rigorous training exercises she practiced daily.

"Hey, Mom," said Darek, giving her a brief hug when she was within hugging distance before pulling away. "Where is the Superior?"

Mom scratched the back of her neck. "He's almost ready to come down. He just needs to do a few more things. I was going to stay and wait for him, but he told me to go down and he'd catch up later."

"So wait," said Aorja, glancing up at the tower on top of the Arcanium, where the Superior's study was. "Are you telling us that the Superior, who made it mandatory for every student to be down here to greet the Institute mages, is going to be one of the last people here?"

"Something came up while he was getting ready," said Mom vaguely. "One of the gods wanted to talk with him and you know how much those gods hate it when we mortals do not listen to them."

Darek was not surprised. The Magical Superior was one of the few mortals—maybe even the only mortal—who had regular, daily discussions with the gods. This was because of the Magical Superior's deep understanding of magic and even deeper loyalty to the gods themselves. He wondered if the gods actually looked upon the Superior as their equal or not.

Probably not, Darek thought. *The gods are greater than all of us, greater even than the Superior. Still, I do wonder what they wanted to talk with him about today. Did something happen that required them to request the Superior's aid?*

Darek's thoughts were interrupted when someone pointed and shouted, "Hey, look! The Institute mages are here!"

The entire crowd of Academy students and teachers looked in the direction that that student was pointing. Just over the Walls—the massive ice barriers that separated the school from the rest of the Great Berg and were the final challenge that met all potential future Academy students— was a large red thing trailing smoke exhaust behind it that was too far away to make out at first. It was coming fast, however, and it would no doubt be easier to see very soon.

Then an ancient, deep voice called, "Students! I have received a message from the Institute mages informing me that they will be landing their ship in the sports field. We will go down to meet them there."

Darek looked back toward the Arcanium and saw the Magical Superior himself standing on the top steps. As always, his gray skin, hairless head and face, and long wand —more like a staff, really—made him look as ancient as the gods themselves. The newest thing on him were his auburn robes, which were obviously freshly cleaned and scrubbed. Darek could even smell the scent of soap wafting on the wind from them.

The Magical Superior disappeared and then reappeared at the bottom of the steps in front of the students and faculty. He gestured for them to follow him and, before anyone could oblige, he was already on his way down to the sports field, walking with a quickness and lightness that Darek had never seen in the Superior's step before. That made Darek wonder why the Magical Superior was so eager to go down there and see the Institute mages.

Maybe he's trying to make up for being late, Darek thought.

He had no time to ponder that mystery further, however, because the other mages, including Mom and Aorja, were already following the Magical Superior in the direction of the sports field, which was located on the western side of the school grounds down a slope behind the dorms. He quickly caught up with Mom and Aorja, but he kept his eyes on the red airship in the skies above, which was drawing closer and closer to the sports field every second.

By the time the North Academy mages had reached the edge of the sports field, the red airship was landing. The Magical Superior gestured for the Academy mages to stand back and wait until the airship had shut off, but that was fine by Darek because it gave him an opportunity to observe the first airship he ever saw in person.

It was shaped like a beetle, although it lacked the beetle's horn on the front. Four legs popped out of its underside to act as landing gear, while smoke and flame from behind it filled the air and obscured the engine. Words written in some language—probably Aqua, seeing as the Institute mages were aquarians, although not being an expert on aquarian languages, he could not be sure—were painted on the ship's side in big blue paint. The cockpit was like a beetle head, but the glass on it was tinted so darkly that it was impossible to see the pilot or anyone else who might have been sitting in there.

But what stood out the most to Darek was the sheer noisiness of the ship. In all his life, Darek had never heard anything quite as loud as the engine of that ship. It was like a thousand bombs were going off at once, multiple times, with a couple hundred gunshots added in for good measure. It was so loud that Darek couldn't even hear himself think, much less hear what anyone else was saying.

In fact, the ship was so loud that it honestly scared him. He stepped behind Mom and Aorja, neither of whom seemed to notice his fear (thankfully), and tried not to look scared at the airship's excessively loud engine. He just hoped that if anyone looked at him, they would not think he was afraid of what was probably a harmless machine (harmless from a distance, at least).

A few minutes after the airship touched the ground, the engine finally began to die down with a whine until eventually, it went completely silent. Darek still couldn't see whoever was inside the cockpit, but he thought he spotted some movement within, as though the pilot, whoever he or she was, was getting up.

Then, about a minute after the engine died down, a platform began to lower from the underside of the ship. It lowered slowly but surely, until the platform landed on the ground underneath the ship. There were about a dozen or so aquarians standing on that lift, but the underside of the airship was dark, making it difficult to tell from a distance what they looked like exactly. Once the lift touched the ground, however, the Institute mages walked out from the shadows of the ship's underside into the light of the sun.

Forgetting about his fear of the airship, and excited to see the guests, Darek pushed past Aorja and Mom and the other students until he got to the front of the welcome committee. When he did, he stopped and observed the Institute mages as closely as he could from his current position.

The Institute mages did not look much like mages to him. Instead of wearing mage robes, they wore skintight diving suits that didn't restrain their movements. Their diving suits were green and silver, which he figured were probably the colors of their school.

Another thing Darek noticed was how none of them seemed to have wands of any sort. That struck him as odd. All mages were supposed to use wands. While it was possible for a mage to use magic without a wand, wands helped a mage control and channel their magic, which was why very few went without them. That these Institute mages apparently had none of their own confused Darek more than anything, although he could not guess where they could keep their wands if they had had any.

Instead, Darek noticed what looked like bracelets, each one filled with a different colored stone, attached to the bodies of the Institute mages in various places. Some had the bracelets attached to their wrists, while a few had them on their ankles, and others in other parts of their body (such as the jellyfish-like mage who had his bracelet wrapped around his neck like a collar).

Maybe those stones are what they use to channel and control their magic? Darek thought. *I should ask the Superior about that later. He'll probably know.*

Then there were the Institute mages themselves. As a group, they looked far bigger and stronger than the Academy mages. In a one-on-one fight with no magic, Darek wasn't sure that he or any of the other Academy mages could even defeat the Institute mages. He found their inhuman faces—which resembled sea creatures ranging from goldfish to manta rays and everything in between—disturbing, despite the fact that none of these Institute mages appeared threatening or even unkind in any way.

Another thing he noticed about the Institute mages was that he couldn't sense their magical auras. That was strange. All mages gave off magical auras that could be sensed by other mages. Yet these Institute mages, apparently, either did not have magical auras at all or had somehow figured out a way to hide them from him and possibly the others as well. It made it difficult to gauge how powerful the Institute mages were, a fact which unsettled him.

At the head of the group was an older female aquarian, much older than the rest based on how bent over she was and how slowly she walked in comparison to the others. Her diving suit, too, was different, being much looser around her body and being colored a solid green rather than green and silver like the attire of her students. Her head was vaguely whale-like in appearance, although she was nowhere near as large as an actual whale. She did, however, have a piercing, intelligent look in her eyes, one that made Darek understand that he couldn't fool her even if he had been planning to. She had a small bracelet around her left wrist with a rainbow-colored stone set within it.

The Magical Superior spread his arms wide as the Institute mages approached. "Welcome, welcome, mages of the Undersea Institute. I am the Magical Superior, the headmaster of North Academy, and behind me is the entire North Academy student body and faculty, aside from a handful of sick students who could not recover in time to welcome your arrival, although rest assured that they would be here to welcome you just like the rest of us if they were feeling well."

That reminded Darek of Jiku, causing him to look around the crowd for any sign of his old friend. Seeing no sign of Jiku's balding gray head anywhere, Darek turned his attention back to the Magical Superior, who had walked up to the leader of the Institute mages and kissed her hand in greeting, although she did not look very thrilled about it.

"My students and teachers," said the Magical Superior, turning to face the Academy mages, "may I introduce you to the Grand Magus and Archmage of the Undersea Institute, the intelligent and powerful Yorak? She and I are old friends who have known each other for years, but I believe this is the first time she has visited this school as the head of another."

All of the Academy mages bowed their heads at Yorak, which was a sign of respect usually reserved for the Superior himself. Yorak, to her credit, returned the head bow, which meant that she was perhaps not quite as unfriendly as she looked.

"Yes," said Yorak. She spoke surprisingly clear Divina, lacking that odd gurgly accent that Darek had been told all aquarians who learned Divina as their second language had. "My students and I appreciate the welcome party and are eager to learn more about our human counterparts in order that the bonds between our schools may be—"

She stopped abruptly, even though no one had interrupted her. A frown appeared on her whale-ish lips as she looked up over the heads of the Academy students, her eyes on something behind them. The mage who stood at her side, a younger female with a goldfish-like head, was also staring up at whatever it was that caught their attention.

Puzzled, Darek followed Yorak's gaze and realized that she was staring up at the Third Dorm. His dormitory, actually, the one where hc, Jiku, Aorja, and the other half dozen students who lived there slept at night and had their meals together and studied together.

"Yorak?" said the Magical Superior, his voice sounding a little concerned. "What do you see?"

"Nothing," said Yorak. "But do you feel that?"

The Magical Superior went silent and seemed to be trying to feel whatever Yorak felt. Then his eyes widened and he said, "What is—"

And then—right in front of Darek's startled eyes—the roof of the Third Dorm exploded.

Chapter Two

"Durima, come on" said Gujak's voice, echoing off the tall Walls. "We have to get moving. Master made it very clear that he wants us to complete the mission as quickly as we can, otherwise he'll be very angry, and you know what he does when he gets angry."

Durima dug her claws into the icy rock that made up the Walls and grunted. She tried not to look over her shoulder at the hundreds of feet of rock that she had already scaled, as she knew she would get dizzy and if she got dizzy she would probably fall to her death, which would definitely anger Master.

So she focused on her partner, Gujak, who due to his light weight was far ahead of Durima. Looking more like a walking, talking tree than a katabans—also known as minor spirits that served the gods—Gujak was clinging to the Walls with his root-like fingers, looking down at her with an impatient expression on his face. He was only a couple dozen feet from the top of the Walls by now, but it was clear that he wasn't going to complete the treacherous climb until he was sure that Durima was right behind him.

It wasn't her fault that she wasn't as fast as he. Gujak was only a century old, but he acted half his age, whereas Durima was three centuries old, a veteran of the Katabans

War, and still suffering from a stab wound in her right shoulder she had taken from an enemy during the War. Granted, the wound had healed, but every now and then pain in her shoulder would erupt, the pain so bad it sometimes immobilized her or made her flashback to the War.

Durima shook her head. Thinking about the War was guaranteed to bring back those old memories that she had done her best to ignore since the War's end twenty-four years ago. She had to focus on the present.

So she shouted at Gujak, "It will be fine. Master said he didn't expect us to complete the mission soon anyway. Just hold your horses. I'll be there eventually."

Gujak frowned. "It sure would have been easier if we could have used something like that airship that flew by earlier to get up here, wouldn't it?"

Not understanding why Gujak chose to bring that up, Durima resumed climbing up the Walls, saying as she did so, "You mean that big, red noisy machine built by mortals? The one that was probably seen by every living thing in a fifty mile radius? Yeah, that would have been helpful for sneaking into the most heavily-fortified magical school in the world."

"You know what I mean," said Gujak. "And why are we climbing the Walls instead of using the ethereal to enter the school directly? That would have saved us hours of time, wouldn't it have?"

Durima finally caught up with Gujak and stopped to look at him. "Don't you remember? The mages have somehow blocked us katabans from using the ethereal to enter the school directly. I imagine only the gods can use it to enter, and since we aren't gods, we have to enter the old-fashioned way."

"That's right," said Gujak. "But how do you block the ethereal? I thought humans weren't even aware of it. Aside from that one Carnagian king, what's his name, Mal Lock or whatever?"

"I don't know," said Durima, shaking her head. "You think I have time to keep track of all of those mortal kings and what they do or don't know about us? Anyway, we've almost reached the top. If we're in such a hurry, like you said, then we don't have time to sit around and talk."

"You're right," said Gujak. He looked back up at the top of the Walls, which were not very far away now. "Follow me."

Gujak immediately resumed climbing, moving as nimbly across the icy, rock surface of the Walls as a mountain goat. Durima followed, although she had to move more slowly because a powerful gust of ice-cold wind blew through, which threatened to dislodge her due to her massive bulk.

As they climbed, Durima reviewed the reason their Master—the deity known as the Ghostly God, God of Ghosts and Mist—had sent them to the mortal school known as North Academy. She felt it was important to review now that they were so close to their goal, as it would be easy to forget why they were climbing the Walls in the first place due to the sheer difficulty of the climb.

Master had sent them here for a simple reason. The

school, due to the fact that it was so remote and separate from the rest of mortal civilization, had its own graveyard, which, as Durima understood it, was where students and teachers who died there were usually put to rest. Master had told her and Gujak to search for the grave of some mortal named Braim Kotogs, which they were supposed to dig up, and then leave once they found it, but without letting the mortals know that they were there.

Why Master wanted them to do that, Durima didn't know. The Ghostly God, after all, was not the God of the Grave. He dealt with what happened after the body was buried, not before. Then again, Master had been acting stranger than usual lately. For example, in the last couple of months he had taken as a pet a giant, purplish-black snake that he called 'Uron,' which never left his side. That was an odd move because Master had never struck her as the type to keep or even want a pet, but she had not questioned the move at the time because she knew better than to question Master's actions, no matter how illogical they may have seemed to her.

Gujak had noticed how strangely Master had been acting as well, but he questioned it even less than she. When Durima had admitted to him how puzzling it was for Master to take on a pet, he had brushed off her concern as nothing. She supposed it probably was, seeing as she had grown rather paranoid after the War and often read more into a situation or someone's actions than there really was.

Still, as Durima grabbed the edge of the Wall and hauled her bulky, bear-like body on top of it, she found herself thinking about Master's strange decisions anyway. He never did anything without reason, but what that reason was in this case, she had no idea.

Now that she and Gujak were on top of the Wall, Durima stood up to her full height, brushing the snow and ice off her shoulders as she did so. She could now see the entire layout of the school below, which was laid out in the bowl-shaped canyon made by the Walls, looking like a bunch of toy buildings from this distance.

That was when she noticed one of the buildings near the center of the campus grounds was on fire. She and Gujak had heard an explosion a couple of minutes ago, but it had never occurred to Durima to think that the explosion had been accidental on the mages' part. She saw dozens of mortal mages—most human, although some appeared to be aquarians—fighting to put out the flames and smoke, although a good chunk of the mages were apparently too surprised by the abrupt, sudden explosion to act, because they just stood by and watched as the other mages tried to put it out.

"What happened down there?" said Gujak, putting his hands over his eyes. "A spell gone wrong?"

"No idea," said Durima, panting from the long climb. Her eyes focused on what appeared to be a small, enclosed graveyard behind the largest building all the way on the other side of the canyon. "It's a great distraction, though. We should take advantage of it and get down there to the graveyard before the mages recover and get their bearings back."

"Good idea," said Gujak. He looked around at the Wall beneath their feet. "Um, how do we get down there? Do we have to climb again?"

Durima scanned the Wall until she noticed a pathway leading down to the bottom of the valley. "That looks like a path we can take. Come on."

Before either of them could take a step toward the path, however, Durima's enhanced hearing picked up the sound of metal scraping against ice. She stopped and looked around, but she did not see anything else on the Wall besides Gujak.

"Did you hear that?" said Durima, looking at her partner. "I thought I heard metal scraping against the ice."

"I didn't hear anything," said Gujak. "You're probably just imagining things. Let's—"

Without warning, something invisible slammed into Gujak's face. The blow knocked him flat off his feet and sent him sliding across the ice, almost off the edge of the Wall, but he stopped against a rock protruding out of the ice just in time. Of course, he was too dazed by the blow to get up.

"Gujak," said Durima, tensing as she looked around for their hidden attacker. "What was that?"

There was that sound of metal scraping against ice again, but it was far closer this time, almost right behind her. Durima ducked and felt the air of something heavy pass over her. She responded by whirling around and punching the spot in the air where she thought her assailant was.

It was a direct hit. Her massive fist struck something hard and metal, making a clanging sound that made her cringe. It was only for a moment, however, because in the next moment her fist was touching air and she heard something heavy crunching backwards across the snow and ice. She even saw its footprints now, which were large and clawed, but they were not much of a clue as to the creature's identity, whatever it was.

Durima wasn't about to let that thing get away, however, just because she didn't know what it was. Although she was no mage, Durima, like most katabans, did know a thing or two about magic, enough to be able to slam her fists into the ground and activate her geomancy.

The Wall rumbled under her feet as she searched for the stone she needed. She found it easily and channeled more energy into it. In her mind's eye, she saw the stone rising rapidly from within the walls and could even hear it breaking through the ice.

Then a massive fist-shaped stone pillar burst out of the Wall, sending chunks of ice and rock flying everywhere. The giant fist-shaped pillar bent forward and slammed into the invisible creature, creating another loud clanging noise that made Durima cringe again.

This time, she must have hit it hard enough, because the creature's form flickered for a moment before its invisibility melted away, revealing the strangest 'creature' that Durima had ever seen in her life.

From head to toe, the creature was completely metal. It was not some kind of animal wearing metal armor; it was literally constructed out of metal, similar to the automatons used by the Mechanical Goddess in the southern seas. It looked like an upright lizard, using its front legs to hold back Durima's giant stone fist. Its tail whipped through the air so fast that it was almost impossible to follow, while its eyes glowed yellow. Its 'skin' was serrated and had what appeared to be open vents on its stomach, though what those vents could be used for, Durima didn't know.

Nor did Durima know why the North Academy mages had an automaton apparently acting as the school's bodyguard. She had thought only the Mechanical Goddess had access to such tech, but then she supposed that it didn't really matter because the machine was trying to kill them and *would* kill them if Durima and Gujak didn't kill it first.

So much for a stealthy entrance, Durima thought as she put more focus and energy into the stone fist. *Might as well have walked right into the school itself and shouted, 'Hey, we're going to desecrate the grave of one of your fellow mages and then leave, if that's all right with you.'*

She could feel the pressure of the stone fist bearing down on the lizard-like machine. The automaton was much stronger than it looked, however, because it was holding its own against the stone fist, despite the increasing pressure of Durima's creation. Whoever had designed the automaton had obviously done a good job, much to Durima's frustration.

Still, even the best machine was no match for magic. She just needed to apply more pressure onto it and sooner or later the damn thing would fall apart. Of course, that might be noticed by the mages, which would undoubtedly put a dent in her and Gujak's plans, but right now Durima didn't have the time or energy to worry about that, not when there was this mechanical monster that needed to be crushed.

So Durima poured more magical energy into the fist, making it stronger and stronger. She knew that she was getting weaker, but she didn't think it would be very long before the automaton broke first. After all, magic always won against mortal technology, no matter how good it was.

Much to her astonishment, however, a drill popped out of the automaton's forehead. The drill looked too small to be able to do much, but the automaton slammed its head into the stone fist anyway. It actually managed to move the fist back a few feet before Durima reasserted her dominance and began pushing back again.

That was when Durima noticed the cracks beginning to form in the fist's surface. The cracks started out small, but grew larger and larger with each passing second, until the fist was beginning to shake and shudder with repression. It occurred to Durima that the fist was going to explode, but before she could reinforce it with more magic, the stone fist did just that.

Chunks of rock flew everywhere as the automaton staggered forward, pulled forward by the momentum of its attack. The drill was still spinning in its head, making a loud whining noise as the automaton fell on all four of its legs. Although the automaton was clearly incapable of feeling emotion, the way it looked at Durima made her think that it was glaring at her.

Damn it, Durima thought. *Now might be a good time to run.*

Not that she could act on that thought. The Ghostly God would be extremely displeased if Durima and Gujak returned now. No doubt he'd punish them both severely, maybe even kill them outright. She remembered how much he emphasized the seriousness of the importance of this mission and exactly what he said he would do to them if they failed.

Shuddering at the thought, Durima slammed her fists together and charged at the automaton, fists swinging through the air. The automaton charged at her, the drill in its head extending until it was almost as long as a sword.

Right before she crashed into the automaton, Durima launched herself into the air and brought both of her fists down on its back. She did it as hard as she could, putting every last ounce of her strength into this blow.

The automaton's back crumpled under the impact of her fists, causing the automaton itself to collapse under her weight. Durima then began pounding her fists into it, smashing through its thick metal coat, aiming for any spot that looked fragile and important. She even managed to tear out some wires, although when she grabbed them, they sent electrical jolts through her body that forced her to let them go.

But she still pounded away at the machine, which no longer moved underneath her. She wasn't even thinking as she slammed her fists into the same spot over and over again. She had lost complete control of herself and didn't even realize that the automaton was down for good until Gujak grabbed her shoulder and said, "Durima, stop. The machine is down. You can stop killing it now."

When he said those words, it was like he had turned on a light switch in Durima's mind. Suddenly, she became more aware of her fists, which were bruised and bloody from all of the smashing. The cold wind nipped at the sensitive, cut-up skin of her fists and the smell of frozen metal mixed with her blood entered her nostrils.

Taking a deep breath, Durima ceased pounding away and looked at Gujak. Aside from the dent in his face from where the automaton had hit him, he looked as fine as ever, although he must have been lying prone for longer than Durima had thought because he now had a thin layer of ice covering his chest and there were little piles of snow in the nooks and crevices of his tree-like body.

"What happened?" said Gujak. He put his hands on his chest. "Were you destroying that machine because you really, honestly cared that much about me?"

The honest answer was no, but Durima was too tired to respond. She just stared at the broken machine that lay underneath her, trying to figure out what had come over herself.

It's been a long time since I last attacked anything quite like that, Durima thought. *Since the Katabans War, actually.*

Now it all made sense to her. Her war instincts had kicked in, or what she called 'the Demon.' It was a side of herself that she had discovered during the War, one that she rarely entered consciously or willingly. The Demon came out whenever she was under great stress. It made her violent, mindlessly so, and mercilessly cruel to whoever was unlucky enough to be the object of her wrath when she became the Demon.

It had been years since she had last become the Demon. She had done her best to avoid getting into high stress situations and had been so successful at that that she realized she must have forgotten the Demon even existed.

Gujak knew about the Demon because Durima had a reputation as the Demon leftover from the War. Still, the poor naïve fool didn't seem to grasp that he had just witnessed that side of herself take over.

He's lucky he didn't get in the way, Durima thought. *Otherwise, he would have ended up looking just like this automaton, except bloodier.*

Standing up, Durima held up her fists as she said, "It's not a problem. You know some healing magic, yes? Could you heal my fists for me?"

"Sure thing," said Gujak, touching her fists with his hands. "Here we go."

A brief flash of light emitted where Gujak's hands met Durima's fists. When the light faded, Durima's fists were whole again, although they were still covered in the blood from earlier. Sadly, she didn't have a towel to wipe with, so she wiped her fists on her fur instead.

"Thanks," said Durima to Gujak. "That was—"

"Hold it right there, invaders," said an obnoxiously loud voice, causing Durima and Gujak to look up in surprise. "Don't move a muscle or I, the great Junaz, will blow you both to the Heavenly Paradise!"

Standing not far from them was a human mage, a male one by the broad size of his shoulders and the deepness of his voice. He wore completely black robes that went down to his ankles, with equally black boots poking out from underneath them. He had a shock of golden brown hair peaking out from behind some kind of wooden mask that resembled a fox's face.

The mortal mage was aiming a wand at them, which was painted silver, like he was going to do exactly as he said if they did not obey his commands.

"Durima, who is that?" Gujak muttered, looking at the strangely-dressed man like he had never seen anything quite like him before.

Durima shook her head and replied, in a similarly low voice, "No idea. Never seen him before."

"Conspiring among yourselves?" said the man who had called himself Junaz. "Cease that deceptiveness at once, you fiends. For I, the great Junaz, will shine a light on whatever darkness you are trying to hide in."

"I think he's crazy," said Gujak. "Definitely crazy."

It was hard to tell Junaz's expression, but he did tilt his head to the side and say, "What language do you speak? Sounds like clicks and whistles to me."

Of course. This Junaz—whoever he was—was a mortal, and few mortals understood the language of the katabans, although most katabans understood the human version of Divina well enough. Durima had never heard a mortal describe it that way, however.

"I suppose it doesn't matter," said Junaz, shaking his

head as the tip of his wand began to glow. "Do you two know who I am? I am the great Junaz, devoted follower of Nimiko, the God of Light, and the luminimancy teacher at this great school. In addition, my knowledge of the mechanical arts is second-to-none at North Academy and I have personally worked on the great armadas that patrol the skies of Shika."

None of that meant anything to Durima, although she knew who Nimiko was, having done a few small tasks for him over the centuries. She doubted that would make Junaz leave them alone if she told him, however, because she was under the impression that, like most mortals, he was too stupid to understand when he wasn't wanted.

"Why is he wearing a fox mask?" Gujak asked, taking a step back as if he was afraid of the strange mortal. "Is he trying to hide something?"

Durima shrugged. "You think I'm an expert in human behavior?"

Then Junaz gestured with his wand at the destroyed automaton. "Do you know what you did? That was once Guardian, a gift from King Malock himself, which acted as one of the school's many, many defenses. It had been my job to maintain Guardian—as I said, I was once a top engineer in the Shikan air force—and now you have ruined it for no reason I can see other than it was doing its job."

"It tried to kill us," Durima muttered, although she didn't expect this Junaz character to understand, or if he did, to care.

"The only reason I came out here today, despite the

current crisis in the Third Dorm, is because I sensed that Guardian was fighting intruders and was losing," said Junaz. "It appears my senses were correct. As always."

"Does he ever stop talking?" Gujak wondered. "You know, we probably could walk away very slowly and he might not notice until we're actually gone."

For one, Durima agreed with Gujak, while Junaz was still speaking. "I don't know who you two are, or for that matter, *what* you two are, but I do know this: You both are clearly up to no good. I will capture you both so you may not succeed in whatever wrongdoing you are planning."

Durima snorted. This pathetic, tiny human was going to try to bring her and Gujak in? Sure, Durima was still tired from fighting the Guardian, as Junaz called the hunk of junk she had just finished tearing apart, but she knew how squishy and fragile humans could be. That Junaz wore a fox mask, of all things, only added to her incredulity at his confidence in his ability to defeat them.

Standing up, Durima said, "Then bring it, Fox Mask. Or are you just all hot air, like most humans tend to be full of?"

Of course Junaz didn't understand a word she said, but he said anyway, "I don't know what you just said or if you said anything at all, but enough idle chitchat. Prepare to be defeated, monsters."

Junaz did a bunch of complicated movements with his wand, almost like a swordsman slashing with his sword. He did the movements so quickly that Durima could barely follow, but she didn't need to see what he did in order to see the results.

A burst of light—brighter and hotter than any Durima had seen before—erupted from his wand. It hurtled across the Wall toward them and slammed into both Durima and Gujak before they could move.

It was like being hit with a sledgehammer. And like being hit with a sledgehammer, Durima immediately lost consciousness.

Chapter Three

Darek didn't even hesitate when he saw the Third Dorm's roof explode. While the rest of the students from both schools just stared at the column of flame and smoke in horror and shock, Darek teleported up from the sports field to the back of the Third Dorm.

He ran around the building until he reached the front door. Yanking the door open, Darek was met by clouds of black smoke pouring out of the open doorway like water bursting from a dam. Coughing and wheezing, Darek pointed his wand at his face and created an air bubble around his head. Immediately, the smoky smell faded from his lungs and nose, allowing him to breathe again as he dashed into the Third Dorm.

There was a reason Darek had not hesitated to act. The Third Dorm was his dormitory, the place where he and his fellow dorm mates stayed. Most of his things were in there, after all, so he was determined to put out the fire and save as much of his stuff as he could.

Of course, he also wanted to make sure that no one else was in here. He doubted there was, seeing as the Magical Superior had made it clear that any students who stayed in their dorms in lieu of greeting the Institute mages would be disciplined, but he just had to be sure.

When he entered the Third Dorm itself, he had little time to think about his motivations for running into a burning building. The air was hot and oppressive, like walking into an oven, with flames licking at the walls, floor, and ceiling. A chunk of the ceiling had fallen down and crashed onto the coffee table in the center near the burning sofa. The stairs leading up to the second floor were blocked off completely by a chunk of debris from the ceiling, but it was clear based on the position of the explosion outside that the explosion had started in one of the dorm rooms on the second floor, which meant that Darek had to get up there quickly to put it out.

Keeping his head down, Darek ran over to the stairs and waved his wand. The flames parted just long enough for him to jump through them and land on the other side of the stairs. As soon as his feet touched the ground, he was off, running up the stairs to the second floor even as the heat grew worse.

Upon emerging on the second floor, Darek immediately spotted the room in which the explosion had started. He knew that it had to be the room where the explosion had started because the door had been blasted off its hinges, leaving an open doorway in which smoke and fire bellowed out.

Even worse, Darek recognized that open doorway was the doorway to his own room. That meant that the explosion had started in his and Jiku's shared room, although why or how, he didn't know.

Regardless, Darek knew he had to act right away. He ran

toward the open doorway to his room and waved his wand. As he did so, a powerful gust of wind blew from nowhere, tearing through the smoke and giving him a brief glimpse of the inside of his room before the smoke returned and obscured his vision.

Don't have much time, Darek thought. *Air bubble is getting thinner. Gotta get out of here before it goes away completely. Fire's too strong for me to put out on my own. I will have to let the others deal with it.*

Right before he tried to leave, Darek heard the crashing of something nearby. Looking in the direction he had came, he saw that another chunk of ceiling had fallen in front of the stairs, effectively blocking off all escape routes. Not only that, but the flames had grown as well, growing far too large for him to control. They licked at the floor and what was left of the ceiling, leaving burn marks wherever they touched.

Can't escape through the stairs, Darek thought as he walked backwards, his eyes beginning to burn due to the thinness of the air bubble. *Must—*

"Help!" a familiar, old voice shouted. "Someone, help me! I'm stuck!"

The voice was immediately cut off by hacking and wheezing. Darek had no trouble recognizing that voice as belonging to Jiku, who based on the sounds of his shouts for help was lying somewhere in Darek's room. That made sense, seeing as Jiku and Darek were roommates as well as dorm mates, but at the same time he wondered what Jiku was doing back here in the first place.

Doesn't matter, Darek thought. *I just need to rescue him before he dies. That hacking and wheezing doesn't sound good at all.*

Feeling his air bubble thinning with each passing second, Darek dashed back toward the doorway to his room. The thick smoke and burning flames continued to block the entrance, but he waved his wand again, sending a powerful gust of wind that cut through both like a sword, giving him just enough time to jump through the gap and land in the room.

Panting, sweat running into his eyes, Darek looked around, scanning the place for any sign of Jiku. It was hard because the smoke was still thick in here, but then he noticed the familiar red boots of his friend poking out through the smoke.

Not saying anything—after all, talking wasted clean breathing air and he could not afford to waste even one ounce of that—Darek moved forward, ignoring the burning smoke that burned his hands. As he did so, he realized that a large chunk of the ceiling had fallen on Jiku's chest, pinning the middle-aged man to the floor.

Damn it, Darek thought. *How am I supposed to move that?*

He raised his wand to try to move the chunk of burning debris with telekinesis, but then without warning a flame leaped out from his own bed nearby and struck his wand hand. Instinctively cursing, despite how much air that movement wasted, Darek clutched his now burnt hand as his wand disappeared somewhere in the smoke and fire all around him.

No time to find it, Darek told himself as he moved closer to the chunk of rock on Jiku's chest. *Just use your magic as best as you can without it.*

Of course, it was not that easy. Darek hadn't had much experience going wand-less. He could do it, but it would be like trying to walk without shoes in the middle of a furnace.

He would *have* to do it. For Jiku.

Raising his hands—including the one that still burned—Darek focused on moving the damn ceiling chunk that lay on Jiku's chest. Without the wand to help him focus, it was like trying to move a boulder with his teeth. It didn't help that his air bubble was so thin now as to be practically nonexistent, and the smoke was in his eyes making it hard for him to see.

But then, much to his amazement, the ceiling chunk did in fact wobble before completely rolling off Jiku's body. Darek grimaced when he saw the burnt mark on his friend's chest and almost became depressed when he realized just how still Jiku was.

Yet Darek didn't give himself time to worry about his friend. He got down on his hands and knees, burning them against the hot floor, and grabbed Jiku's hand as the last of the air bubble gave out.

Suddenly, thick, hot, black smoke filled Darek's lungs, making him hack and wheeze as much as Jiku had earlier. Tears formed in his eyes as the smoke burned them and unless he was mistaken his robes felt like they had caught fire.

Must ... get ... out of here, Darek thought. *Must teleport.*

Now.

Darek had never teleported without a wand and wasn't even sure if he could. Nonetheless, with the smoke rapidly filling his lungs and with Jiku comatose, Darek had to give it a try.

Closing his eyes, Darek focused entirely on the courtyard of the Arcanium. He thought about it with all of his heart and soul until he could practically taste the soft green grass in front of it.

Then he focused on actually being there. He focused on the place as best as he could, trying to forget everything else, trying to even forget his own burning hand and missing wand. The Magical Superior had often told him that complete focus was necessary in order to teleport in stressful situations, but Darek found that much harder to do than he thought it should be.

And then, without warning, the smoke, heat, and hard stone floor under his knees vanished, replaced with a light, cool breeze and soft grass under him.

Gasping for breath, opening his eyes, Darek saw the steps of the Arcanium before them and then looked down at Jiku. His heart failed him at the sight of his friend's appearance.

Jiku looked like he had been burnt to a crisp. His face was burned black in several places, his robes had burned holes in them, especially in the chest area, and his silver-gray hair was now blackened around the edges. He looked like the corpse of a burn victim, which was very nearly close to what he was.

Raising his hands to cast a healing spell (despite having zero experience healing burns, much less wand-less), Darek was interrupted by the sound of people running toward him. He looked over his shoulder and saw the Magical Superior, Archmage Yorak, an aquarian who might have been Yorak's assistant, Mom, and Aorja running toward him. Behind them, the students from both schools were fighting the burning Third Dorm with their magic, while the teachers supervised and helped. They seemed to be having trouble with the fire, but it didn't matter to Darek because the flames did not seem to be spreading to the other dorms.

It was the Archmage who reached Darek first, well before the other three. She pushed him aside rather roughly for a woman her age, fell to her knees at Jiku's side, and said, "How long has he been out?"

"I don't know," said Darek, feeling annoyed. "Maybe ten minutes at most."

"Ten minutes," the Archmage growled. "That's not good. Listen, I know some healing spells that should hopefully take care of the worst of his wounds. Just stay back and let me cast them, okay?"

Darek bit his lower lip, but when he looked at Jiku again and saw how terrible his condition was, he nodded. Scrambling to his feet to get out of the way, Darek watched as the Archmage held her hands over Jiku's body.

The stone inside the Archmage's bracelet began to glow. Magical energy flowed from it through her hands into Jiku's body. It was a mesmerizing experience, as Darek had never seen an aquarian mage cast a spell before. It was hampered somewhat by his lungs, which were still burning from the smoke he had briefly inhaled, causing him to hack every now and then, but he would have those looked at later, after Jiku was fixed.

By the time Yorak finished healing Jiku, the others had arrived. While the Magical Superior went to inspect Jiku and Yorak's assistant helped the Archmage stand, Mom and Aorja went to check on Darek. Mom in particular fussed over his appearance and health, despite the fact that he was perfectly fine aside from his aching lungs, and he told her so.

Nonetheless, Mom being Mom, she said, "I know you are fine, Darek, but I wanted to make sure that you actually are fine. You ran into a burning building, for the gods' sake. That's not something most people can do without suffering some serious consequences, even if you used magic to protect yourself from most of them."

Darek rolled his eyes, but then clutched his hand as soon as the burn flared again. Without so much as a warning, Yorak pointed at Darek's hand, her stone glowed, and the burning went away as if it had never been there at all. He opened his mouth to thank her, but now Yorak and the Magical Superior were talking and he didn't want to interrupt their obviously important discussion, whatever it might have been about.

"How do you feel?" asked Aorja, putting her hands together in concern. Her guitar was no longer with her; perhaps she had forgotten it in the rush of things. "Can you still breathe?"

"Yes, I can," said Darek, waving off her concern. "You should be focusing on Jiku. He's the one who was in the midst of the explosion. I'd be surprised if he survived this."

"He will," said the Magical Superior suddenly, causing Darek, Mom, and Aorja to look at him. "Yorak confirmed that he will live. He will have to rest for a few hours, however, as the spells she cast on him work best when the target is asleep. We will need to transport him to the Arcanium until he wakes up."

"Oh, that's wonderful to hear," said Aorja with a sigh. "I was worried that the old coot wasn't going to make it."

"He wouldn't have, had not this young man saved him," said Yorak, nodding at Darek. "What is your name?"

"Darek Takren," said Darek. He gestured at Jiku. "And he's Jiku Nium. Once he awakes, I'll be sure to let him know that you saved his life. Jiku always liked to thank people who helped him, so I'm sure he will be anxious to thank the person who saved his life later."

"That would be you, wouldn't it?" said Yorak, looking at him like she wasn't sure that he had been paying attention. "After all, it was you who ran into that burning building and saved him, yes?"

"Yes, but I didn't even know he was in there and you were the one who actually healed him anyway, ma'am," said Darek. "I just heard him calling for help. I originally ran in there because I wanted to make sure that there was no one in there and wanted to see if I could save any of my possessions."

"Jiku's been missing all morning," Aorja added. "None of

us knew where he was until now. We thought he might have been in the Arcanium, sick."

Yorak turned to look at the Magical Superior, a questioning expression on her face. "Superior, why was one of your students inside his dorm room, rather than outside waiting to greet the rest of us?"

The Magical Superior stroked his chin, his eyes darting between the unconscious Jiku lying on the grass and the burning Third Dorm, which the other mages finally seemed to be getting under control, if the rapidly decreasing size of the flames and smoke was any indication. "I do not know the answer to that question, Yorak. This should not have happened. At this point, I know as much as you do about this situation."

The silent aquarian with a goldfish-like head—perhaps Yorak's assistant, who had up until this point been completely silent—pointed at Jiku and looked at Yorak. Yorak returned the look and stared at her assistant for a few seconds before returning her gaze to the Magical Superior.

"My pupil, Auratus, wants to know why we don't just read your student's mind to find out what happened to him," said Yorak. "Which I think is a good point."

"Because that would break the Telemancy Rules of Ethics," said the Magical Superior. "Rule Number One is that you cannot use telemancy to read someone's mind without their permission except in emergencies."

"That one of your dorm buildings was blown up, and two of your students nearly killed as a result, does not count as an emergency?" Yorak asked, her voice skeptical. "Superior,

I would think that this calls for an emergency of the highest order. There is clearly someone here in the school who is trying to cause harm."

"That is an odd conclusion to jump to, Yorak," said the Magical Superior, leaning on his staff. "Jiku may have started the explosion accidentally. It is not unheard of for students here to try spells above their ability and which they do not understand. The consequences are usually even more disastrous than this."

"But this is different," said Mom. She didn't seem at all intimidated by the looks that the two most powerful mages in the world were giving her, but then again, Mom had always been harder to intimidate than most people. "I know Jiku. He's an expert pyromancer. He could handle an explosion like that just fine. And anyway, he was far too responsible to cast an explosion in his own dorm room like that."

"Mom's right," said Darek, nodding. "Jiku's one of the more advanced students. I can't see him doing something like this, not even accidentally. Someone else had to do it."

"But who?" Aorja wondered, looking at Jiku with worry on her features. "Who would have even tried to do something like this? Is there a spy among us?"

"If there is, then what is to stop that spy from striking again?" said Yorak. "And maybe even putting my students at risk? Superior, I appreciate the gesture, but it may very well be time for me and my students to head back early. I do not want to put any of their lives at risk if there is a mad bomber running around blowing up dormitories."

Much to Darek's surprise, the Magical Superior actually grabbed Yorak's arm and looked at her pleadingly. It was odd because the Magical Superior rarely ever made physical contact with anyone, even with his own students. The pleading way that the Superior looked at Yorak was bizarre, too, which made Darek wonder just how close the two were and what the exact status of their relationship was.

"Please, Yorak, don't leave just yet," said the Magical Superior. "You just got here. Besides, we don't have all of the facts yet. We still need to examine the remains of the Third Dorm to find out who did it. It may be that this was a singular event, but rest assured that we *will* find out who did it and we *will* keep your students as safe as ours, if not safer."

Once again, Darek was struck by the Magical Superior's behavior. He spoke with the kind of conviction and attitude that Darek had never seen the Superior speak with before. It was like Skimif, the God of Martir, had taken the Superior's soul and replaced it with someone else's. He wondered if this was the same Magical Superior he had known for the last thirty years or if this was some kind of imposter pretending to be him.

Even odder, Yorak didn't shake off the Magical Superior's hand. She just gave him a hard, skeptical look, as if she had been told this before and didn't quite believe it. Her pupil, Auratus, stood at her side, but whether she believed the Superior or not, it was impossible to tell.

"All right," said Yorak with a sigh. "I have always had a hard time saying no to you, Superior. I suppose we'll stay for now. But if something else like this happens, I will not hesitate to gather up my students and go back to the Institute. Understood?"

"Completely," said the Magical Superior as he let go of her arm. "Of course. I would do the same in your situation. I won't even try to stop you if you decide to do that."

Darek tilted his head. Clearly, the Magical Superior and Yorak must have known each other in the past, but that didn't explain where and how they met or what their relationship had been, exactly. It was probably none of his business, but seeing them treat each other like old friends still incited his curiosity and made him wish that he was a better dictamancer. Then he would be able to look into their past and see what happened back then.

"I have no trouble believing that, Superior," said Yorak. "But I do have trouble believing that this school is as safe as its reputation suggests."

"Don't worry," said the Magical Superior. "This is the first time that something like this has happened in years, in decades even. I will personally investigate the matter and bring to justice whoever did it and thought they could get away with it. Guaranteed."

Next to Darek, Aorja rubbed her arm, like the situation was making her uncomfortable. She kept glancing at Jiku, no doubt wondering how he was feeling and whether he was going to be all right. Mom had her arms folded across her chest, her sharp eyes focused almost entirely on Yorak. Darek knew that look well, for it was a look Darek had seen Mom give to many people over the years and it always meant that she didn't trust the individual in question, at least not entirely, although why Mom looked at Yorak, of all people, with that look, he didn't know.

It's not like Yorak is behind the explosion, Darek thought. *Is she just upset that Yorak thinks the school isn't safe or something?*

At that moment, a familiar, overly-loud voice shouted, "Superior! I have urgent news to deliver to you right away!"

Darek looked up the steps of the Arcanium and groaned inwardly. A tall man, wearing black robes, with that stupid fox mask on his face, was running down the steps of the Arcanium toward them. He ran so fast that he seemed to be flying across the Arcanium's courtyard, his wand attached to his belt bouncing at his side.

"Who is that?" said Yorak, blinking at the sight of the strange man.

"Junaz Esperon," said the Magical Superior, sounding a little bored. "The luminimancy and metamancy teacher. He's ... unique, to put it lightly."

"Why is he wearing the face of a beast?" said Yorak.

"He's crazy," Mom confirmed.

"Actually, it's because he thinks it will give him the cleverness of a fox," said the Magical Superior.

"Like I said, he's crazy," said Mom.

Darek had to avoid laughing at that, although a smirk crossed his lips involuntarily.

"He's also a very good teacher and mechanic," said the Magical Superior. "I was wondering where he was. He must have found something important if he was not present to greet you."

In less than a minute, Junaz was before them. His hands on his knees, he panted and had to push his long, dark hair out of his eyes in order to see through the slits in his mask. It was like he had run a mile, although the distance from the Arcanium to their current spot was not very long.

"Magical Superior, sir," said Junaz in between panting. "I captured two intruders who were trying to break into the school without us knowing. I believe they are the culprits who caused the explosion of Third Dorm in order to distract us from their real plan."

"Really?" said the Magical Superior. "That sounds almost too good to be true. Who are they?"

"I have no idea," said Junaz, shaking his head. "One of them resembles a huge bear, with fists as big as boulders and fur as red as heatstone. The other looks like a walking, talking tree, but I suspect neither of them are quite what they appear."

"So a giant bear and a talking tree tried to blow up the Third Dorm so they could sneak into the school without anyone noticing?" said Mom. "That's the craziest thing you've ever said, Junaz, and that's after you told me, when I first met you, that that fox mask of yours makes you as clever as the real thing."

An offended look flashed in Junaz's eyes as he said, "Sorry if that offends your narrow view of the world, Jenur, but it is quite true. They even succeeded in destroying Guardian. Trust me, I would never lie about that."

"If they destroyed Guardian, then they're definitely a

threat," said Aorja. "That thing is supposed to be unbeatable, isn't it?"

"Yes," said the Magical Superior. "So Junaz, where are these two intruders you spoke of?"

"I put them in the catacombs, sir," said Junaz, pointing at the ground beneath their feet. "Locked them up in the cells. They are not yet conscious, but I believe they will soon awake any minute now."

Darek grimaced, although no one seemed to notice. The catacombs were a series of underground tunnels and caves that ran underneath the entirety of the Arcanium. They had been built by the founder of North Academy, whoever he was, but their exact purpose was unknown, although nowadays the teachers used them to store supplies and important objects they couldn't store anywhere else.

Darek had never liked the catacombs. They always seemed far too sinister for his taste, especially the jail cells. He didn't even know why the tunnels beneath a school would need prison cells in the first place; after all, to his knowledge, they had never even been used until today.

"Then I will go down there to speak with them right away," said the Magical Superior. "We will find out if they are involved with the explosion of the Third Dorm, and if they are not, why they tried to sneak into the school in the first place."

"I wish to come with you, Superior," said Yorak. "If these two intruders are behind this tragedy, then I would like to know if they have any other terrible plans up their sleeves. For the safety of my students."

"Very well," said the Magical Superior. "But first ..."

The Superior looked at Darek, Mom, and Aorja. "You three, take Jiku to the medical wing of the Arcanium. He should be resting on something better than the grass." Then he looked at Junaz. "Junaz, you will take me and Yorak down to the catacombs and show us where you put the intruders."

"Yes, sir," said Junaz, bowing.

Yorak gestured at her pupil, Auratus. "Auratus, I want you to go and find out if the other students have found any clues among the debris of the Third Dorm. Please also tell the others that the intruders have been caught, but that the students should be prepared to leave at any time just in case."

Auratus did not respond to that verbally. She simply saluted Yorak and then ran off toward the Third Dorm without hesitation. She ran somewhat awkwardly across the grass, like she wasn't used to running on land.

"Now then," said the Magical Superior to Junaz. "Take us to the intruders. If they are truly the ones behind the explosion, then they are a clear threat to the students from both schools. And I do not tolerate threats to my students from anyone, no matter who they might be."

Chapter Four

Durima's head hurt. Her arms hurt. Her legs hurt. Her back hurt. And every other part of her body hurt. Even worse, she could not remember why they hurt. They just did. Maybe they had always hurt and she was just realizing it now. She was getting on in years. Most katabans only lived to be five hundred, after all, although that may have been because most katabans got killed on missions for their gods or in some cases by the gods themselves. As a matter of fact, Durima did not know what the maximum age for a katabans was. She knew that the Katabans Council, the group who organized katabans society and enforced the rules all katabans followed, had several members who were older than five hundred and who seemed to be in good health still.

Maybe we don't die at all, Durima thought. *After all, it's not like these are our actual bodies. These suits of flesh are nothing more than forms we take on whenever we have to enter the physical world, to be discarded or swapped out at will.*

Then Durima shook her head and her memories came back to her. The automaton ... the strange mortal ... the flash of light that had hit her and Gujak with the force of a sledgehammer ... it all came roaring back to her in an instant.

Her eyes flickered open and she saw that she was lying on the floor of what appeared to be a cave. Putting her left hand flat on the ground, Durima tried to find out where she was.

She sent a brief burst of geomancy into the earth, sort of like a sonar blast. Then the burst returned to her and she found out that she was still in North Academy's general area. Unfortunately, she was underground, deep underground if the signal was any indication, and she was apparently alone.

Sitting up, rubbing the back of her head, Durima looked around at her cell. It must have been designed for someone much shorter than her, because the ceiling was low over her head and the walls were too narrow for her liking. There wasn't much room for her to move and stretch, despite the fact that her arms and legs were not particularly long.

A set of tall, metal bars stood before her, the only thing standing between her and freedom. They looked old, even ancient. Though Durima was still in pain, she didn't see any reason she couldn't knock these bars out with one good punch from her fists. Then she could find Gujak and they could continue with their mission.

So Durima stood up as much as she could (although she had to crouch to avoid scraping her head against the ceiling) and walked over to the bars. Pulling back her fist, she slammed it directly into the bars as hard as she could.

To her encouragement, the bars actually bent inwards. They didn't break or go flying, but it was an encouraging sign, making her rear back again to punch it again.

Then, before her startled eyes, the bars began to fix themselves. Slowly but surely, the bars bent back to their original shape, leaving no sign at all that they had just been bent inward not one minute earlier.

"What the hell?" said Durima. "What is this? More mortal magic?"

"Durima?" said Gujak's voice, which sounded like it was coming from the cell next to hers. "Are you awake?"

"Yes," said Durima, not bothering to hide the frustration in her voice. "You as well?"

"Yep," said Gujak. "But my head hurts. I think I took the brunt of that strange mortal's attack."

"I'm willing to bet that you didn't," said Durima. "But it doesn't matter. How long have we been down here?"

"I don't know," said Gujak. "There aren't any windows or anything to let the sun shine in, so I don't know what time it is or how many hours have passed or anything. I've just been sitting here in the dark for a while trying to think of a way to escape."

"Have you tried using the ethereal?" Durima asked.

"The ethereal doesn't go down here," said Gujak. "Trust me, if it did, I would have gotten out of here long ago."

Durima cursed. Of course. She had forgotten that the ethereal—that second plane of existence accessible only to gods and katabans—did not, for whatever reason, extend underground. It only allowed people traveling upon it to appear on the surface. Why this particular limitation existed, she didn't know, but she suspected that the Powers must have built it into the ethereal when they were laying the foundations of Martir eons ago.

"It doesn't matter," said Durima. "I think we'll be able to get out of here pretty easily. Human-made prisons are almost always designed for humans, not katabans like us."

"There's something different about this one, though, Durima," said Gujak. "The magic here is stronger than the average human prison. I think there are a bunch of spells keeping us in, even if we can't see or sense them. Did you see what happens when you dent the bars?"

Durima scowled. "Yes. I just found that out for myself."

"There might be other ones like that around here," said Gujak. "Maybe even worse. I've heard rumors of mortals casting all kinds of terrible spells on the places that they want to keep others out of. I don't want to get blown up or turned inside-out."

"Mortal magic is weak and ineffectual," said Durima. "It's only a pale imitation of godly magic, after all. If it was so great, mortals wouldn't even bother with non-magical ways of dealing with their problems."

"If you say so," said Gujak. "Still doesn't get us out of here, though."

"That's because I will get us out of here," said Durima. "Just hold tight for a moment. I've been in worse situations before."

That was perfectly true. During the Katabans War, Durima had once been captured by enemy soldiers. They had tossed her into a deep pit, with slimy, unclimbable walls, where they had left her to die. She had managed to escape by using her geomancy to create a pillar of stone that rose from the pit, but it had still been quite the bleak situation at the time.

"But ... what about Master?" said Gujak. "He probably knows that we were captured. Do you think he'll punish us for taking so long?"

Durima shuddered. "No doubt. Master has never been particularly forgiving of failure. That just gives us all the more reason to get out of here."

"Do you think he'll put us in the Mind Chamber?" said Gujak, his voice almost panicking. "I can't handle the Mind Chamber again. Just that one time was enough. I don't know how you managed to handle it five times."

A primal fear rose in Durima's chest when she thought about the Mind Chamber, forcing her to repress her memories to avoid losing control. She needed her wits about herself if she and Gujak were going to get out of here at all.

"Let's try to think positive thoughts for now," Durima said. "If we get out of here speedily, Master might be willing to forgive us for our failure or at least lighten our punishment. Maybe he will just take away our meals for today."

"I hope that's all he does," said Gujak.

She didn't like his bleak tone because it was making her nervous. So she decided to focus on the situation at hand, to be totally in the present, as she had learned to do during the War. It was the only way she'd get out of here.

At least there isn't any slime here, Durima thought,

tapping the ground with her foot. *Maybe I can dig my way out.*

Before she could test that idea, the sound of footsteps—at least three sets of feet, hard to tell with the way they echoed off the narrow tunnel walls—filled her ears. She looked to the left at the rock wall that separated her cell from Gujak's, but it wasn't until a bright white light began to shine down the hallway outside the cell that Durima realized that someone was coming to visit them.

She backed up against the back wall, waiting for whoever was coming. Reaching out with her magic senses, Durima sensed three magical presences. One was a normal mortal mage, but the other two practically dwarfed his power. They weren't quite on the same magical level as the gods, but they were far stronger than that of any other mortal she had felt before. In fact, these two presences were so powerful that they even dominated Durima and Gujak's combined power.

What kind of mortals are these? Durima thought. *I didn't know mortal mages could even be that powerful. I will have to tread as carefully around them as I tread around Master. Well, maybe not that carefully, as they are no doubt fairer and more merciful than him, but I still cannot let my guard down.*

A minute or two later, the three mortal mages stood in front of her cell. One was Junaz, who was the owner of the average magical energy level. He still wore that strange fox mask. He was also the source of the light, which shone like a star on the tip of his wand.

The other two mages, then, were the sources of the

supreme magical presences she had felt. One was an old human, very old based on the grayness of his skin. He leaned on a tall staff that resembled an unusually long mage wand, but despite his old age, he radiated so much power that Durima knew he was not the kind of person you messed with.

The other one standing next to him was a female aquarian who appeared just as old as the elderly human. Like the old human, the old aquarian radiated a powerful magical presence that left no doubt as to her power level and energy. The two of them together were almost enough to match the magical presence of a god.

But for all that, Durima had no idea who either of those two mages were. They were clearly important, probably authority figures of some kind, but she paid so little attention to the mortal world that she did not know how important or well-known they were. Unlike Junaz, they were wild cards, which gave her even more reason to tread lightly.

Then, much to her astonishment, the old human spoke in perfect Godly Divina. "You and your friend are katabans, yes?"

Durima was so surprised that she had to say, "Yes, we are. How can you speak Godly Divina so perfectly? I know you mortals can speak in your bastardized version of Divina, but I thought you mortals were incapable of speaking the divine tongue."

The old man smiled. "I am the Magical Superior of North Academy. The gods prefer to speak with me in their own tongue, so I learned it. Yorak here also knows it, but alas, Junaz does not, so he has no idea what we're saying."

Durima already knew that Junaz, who appeared baffled by what to him was an incoherent conversation of nonsense and gibberish, didn't know Divina, but knowing that the old female aquarian did just made the situation that much more difficult. She had thought she might be able to fool the human, but with that old aquarian there—who had the eyes of a hawk—she began to doubt her own abilities.

"Wait," said Durima, squinting at the Magical Superior. "You are the famous Magical Superior of North Academy, one of the strongest mortal mages in all of Martir?"

"Indeed," said the old human. "The one and only. And this is Yorak, the Archmage and Grand Magus of the Undersea Institute, also a powerful mage in her own right, equal in power to my own."

"I've heard about both of you," said Durima. "You are the two most famous mortals in the katabans world due to your unique connections to the gods among your kind. I never thought I'd live to actually meet either of you. And to be honest, both of you are much older than the rumors suggested."

"Enough chitchat," said Yorak. She, too, spoke Godly Divina as fluently as the gods; in fact, Durima thought Yorak spoke it better than most katabans based on those two words alone. "We're here to find out why you two were caught trying to break into North Academy. What were you planning to do? Harm our students? Steal a treasure of important value? What?"

"We didn't mean it," Gujak suddenly spoke up in a pleading tone. "Please don't kill us. We're not up to anything bad. Just let us go and we'll never bother you again ever."

Durima cursed. This was another reason Durima didn't like being captured. Gujak was a coward of the highest order. More than once over the years he had broken down and pleaded for mercy from their enemies. It was also why she was grateful that Gujak had not been fighting at her side during the War. He would not have been able to handle the stress.

Junaz was looking at Gujak's cell with a puzzled expression on his face, no doubt wondering what the heck Gujak had just said, but the Magical Superior said, "Kill you? Why would we ever do that? We have captured you, which I think is punishment enough for now."

"But that confession does offer us a glimpse into your true reasons for being here," said Yorak with a smug smile on her face. "Why else would your friend blubber about us killing you two unless he knew that you two are up to no good? Tell us how you blew up the Third Dorm without having to be there. Do you have a spy among the students? Or was it some kind of magic?"

Durima frowned. She had no idea what the Third Dorm was, but she did recall seeing, from atop the Walls, one of the buildings on the campus grounds on fire. She figured that that had to be what the Archmage was talking about, but she was just as ignorant about its cause as Yorak was.

So Durima said, "I have no idea who started the

explosion or why it happened. It would have been a great distraction if we hadn't been caught by fox mask there."

She said that while pointing at Junaz. Junaz looked at the Superior and said, "Why is she pointing at me? Is she threatening me?"

The Magical Superior switched to the mortal tongue, saying as he did so, "No, Junaz, she is not threatening you or anyone else. She's just complaining about how you and Guardian managed to capture them."

Through the slits in his mask, Junaz's eyes looked smug and satisfied. "Well, it was quite easy. Despite their obvious strength, these katabans stood no chance to my luminimancy. They didn't even put up a fight."

Durima growled at him threateningly, seeing as she couldn't actually speak mortal Divina well enough to communicate her thoughts to him. Junaz shrank back the minute he heard her deep-throat growl, which was an amusing sight to Durima, causing her to chuckle.

"Jumpy one, aren't you?" said Durima to Junaz, even though she knew he couldn't understand a word she said. "Do you teach the students here how to run and hide from big scary monsters that could rip their heads off their shoulders?"

"Katabans, be quiet," the Magical Superior said, a hint of a threat in his voice. "I will not have you scaring and threatening my teachers. I do not tolerate that kind of behavior from anyone in my school."

Durima rolled her eyes, but said nothing else to Junaz. As much fun as it was to threaten and scare the dumb mortals, the Magical Superior's power level was so high that she knew better than to go against whatever he said. Any mortal who wielded that kind of power was the kind of mortal worth listening to, even for a katabans like her. She knew enough about power thanks to her relationship with Master to respect anyone who had more than her.

"Fine," said Durima. "But that doesn't mean I have to respect him."

"I'm not asking you to respect him or anybody else," said the Magical Superior. "I am only asking you not to threaten him in my presence."

"And why do you care?" said Durima. "The idiot can't even understand what I'm saying."

"Because he is one of my teachers and I do not tolerate threats against my faculty," said the Magical Superior, his voice hard. "Now, let's move on. What are your names?"

"Why do we have to tell you that?" said Durima. "Our Master told us not to tell anyone who we are or what we're doing here."

"So you have a Master," said the Magical Superior. "Who is this Master of yours? Why does he want you to keep your reason for being here a secret?"

"I will not tell," said Durima, folding her arms across her chest. "I will never tell. I shouldn't have even told you that much."

"No, keep talking," said Yorak, gesturing at Durima to continue. "We're perfectly fine with you voluntarily telling us all about your Master and his plans. It suits our designs perfectly."

"That is exactly why I am not going to talk about it anymore," said Durima. "I fear Master more than you."

"Your Master must be very powerful if you fear him more than us," said Yorak. "The Superior and I are the two most powerful mages in the world. If we wanted, we could annihilate both of you without even thinking about it."

"But you won't," said Durima. "Otherwise, you would have done that already, rather than toss us into a couple of tiny cells deep beneath the earth."

"Don't push your luck," said Yorak. "I am *not* in a good mood right now and I am more than willing to do whatever I need to in order to find out who is threatening the lives of my students and the Superior's students."

"Calm down, Yorak," said the Magical Superior, putting a hand on her shoulder. "The katabans is correct that we are not going to kill her. While I am no fan of either of these two, killing them would undoubtedly bring the wrath of their Master upon us, their Master who in all probability is a god himself."

Durima saw an opening and went for it. She wrapped her claws around the bars of her cell and said, "Yes, Master is a god. A powerful god, too, one who could easily crush you mortals underneath the heel of his boot. I will not reveal his identity to you, but I will tell you that if you respect the gods at all, you will let me and my friend go free so we may complete the mission that we came here to do."

She said that because Durima understood that these mages, more than any other kinds of mortals, respected the gods. Magic flowed from the gods like water from an underground spring. The only reason these mages could use magic at all was because they had devoted themselves to this god or that god. Mages were not known as the People of the Gods for no reason. By playing on the mages' inherent respect—and by extension, fear—for the gods, Durima was practically guaranteed to win her and Gujak their freedom without much work.

It's such a brilliant plan, Durima thought. *Why didn't I think of it earlier? Would have been far more effective than insulting and threatening a dumb mortal who can't even understand what I'm saying.*

Her grin faded when the Magical Superior shook his head. "No."

"No?" said Durima, her grip on the bars lightening. "But … you respect the gods. Aren't you afraid of displeasing my Master? He will not be at all happy to learn that you are getting in the way of his will."

"I understand exactly what might happen if I continue to refuse to let you go," said the Magical Superior. "But this is not the first time I have defied the gods. I feel like too much has happened with too few answers to trust that you two are not up to any wrongdoing."

"By accusing me and my friend of being up to no good, you are accusing our Master of being up to no good as well," said Durima. She brought her face closer to the bars, glaring at the Magical Superior. "Are you sure you want to imply that a god could possibly be at fault? That's dangerous territory, you know."

The Magical Superior returned her gaze with a strong

one of his own, despite his weak human body, and said, "My loyalty is first and foremost to the students of my school, who I have sworn to protect and defend at all costs. If your Master truly is a good god and has no ill intentions for us, then I will free you two personally. For now, you must stay there."

"We still won't talk," said Durima. "Neither of us will. You cannot make us."

"I won't," said the Magical Superior. "Neither will Yorak or Junaz. Instead, I will go and find out myself who your Master is and what he is planning to do here."

"And how, may I ask, do you intend to do that?" said Durima. "Ask every single god in the Northern and Southern Pantheons until you find him? Seems awfully impractical to me, even for someone as magically-talented as you are."

"Of course I am not going to use such an impractical, time-consuming method," said the Magical Superior. "Instead, I am going to return to my study, where I will contact the only god who knows exactly what is going on at all times in every part of the world. Including who your Master is and what he is doing at this very moment."

"Who is that?" said Durima.

"That is not information you need to know," said the Magical Superior. "Though to be perfectly honest, I thought you would know, seeing as the god I am thinking of is by no means an obscure one."

Durima took her claws off the bars of her cell and sat back. "So is that it? Just going to leave us here to rot until you find out who our Master is?"

"You are hardly going to rot," said the Magical Superior. "You will simply remain down here until I get the information I need. Then I will decide whether to free you or not."

Durima huffed. "Fine. But when Master comes here, looking for the mortal stupid enough to defy his will, I will make sure to point in the direction of your study."

The Magical Superior opened his mouth, likely to say something stupid, but then the ceiling shook above their heads. The three mortals looked up as dust fell from the ceiling. Durima also looked up, as she had no idea what was causing the ceiling to shake.

"What's going on out there?" said Yorak. "Superior, is this normal or is it another explosion?"

"I don't know what it is, Yorak," said the Magical Superior as the ceiling shook again. "We must return to the surface immediately. If it's another attack, then we have to make sure that our students are safe."

The Magical Superior looked at Durima with hard eyes. "You and your friend stay put until we return."

Durima held up her hands as another layer of dust fell and landed on her shoulders and head. "It's not like I can open the door and waltz on out, although rest assured that I would like to do so."

The Magical Superior didn't seem happy about what she said, but he didn't push the subject. He went walking back in the direction they had came, with Junaz and Yorak following closely behind. Soon the entire catacombs was engulfed in the darkness from before, only this time, the ceiling shook and dust continued to fall with every tremor.

Oh, Master, Durima thought, wincing at a particularly violent shake. *I just hope that whatever you've done, that it will not cause the ceiling to fall in on and kill us.*

Chapter Five

A few minutes prior to the tremors ...

Darek and Aorja sat on either side of Jiku's bed, looking at their friend, who still lay unconscious in the medical wing of the Arcanium. He lay underneath heavy blankets, which were white as snow, with the sheets pulled up to his chin. His chest rose and fell under the blankets, a sign he was breathing, that he was still alive, that he would survive.

It had only been minutes ago that Eyurna, the head panamancer and doctor of the medical wing, declared that Yorak's magic had done the job and that Jiku was indeed going to be fine as long as he got enough rest. She had allowed Darek and Aorja to stay by his side because they were his friends and because she had some other work to attend to that was more urgent.

Neither Darek nor Aorja had spoken much since then. They had been too busy worrying about Jiku, although Darek had from time to time occasionally wondered who had started the explosion and whether the other mages had yet found any clues pointing to the identity of the bomber. For that matter, he wondered how the Magical Superior's interrogation of the two intruders was going.

So much has happened just within the last hour, Darek thought. *I wonder what it all means.*

Mom had stayed just long enough to make sure that Eyurna was going to confirm Jiku's health. Then she left, telling him and Aorja that she was going to go see the progress of the other mages. She said she would be back if she had any news, but since that had been about ten minutes ago already, Darek assumed that she was probably not going to return any time soon.

Darek looked around the medical wing again, just to get his mind off the stressful events of the day. It was a long room with about two dozen beds on each side, with tall, curtained windows between each bed. The ceiling and floor were white, while the curtains had flowery designs that were supposed to calm the patients. Eyurna's office was located at the end of the room, while thick chandeliers hanging from the ceiling illuminated the place during the night. Currently, the open windows offered an excellent amount of daytime illumination, the sunlight reflecting off the white sheets, but not in a way that hurt Darek's eyes.

Then he looked at Aorja. She had her guitar at her side, but it was still inside its case. She had said she was going to play it the minute Jiku woke up, but she looked so worried about his health that it seemed unlikely that she would remember to do that even if Jiku awoke soon.

That wasn't surprising. Aorja was always worrying about him and Jiku and their other friends. She wasn't training to be a panamancer—she always said that she couldn't handle working with sick people all the time—but she was so compassionate that she might as well have been one.

I'm glad we're friends, Darek thought. *Me, Jiku, and Aorja. It certainly makes it easier to handle events like what happened today.*

At that moment, his thoughts were interrupted by the sound of the door to the medical wing opening and closing. He looked in the direction of the door and almost started when he saw who was walking up the path between the beds.

It was two of the Institute students. One was manta-like in appearance, with thick goggles strapped over his eyes and an armband wrapped around his right arm, which had a glowing green stone in it. He walked extremely awkwardly, lifting his feet too high and bringing them down too fast, which made him look like he was stomping. He seemed unused to walking on land, which made sense, seeing as the Undersea Institute was located underwater.

The other student had a goldfish-like head and a deep black stone embedded in the anklet on her left ankle. Unlike her fellow student, she walked across the stone floor with ease, though as she sometimes almost tripped, it was pretty clear that she was not exactly used to walking on land, either.

Of the two, the goldfish-headed one looked the most familiar to Darek. He remembered that she was called Auratus, the silent pupil of the Grand Magus Yorak. What these two were doing here, Darek didn't know, although neither of them appeared hostile.

Still, he stood up when they approached and said,

"Hello. What are you two doing here?"

Auratus said nothing, but the manta-like mage said, in broken Divina, "Here to see student. Want to make sure he is okay."

"Oh, he's going to be fine," said Aorja, brushing her long blonde hair out of her eyes. "He just needs rest is all. It's thanks to your headmistress, actually, that he's going to be okay."

"That's good," said the Institute mage. "Grand Magus very smart and talented. Of course."

He said that with obvious pride, his chest puffed out. Auratus, standing next to him, looked proud of her headmistress as well, although it was hard to tell because she was so quiet and her goldfish-like face made it difficult to read her facial expressions.

"Say, what are your names, anyway?" said Darek. He held out a hand. "I'm Darek Takren and this is Aorja Kitano. You are—?"

The two Institute students stared at Darek's outstretched hand like they had never seen such a thing before. It confused Darek for a moment before he realized that aquarians might not greet each other with handshakes, but he had no idea how they greeted each other and he felt too embarrassed to ask them.

So, lowering his hand, Darek said, "Just a human way of greeting someone new. Anyway, you can just tell us your names."

"Okay," said the male student. "I Kuroshio. Botamancer. And this Auratus, personal pupil of Archmage."

"I already knew her name," said Darek. "She was there when I rescued Jiku here. Why doesn't she introduce herself, though?"

Auratus looked down at her feet, almost like she was embarrassed, while Kuroshio said, "She ... what's the word. She is mute. Can't speak."

"Oh," said Darek. "I'm sorry to hear that. Has she always been that way or—?"

"Been that way for long time," said Kuroshio. "But not forever. Not subject she like to talk about."

Auratus gave Kuroshio a grateful smile, although Darek didn't understand it. He wanted to find out more about how she lost her ability to speak, but before he could, Aorja asked, "So how does Auratus communicate if she can't talk?"

Kuroshio tapped the side of his head. "Telepathy. Sends mental messages to people. Sometimes sign language, but telepathy more reliable."

"Oh," said Aorja. "I've heard of those types of mages. They're usually audimancers, aren't they?"

"Auratus not audimancer," said Kuroshio, his tone sharp. "Fuscimancer. Controls shadows. Good at telemancy as well."

Granted, Darek was no expert at understanding aquarians, but he knew the 'this is not a subject that you want to talk about' tone very well. Clearly, Auratus was sensitive about being accused of being an audimancer, though why, he didn't know and he didn't think Auratus or Kuroshio would be willing to elaborate. He had a feeling that it wasn't really any of their business, although he really wanted to know more about it. Maybe he could find out more about her, subtly.

"Oh, fuscimancy?" said Aorja. "That makes her a servant of Ooka, the God of Shadows and Knives, yes?"

"Yes," said Kuroshio. "She very good. In training to one day replace Yorak as Archmage."

"Then she must be very good," said Darek. "The Magical Superior used to have a pupil years ago, but then he was killed and the Superior has gone without one since."

"Why?" said Kuroshio. "Need successor, right? Why go without pupil?"

Darek shrugged. "It happened when I was very young, so I don't recall all of it. I've never talked about with the Superior and he hasn't shared his reasons for doing it, but there have always been rumors about him picking a new one every year, although he has yet to do it."

"Hmm," said Kuroshio, scratching his arm. "Interesting."

That was all he said on the matter before lapsing into silence. Neither of the two aquarians said anything else and for a moment, Darek was too absorbed by the awkwardness of the moment to know what else he should say.

Then Aorja spoke up, pointing at Kuroshio's armband. "Why do you aquarian mages use stones to cast spells instead of wands?"

Kuroshio put his hand over his green stone. "More practical. Easier to use underwater. Stone channels magic better than wood."

"But how does that work?" Aorja asked, leaning forward, her eyes darting from Auratus's anklet to Kuroshio's armband. "I know that technically anything can be used to channel magic, but I was always told that wands were the best because they were specifically designed to channel the divine energy. Never occurred to me to use a stone."

Kuroshio stared blankly at Aorja, which told Darek that he clearly had not understood most of what she said. It made him wonder just how much Divina that Kuroshio understood. For that matter, he wondered how much Auratus understood, who due to her inability to talk was even more of an enigma than Kuroshio.

So Darek said, in a slower voice than Aorja, "Aorja wonders how your magical stones work. She says that wands were designed for magical use, which is why we think they're better."

Kuroshio's goggles made it difficult to tell if he understood Darek's explanation at first, but then he nodded and said, "Ah. Well, stones very good. Mined from ocean floor. Can store magic energy. Useful."

His broken Divina was hard to understand, although Darek thought he got the gist of it. "So these stones are different from normal stones, then?"

Before Kuroshio could answer, a small tremor shook the floor beneath their feet. Darek and Aorja looked down at the floor and so did Kuroshio and Auratus. Another tremor followed, this one stronger than the last.

"What that?" said Kuroshio, looking up at Darek and Aorja with panic in his eyes. "Earthquake?"

Darek shook his head as another tremor made Jiku's bed shake, although Jiku himself did not move. "Can't be. We never have earthquakes around here. This is something else entirely."

"Geomancer?" said Kuroshio, looking from Darek to Aorja and back again. "One of your fellow students?"

Another tremor happened before Darek could respond, this one so abrupt that it almost threw him off his feet. He grabbed the railing of Jiku's bed to steady himself, however, and held it tightly as he stood up to his full height again.

"I don't think so," said Darek. "We should go check, however, just to be—"

For the fourth time, the medical wing was shaken by another tremor, but this time, it was enough to cause the chandeliers overhead to sway. Darek doubted they would fall—the entire Arcanium was reinforced by an ancient magic designed to keep the place from falling in on itself in the event of some disaster like this—but seeing the chandeliers swaying set him on edge anyway.

"Come on," said Darek as he pushed away from Jiku's bed. "We're going to go find out what's going on out there and deal with it, if possible."

Bursting through the front doors of the Arcanium and out onto the front steps, Darek found the cause of the tremors immediately, although he had a hard time understanding what he was looking at, at first.

The creature had the giant wings of a bat sprouting from its shoulders, with a long, lion-like tail that whipped through the air. Its hind legs were short and stubby, like the legs of a zinyu, and its body was covered in fur like a thick coat. It had the face of a tiger, but the strangest part of all was its 'arms,' which were essentially pile drivers that it used to beat against the earth. Every time its 'arms' slammed into the ground, another tremor shook the school, easily identifying the monster as the source of the tremors.

"What in Skimif's name is that?" said Aorja, her eyes widening as she drew her wand for battle.

"Chimera," said Kuroshio. "Created creatures. Very rare, though."

Darek had heard about chimeras. Like Kuroshio said, they were very rare, and when they did exist, their appearance was often radically different from one another. Chimeras were creatures created by biomancers, although due to the difficulty of such a feat, they were rarely seen. The gods could create chimeras as well, although those were even rarer.

Not that the rarity of such creatures mattered at the moment. After all, there was currently one right in front of them at this very moment apparently trying to destroy the foundations of the school itself. There was no time to sit around and think or talk about the history of chimeras or anything like that.

About the only thing that registered on Darek's mind was that none of the other students or teachers had yet to show up, despite the fact that the chimera was not even trying to hide. He figured that the others would be here soon, but until then, it would be up to him, Aorja, Kuroshio, and Auratus to deal with it.

"I don't care what it is," said Darek as he reached for his wand before remembering that he had lost it in the fire of the Third Dorm, and cursing in his mind. "It's clearly up to no good. Let's show it what happens when you mess with the Academy and the Institute."

Although he was wand-less, Darek teleported down the steps to the commons area without waiting to see if the others were going to follow. As soon as he reappeared on the grass, he pointed his hand, which was now glowing an icy-blue with the ice energy he was channeling through it, at the chimera and flicked his wrist.

The chimera—which had completely ignored him in its desire to destroy the school—suddenly became encased in a thick block of ice up to its neck. The chimera roared in shock and anger before its deep black eyes fixed on Darek. It gave off a low, powerful growl that would have sent Darek running if the school itself had not been at stake here.

What's it gonna do? Darek thought with a smile. *It's completely trapped inside that ice block. It can growl threateningly all day long and it still won't do a thing.*

His smile vanished from his face, however, when thick cracks appeared in the ice block. A moment later, the ice exploded, sending huge frozen chunks flying everywhere as the chimera stretched its wings and shook its head.

Ducking to avoid one particularly large chunk of ice that went flying in his direction, Darek raised his hand to try freezing it again (he decided that he just hadn't made the ice thick enough the first time) when the chimera vanished.

By Skimif's name, Darek thought, his eyes darting all over the courtyard as he looked for the chimera. *It can teleport?*

At that moment, he heard feet running down the steps behind him. Looking over his shoulder, Darek saw Aorja, Kuroshio, and Auratus running down the Arcanium's front steps toward him. He opened his mouth to tell them to keep an eye out for the chimera when a thick shadow fell over him, followed immediately by a terrible scent, like that of swamp mud mixed with blood.

Turning away from his friends, Darek saw the chimera standing right in front of him. Not only that, but it was raising its pile drivers above his head, clearly planning to turn him into paste.

Darek had no time to attack it or teleport out of its way, so he jumped to the side and landed on his side as the chimera brought its pile drivers onto the ground where he once stood. The ground shook under the pile drivers' impact, making it impossible for Darek to find his footing. He shot a glance at Aorja, Kuroshio, and Auratus, who were thrown off the steps and onto the ground very roughly, although they seemed to be okay.

Getting to his feet now that the ground wasn't shaking, Darek aimed his hand at the chimera once more, but then it vanished again. Cursing foully under his breath, Darek looked around for the chimera when he spotted a dozen or so of his fellow students, along with a handful of teachers, running toward the courtyard where he stood.

A smile spread across his face when he saw them.

Having so many of his fellow students helping, plus some of the teachers, would undoubtedly make it easier to defeat the chimera. After all, the students and teachers in this school were the best of the best. Soon, the chimera would be defeated and everything would be—

He smelled it before he felt it, but when that same scent of swamp mud and blood entered his nostrils, his brain only registered it too late. Something hard and thick slammed into his back, like a thick pillar of stone. It sent him flying through the air, perhaps a dozen feet above the ground. The world spun around him until he landed flat on his back on the grass, the impact knocking the breath from his lungs.

He heard shouting and raised his head high enough to see that the other students and teachers were almost here. He tried to shout to let them know that the chimera was dangerous, but the impact of the fall must have been worse than he thought, because his words came out gargled and distorted.

One of the teachers—a stout, elderly man with spectacles named Noharf Ximin—was in the lead. He drew his wand from the folds of his robes and aimed it at the chimera, but the chimera let out an ear-splitting roar that forced Darek to slam his hands over his ears to avoid losing his hearing entirely.

When the chimera ceased roaring, Darek removed his hands from his ears. His hearing still worked, although when he looked at the students and teachers who had been coming to help, he was puzzled to see them standing just outside of the circle of grass that made up the courtyard.

Many of them were striking some kind of invisible barrier with magical blasts, while a handful had ditched their magic for their feet and fists.

It took Darek a moment to realize what he was looking at. Somehow, the chimera's roar had created an invisible barrier that kept out all of the other students and teachers except for himself. Even Aorja, Kuroshio, and Auratus were on the outside. He saw them doing their best to attack the barrier, but it was clearly no use whatsoever.

Getting to his feet, Darek looked at the chimera, which, unless he was mistaken, appeared more than a bit pleased with its brilliant plan to isolate him from the rest of his friends, fellow students, and teachers. He saw its shiny white teeth reflecting in the sunlight and knew immediately that he was screwed.

Darek's shoulders slumped as the realization hit him. He could still use magic, but using his hands to channel his magic was always a risky move, largely because of the damage it could deal to them. That was another reason why human mages used wands. It was the best way to protect their hands or other parts of their bodies from the negative aftereffects of the spells they used on a daily basis.

Right now, Darek's hands looked fine, although they felt terribly cold and there was a slight bluish tinge to them that did not look natural. Still, as he was on his own, there was no way he could run away and let someone else deal with the chimera. He'd have to deal with it on his own, at least until one of the others figured out how to break down that barrier.

The chimera and Darek began circling each other, neither one taking his attention off the other. The chimera was clearly looking for an opening, just like Darek was, but Darek was not going to let it find one. He would have to distract it until one of the others could find a weakness in the barrier, as he doubted he could defeat it without his wand.

Panting, the sweat running down the side of his head making him feel hotter than he was, Darek tried to figure out the best spell he could use that would damage his hands the least. Pagomancy was his specialty, but it was pretty clear that if he used it more often, he would end up freezing his hands. Therefore, he needed something else.

Unfortunately, he had little time to think about what else he could do, because the chimera teleported again. His senses went into overdrive as he searched for the chimera, but then he realized that it was using the same strategy as before.

Therefore, he whirled around just in time to see the chimera reappear behind him. Without even thinking, Darek slammed both of his fists into the chimera's thick, barrel-like chest. The blow itself did little against the chimera's body, as Darek was not much of a bodybuilder and the chimera's body was like a boulder.

Instead, Darek channeled as much magic as he could through his hands into the chimera's body. He knew he probably shouldn't have, but he focused on his pagomancy, sending cold waves of ice through the chimera's body. He didn't even think about it, just kept channeling more and more ice cold energy as fast as he could.

The chimera must have been shocked that Darek had predicted its strategy because it stood there for a moment as the ice spread across its whole form. When it finally seemed to realize what was happening, it let out a roar of anger, but that roar was soon cut off when the ice formed around its head, completely cutting off its air supply.

Yet even after the ice consumed its head, Darek made it thicker and thicker, remembering how easily it had broken out of the ice block he had encased it in a few minutes ago. This in spite of the fact that his hands were now screaming with pain from the sheer coldness of the ice. He knew he should stop soon, but he was so determined to make sure the monster was actually dead that he didn't let up for at least another thirty seconds.

By the time he was certain that the chimera was no longer a threat, the ice was so thick that the chimera itself was barely visible underneath it. Removing his hands from its chest, Darek took a step back, panting, feeling his magical energy levels at perhaps half their normal levels, if even that.

Then he looked down at his hands and wished he hadn't. His hands were a solid blue, almost as blue as the ocean itself. He couldn't even feel them, although he had no idea if the damage was permanent or if it was temporary. Nor could he move his fingers, which looked more like frozen sausages now than the digits of a human hand.

The air where the barrier had formed shimmered, and the next moment, it was gone. Darek realized that the chimera must have been consciously maintaining the barrier, which meant that if the barrier was gone, then the chimera was well and truly dead.

Yet Darek didn't shout in joy or celebrate his victory. Using up so much power so quickly, in addition to his frozen hands, had worn him out and he could barely stand upright, much less jump for joy at his victory.

He closed his eyes as he fell backwards, his mind fading into unconsciousness well before he hit the grass.

Chapter Six

More dust fell from the ceiling, although Durima noticed that the tremors seemed to be getting rarer and rarer. Either the mages were having success in stopping whatever was causing the tremors or the tremors had been a prelude for something worse.

Either way, Durima thought as she rested her chin in her oversized hands, *Gujak and I are still stuck down here. Stuck like rats in a box.*

When the Magical Superior, Yorak, and Junaz left, Durima had made another fresh attempt to break out. She had tried to bash in the bars with a fist made of rock she had summoned from the ground, but the bars must have been crafted by Grinf, the God of Metal, himself, because they withstood the blow quite easily. And like before, they had bent themselves back into shape. Durima wished she knew what kind of magic the mages used to make such sturdy bars because she believed that the gods should ban its use by the mortals.

That was why Durima had resorted to sitting in her cell, thinking about other escape methods she hadn't tried yet. Gujak had been strangely quiet the entire time, probably because he was convinced that this whole mission was a lost cause. Perhaps he was too busy thinking about what Master would do to them if he found out that they had failed their mission.

He's not going to be happy, Durima decided. *Maybe we're actually safer in these cells than we would be outside, where Master can get us.*

It was an absurd thought, but it had some merit to it, which made their imprisonment seem a little less grim. Still, it was almost impossible not to think about the ways in which Master would punish them for their failure once they escaped, although she did her best to avoid thinking about them anyway.

That was when Durima heard something slithering through the darkness. It sounded huge, much larger than the average snake, and for a moment Durima was worried that the mortal mages had a pet snake that would eat them.

Then she felt that presence. The temperature in the catacombs dropped like a rock. She shivered and heard Gujak do the same. The presence grew larger and larger the closer the slithering sound became. And she knew exactly who was slithering around nearby and that it was no pet of the mages, although it was definitely someone's pet.

It could only be one creature: Uron, the large teleporter snake that was the pet and servant of Master.

That thought should, perhaps, have made her happy, instead of terrified. After all, Uron was on their side. Although the snake had only been working for Master for two months, it had already proven itself a good ally, although not so much a good friend. No doubt Uron would save them from their cells. Still, the snake had always made

Durima uneasy and she didn't look forward to seeing it again, no matter what it was here to do.

If Uron was indeed present—and he was, there was no mistaking that powerful, overwhelming presence that reminded Durima of the gods themselves—then he was probably here to save her and Gujak. Which meant that Master already knew about their failure, which most likely meant that Master was going to punish them dearly when they returned to his domain.

Actually, as Durima listened to Uron's slithering, she was surprised that Uron had come at all. The snake rarely left Master's side. Most of the time, Uron stayed curled up next to Master, like a grotesque dog. Why Master seemed so attached to the snake, and for that matter, where Uron had even come from in the first place, Durima didn't know. She just knew that Uron showed up one day about two months ago and Master had never bothered to explain where he had come from or why he was now Master's pet.

That's because Master would probably not be very happy if we asked, Durima thought. She distinctly remembered Master, on the first day he had Uron, making it clear that asking about Uron was off-limits, but again, he had not explained why, and probably never would.

Her thoughts were interrupted by the sound of the cell door's lock snapping. She heard the door swing open in the darkness and then heard Uron's huge body enter into her cell. With him came that oddly powerful presence, a presence which felt like a dozen gods put together.

That was another thing she didn't understand about the

snake. The most that Master had offered by way of explanation about Uron was that the snake was an unusually large teleporter snake, but he had not explained why Uron's presence was so overwhelming. Animals, even magical animals, rarely gave off as powerful a presence as this.

As Uron slithered around her, hissing, Durima had at one point speculated that Uron was actually a god in disguise. But something about that theory seemed unlikely to her, probably because, while the gods were known to sometimes trick each other for revenge against some slight committed against them in the past, this seemed too elaborate for a god to try to pull off. Besides, with the banishment of Hollech, the God of Deception, Thieves, and Horses, thirty years ago, she couldn't think of any other god who would go to such great lengths to trick Master like this.

She heard Uron stop. Based on what her senses told her, the snake was right in front of her, staring at her. Most likely it was waiting for her to respond, to say something. It was probably magically-linked with Master, now that she thought about it, which would allow the Ghostly God to see and hear whatever Uron saw and heard.

So Durima said, "Thank you for rescuing me, Uron. Have you let Gujak out of his cell yet?"

It let out a low hissing sound that might have been a confirmation or a denial. It was hard to tell with snakes, but especially Uron, who due to its purplish-black skin was practically invisible in the darkness. Considering Gujak was not jumping around shouting in joy, she had to assume that he hadn't been freed yet.

"I suppose I should get up and go, then," said Durima as she stood up as much as she could in her tiny cell, "before the mages stop whatever it is that distracted them in the first place and come back to interrogate us."

Uron did not answer, mostly because it couldn't speak at all. She heard it slither out of her cell immediately and a second later, heard the sound of the lock on Gujak's door being snapped apart. After that, she heard the sound of Gujak's door opening and heard Gujak himself shriek in terror, as if he had been sleeping the entire time.

That explains why he didn't say anything when I was talking to Uron, Durima thought, shaking her head. *What an idiot.*

"Durima?" came Gujak's slightly trembling voice. "Did you know that Uron is here?"

"Yes," said Durima as she stepped out of her cell and stretched her limbs. "He broke me out of my cell first, actually, so I knew about him before you did."

"Oh," said Gujak. "Did Uron give you a message from Master? Because he gave me a folded up paper before he left."

Durima frowned. "A paper? And he left? I didn't even hear him go."

"I know, but he's definitely gone," said Gujak. "I don't know where he went, but I'm guessing he returned to Master. Maybe he only had two things to do and he did them."

"I just don't know about that snake sometimes," said

Durima, shaking her head. "Anyway, what does that paper say?"

"I don't know," said Gujak. "It's too dark. Let me shine some light on it."

A moment later, a pale blue light began shining from inside Gujak's cell. The light was not very strong or bright; however, it was more than enough for Durima to notice that Uron was indeed missing. She did not know if that was a good thing, but she supposed Uron probably had orders from Master to return to him once it had freed them.

Would have been nice for Uron to stay and actually help us, Durima thought, frowning. *But then again, he is Master's special pet and special pets can't be allowed to get themselves hurt doing Master's dirty work, now can they?*

She walked over to Gujak's cage and saw that he was already reading the note. It was a small piece of paper, barely bigger than Gujak's hands. He was reading it by the light glowing from one of his hands, but he didn't seem at all happy about it. His eyes grew wider and wider the more he read, until he was practically trembling in fear, so much so that Durima wondered if he was actually still reading the note itself or if his fear had temporarily shut down his ability to read.

"What does the letter say?" said Durima. "And be quick about it. I don't feel the tremors anymore, which means that the mages have probably dealt with whatever was causing them. Which means it won't be long before they send someone to check up on us."

Gujak looked up at Durima and held out the note to her.

"Read it. Now."

"Read it?" said Durima. "I don't have time to read a note, even one from Master. Weren't you just listening? You can just tell me what it says."

"You need to read it yourself," said Gujak. "I don't want to repeat it aloud. Never know what kind of tricks those mages have that might enable them to listen to us."

Durima let out a drawn-out sigh before cutting it short and grabbing the note. She held the paper under Gujak's light and squinted.

Written in an elegant, easy-to-read script that Durima recognized as Master's handwriting, the note, which was only a paragraph long, read thus:

Do not think that Uron's rescue of you is an indicator that I have forgiven you. When you return from your mission, even if it's successful, I will punish you dearly for your failure. Now burn this note to prevent it from falling into the hands of our enemies.

There was no signature, but there was no need. Durima closed her fist around the note and heated up her hand with some pyromancy she had learned a long time ago. When she felt the paper turn into ashes in her hand, she opened her fist and dropped the ashes onto the floor.

"So he gave us a note only to threaten us with punishment if we fail?" said Durima. "That seems like something he could have told us when we got back."

"He's trying to motivate us," said Gujak, who was trembling in fear. "He wants us to get the mission done now. We must have wasted a ton of time down here being captured."

"Then what are we standing around here waiting for?" said Durima, throwing up her hands. "I certainly don't want to waste even more time down here talking about how Master is angry at us for wasting time."

Durima turned and began walking down the catacombs in the direction that she had seen those three mages walk when they left earlier. Gujak followed, his hand still glowing and illuminating their path, but despite the fact that they were in a hurry, he still seemed to want to talk.

"This must be a very serious mission if Master sent Uron and a note threatening us to complete it," said Gujak. "I thought for sure he was going to demand that we abort the mission and return to his island, but I guess not."

"Why would he ever do that?" said Durima without looking over her shoulder at Gujak. "I can't even remember the last time he called me in from a mission that he wanted me to complete."

"I wonder what's so important about this Braim Kotogs mortal that he threatened to punish us dearly if we failed," said Gujak.

"No idea," said Durima. "Don't really care. Don't have time to care."

It took less time than Durima expected for her and Gujak to get out of the catacombs. She had thought that it would take them hours, but as it turned out, the path out of the catacombs was incredibly straight forward. There wasn't even a locked door to deal with at the end of the path. The catacombs simply opened onto the area behind some of the school's buildings, although as Durima was unfamiliar with North Academy's layout, she was unsure exactly where they were.

Thankfully, North Academy's general layout was easy to navigate. She remembered that the graveyard was just to the north of the Arcanium, and due to the Arcanium's large size, the main building was easy to spot even from their current position.

Yet despite seeing it, Durima and Gujak hesitated. They did not see any of the mages from the school; however, just because they couldn't see them didn't mean that they weren't around. If any of the mages saw Durima or Gujak walking around in broad daylight, that would undoubtedly end with Durima and Gujak back in the catacombs.

So Durima and Gujak moved toward the Arcanium bent double over and doing their best to remain quiet. Thankfully, they did not run into any mages on their way to the graveyard, although they did come across a couple of students behind the Arcanium who were doing things to each other that Durima had heard humans did to each other but which she had never actually seen before. Thankfully, the two students were too enamored with each other to notice Durima or Gujak, and based on the noises they were making, they were unlikely to be much of a threat to their mission for quite a while.

Besides that, the rest of the trip to the graveyard went smoothly, and in a few minutes, Durima and Gujak stood before the waist-high wall and gate that separated the graveyard from the rest of the school grounds. Dozens of large tombstones stood there, many of which were so old that the text carved into them had faded away completely, which made Durima wonder if she and Gujak would be able to identify Kotogs' grave at all.

"We're here," said Gujak, who was talking in a whisper, probably because he didn't want to draw unnecessary attention to themselves (despite the fact that they were alone). "Look at this. They have giant ice Walls and an automaton, plus a crazy mortal wearing a fox mask, to defend their school, but they only have a waist-high stone wall to protect the remains of their dead. They must not value their deceased very highly."

Durima stroked her chin. She did not sense any magical traps; in fact, in comparison to the other high magical levels that seemed to permeate the entire school, the graveyard felt quite ordinary. It was almost as if the mages had cut out a normal mortal graveyard from some town without any magic and plopped it right into their school without bothering to make it magical.

But it didn't make any sense to Durima. Why would these mages, who were clearly obsessed with making their school as ridiculously difficult to get into as possible, leave their graveyard undefended?

Gujak was reaching for the gate, which appeared to have nothing more than a simple metal lock to keep intruders out, but Durima did not have a good feeling about this graveyard at all. She grabbed his arm, causing Gujak to look at her in surprise.

"What's up?" said Gujak. "I was going to open the gate. Do you want us to get seen and captured by the mages again? You remember Master's note."

"Precisely because I remember Master's note that I know that opening this gate now would be a very bad and very dumb idea," said Durima. "Or has the potential to be. I don't sense any magical defenses protecting it, but that doesn't mean we're going to waltz in on an obvious trap."

"What if it's not a trap?" said Gujak. "Durima, you can be kind of paranoid sometimes, you know? Sometimes, things in life are just easy."

"Things in life are never easy," said Durima. "Especially things in life created by mages from one of the most prestigious schools in the entire mortal world. Let me search the area with my geomancy before we so much as touch anything."

Gujak sighed heavily. "Okay. Just be quick about it, all right?"

Durima nodded and crouched to the ground. She put her fists against the ground, which she thought was the most likely place for someone to place a nasty trap for anyone trying to get into the graveyard without the mages' permission.

Like she had done in the catacombs, Durima sent a burst of geomancy energy into the ground. At first, she sensed nothing except for rock and earth. Then it hit something thick and metal, something that clearly was not a natural part of the underground. She could not tell exactly what it was, but it was directly underneath the gate and it appeared likely to pop up out of the ground if Durima or Gujak tried to open the gate. She suspected that the ground under the gate was pressure sensitive and that if they walked on the ground beneath the gate, the trap would activate and do who-knows-what to them.

That by itself would have been enough to prove Durima's fears correct, but then she sensed something else, too. About a dozen long, thick metal columns or spears (it was hard to tell the shape and purpose of underground objects, even when she used her geomancy) were hidden within the walls of the graveyard itself. Springs were hidden under the columns/spears. Which meant that if she and Gujak tried to climb over the walls instead of the gate, they would be skewered like pigs.

And none of these traps are magical in the slightest, Durima thought. *Makes sense. No doubt most magical intruders wouldn't have even thought to check for non-magical traps and defenses when they failed to sense any magical ones. Clever little bastards.*

She did not sense anything else, so she stood up and said, "The gate is booby-trapped. So are the walls."

"What?" said Gujak. "But I didn't sense any magic."

"They're non-magical," said Durima. "Like Guardian. The mages are willing to use just about anything to keep their stuff safe, including non-magical traps and machines."

"Definitely," said Gujak. "So what do we do? Use our magic to destroy these traps?"

"Of course not," said Durima. "I have a feeling that they are rigged to alert the mages if someone tries to destroy them. Remember, right now the mages don't even know we've escaped and hopefully will not know for a while. If we're going to complete this mission without anymore unnecessary problems, then that means we need to figure out how to get into the graveyard without announcing our presence to everyone in the school."

Gujak's shoulders slumped. "Oh, come *on*."

"Stop whining and start thinking," said Durima. "Or do you want to be the one to explain to Master that the only reason we couldn't complete the mission was because we couldn't climb over a waist-high wall?"

"Good point," said Gujak. He then straightened up and smiled. "Wait a minute. I've got an idea about how we can get over that gate without tripping the alarms."

Durima groaned inwardly. Gujak's 'ideas' were often not very well thought out or even particularly clever, such as the time that he had tried to distract a raging herd of baba raga by throwing a stick at them. Nonetheless, every time they found themselves in a situation like this, Gujak was always ready to volunteer his ideas even if they were not wanted. As a matter of fact, Durima thought that sometimes Gujak volunteered his ideas precisely *because* they were unwanted, although she didn't think he was that stupid.

Then again, Nimiko always used to tell me not to underestimate the sheer stupidity of others, Durima thought. *That is rather interesting, coming from a god who's not known for his intelligence or cleverness, but I digress.*

She would have told Gujak off, but he looked so eager

and confident that she decided it wouldn't hurt to let him at least share his idea. Besides, Durima had always found a perverse pleasure in shooting down dumb ideas, so she figured she would get something out of this no matter if the idea turned out to be smart or dumb.

"All right," said Durima. "Shoot."

"Okay," said Gujak, putting his hands together excitedly. "But you know what? I think it would be better if I showed you what I plan to do. It's too complicated to explain and would waste too much time."

"What if it's a dumb idea?" said Durima.

"It's not," Gujak insisted. "I mean, when have I ever come up with a dumb idea?"

Durima gave him a hard look. "The Valley of Death."

Gujak scratched the back of his head. "Well, how was I supposed to know that the volcano there was still active? It *looked* dormant, didn't it?"

Durima sighed. "Okay. Fine. If it fails and we get captured *again*, I am going to ask Master if I can personally punish you."

"There will be no need to do that," said Gujak as he walked up to the front gate. "Stand back and watch the magic. If this plan works, it will be amazing."

Durima did indeed retreat, but not too far back because she wanted to be close enough to take advantage of Gujak's plan if it worked. She kept looking over her shoulder at the Arcanium, wondering when she would hear the mages discover that she and Gujak had escaped and what they would do about that.

As for Gujak, he stopped several feet from the gate; close enough to jump over it if he wanted, but not close enough to step on the pressure switch that would activate the trap. He then crouched down to the ground and began digging a hole in the dirt with his fingers.

"What are you doing?" said Durima. "Playing in the dirt? Is that your grand plan to get us into the graveyard without anyone noticing?"

"I'm not playing in the dirt," said Gujak, without looking over his shoulder at her. "This is all part of the plan. Just be patient. It will make sense very soon, I promise."

Durima was about to ask what he meant by 'very soon' when Gujak plucked off a twig from the side of his head. He dropped the twig into the hole and then covered it with dirt. After giving it one final pat, he stepped back several feet from the dirt and folded his arms behind his back. He stared at the spot that he had re-buried, looking at the patted down dirt as if he expected to learn the secrets of the gods just by staring at it.

"What are you doing now?" said Durima. "Is that your plan? Dig a hole, bury one of your twigs in it, and then stare at it for the gods-know-how-long? I know your ideas aren't exactly always the most brilliant, but this has to be the worst."

"Don't be so quick to judge," Gujak said. "Wait just another minute. It shouldn't be very long now."

"What shouldn't be very long now?" said Durima. "Gujak, you remember that I can't read your mind, right? I've never been very good at telemancy."

"I know," said Gujak. "But you don't need to read my mind because my plan is about to become very obvious to anyone with working eyes."

"That's still too vague for my tastes," said Durima. "Let's try one of *my* ideas inste—"

She was cut off by a rumbling in the earth, which came from the spot that Gujak had buried his twig. At first, it sounded like a volcano was about to erupt, but Durima dismissed that idea right off the bat. There weren't any volcanoes in the Great Berg, not even dormant ones, and if there were any, Durima doubted they would be underneath the school's graveyard.

Yet that didn't explain what was causing that rumbling sound . . at least, that didn't explain what was causing that rumbling sound until a tree popped out of the spot Gujak had dug up. It started off as a single, dirt-covered twig before rapidly growing until, in less than fifteen seconds, a full-grown tree—which towered over both Durima and Gujak—stood before them. And before Durima's startled eyes, the tree began bending over until it was leaning over the gate.

Durima could not help but stare at the tree, while Gujak walked over to it with a big smile on his face.

There's no way that can be an actual, life-sized tree, Durima thought. *It must be an illusion. It doesn't make any sense.*

"Like it?" said Gujak, turning around to look at Durima, the smile on his face growing wider. He gestured at the tree proudly. "If you're confused, all I did was pluck a twig off my body and force it to grow rapidly with a simple growth spell. I could have made it bigger, but I didn't want to attract unwanted attention from the mages, so I kept it as small as I could while making it big enough for both of us to climb."

Durima closed her mouth and shook her head. She stomped up to Gujak and said, "Do you even understand what you did? All it takes is for one—just one—mage to look out the window of the Arcanium or to come visit a deceased one at the graveyard and they'll alert every single mage in the school about the tree that isn't even supposed to be there. Did you even think about your actions or did you just go with the first idea that popped into your wooden brain?"

Gujak cringed under her criticism, but he seemed to have some backbone after all because he said, "I didn't mean to mess everything up. And anyway, it's too late to get rid of it now. I can't just magically make it go away. Either we use it to get into the graveyard now, when the mages don't know about it yet, or we let the mages discover it and discover us. Which choice sounds better to you?"

Durima let out a low growl. "The first."

"Then I don't see what you're so upset about," said Gujak as he began climbing the tree. "We'll find Braim Kotogs's grave and be out of the graveyard in less than ten minutes, I bet."

Durima waited until Gujak had reached the end of the topmost branches and jumped off. He landed on the ground on the other side of the gate, dusting his legs off as he turned to face Durima.

"Come on," he said, gesturing at her to follow. "We don't have all day. There's no time to lose, especially not when Master is expecting us back as soon as possible."

Durima shook her head and grumbled about the stupidity of Gujak's plans, but she nonetheless began climbing the tree anyway. She dug her thick claws into the base of the tree and in a few seconds reached the middle of the tree.

The leaves were itchy against her skin, although the itchiness was lessened by her fur. The uppermost branches did not seem as thick or strong as the lower ones; indeed, when Durima tried to put most of her weight on them, the branches shook a little bit more than she liked.

But Durima figured she could get on them and jump off very quickly if she had to. So she climbed onto the upper branches, steadying herself to keep herself from falling onto the gate below, and then stood up as much as she could. The branches swayed under her weight, but as they did not sway very much, she figured that she was going to be okay.

And then, without warning, the branches snapped under her feet. Taken by surprise, Durima fell straight down. She fell for only a brief period before landing on her back on the graveyard's gate with a loud *crunch,* the fall sending a burst of pain through her back that made her want to scream. The gate crumpled underneath her weight like paper, but that didn't mean it didn't hurt to fall on it like that.

Before she could stand up, however, she heard something moving underneath her, something large, and the next moment the earth exploded around her. Clods of dirt flew through the air, forcing her to cover her face with her hands to avoid getting the dirt in her eyes. The screeching hinges of something metal burst in her ears, followed by the sound of two metal things slamming together and locking in unison. Gujak was shouting in surprise.

All of this happened in perhaps ten seconds, if even that. In no time at all, everything went quiet again and no more earth went flying through the air, so Durima lowered her massive fists and looked around at her current situation.

The gate she had fallen on was broken. Her weight had somehow crushed it, even though the gate had looked solid before. She supposed that she was much heavier than she had thought, although at the moment that was the least of her problems.

The actual problem—aside from her aching back, which had taken the brunt of the fall—was the egg-shaped metal cage that had popped out of the dirt around her. It was covered in earth, making it looking as old and ancient as the underground ruins on World's End, although despite its appearance, Durima doubted it would be easy to break out of.

On the other side of the cage, Gujak was dancing around anxiously, looking at Durima's predicament with big worried eyes and an even more worried-looking frown.

"Oh no," said Gujak. "Oh no, oh no, oh no. This is *not* good. This is *not* good at all."

For once, Durima agreed with Gujak. And for once, she was pretty certain that their mission was going to be a complete and utter failure. And she did not like that at all.

Chapter Seven

"**M**agical Superior, this is the last straw," said Yorak, standing in front of him, her arms crossed over her chest. "I cannot stand by idly while things like this happen to your students, not after you promised me that my students would be safe here."

The Magical Superior didn't cringe under Yorak's harsh tone. He didn't even really look at her. He was instead watching as some of the teachers moved the frozen chimera away from the courtyard, taking it to the catacombs, where it would be kept until they decided what to do with it. Almost all of the students had gathered by now to see what all of the excitement was about, but it would not be long before they had to return to their classes. The Institute students all stood together nearby, listening to the one named Kuroshio as he explained in Aqua what happened.

"Are you even listening to me?" said Yorak. "One of your students almost got himself killed trying to fight a chimera. Don't you even care?"

He knew all about that, of course. The Magical Superior, Yorak, and Junaz had arrived at the courtyard just as Darek Takren had fallen unconscious. Darek's hands had been colder than a cold winter's night in the Great Berg, which had caused the Superior to order Aorja and Junaz to move him into the medical wing right away. At the moment, Eyurna was likely healing him, although he had not heard from her in a while, so he did not know what Darek's current health was like.

"Yes, Yorak, I am listening to you," said the Magical Superior, turning to face her. "I was just thinking about Darek, actually."

Yorak looked skeptical about that claim, but she did not question it, most likely because she knew the Magical Superior well enough to tell when he was lying and when he was telling the truth. "Well, at least that's one thing that's working the way it is supposed to around here. But it doesn't make this school any safer for me or my students."

"I am sorry to hear that," said the Magical Superior. "This attack took me by surprise as much as it did you. I suspect that this attack must be connected to the two katabans prisoners we were speaking with earlier."

"Of course it is," said Yorak. "And it's clear that their 'Master' will stop at nothing to complete whatever his plan is. You know, I think it would just be better if I took my students, returned to the Institute, and let this 'Master' fellow do what he wants."

"But you haven't even been here a day," said the Magical Superior. "Your students and my students have not gotten to know each other very well. Besides, none of your students have been targeted yet, if you haven't noticed."

"Yes, I have," said Yorak, her hands balling into fists. "But who is to say that they won't be targeted next? There's no guarantee that they won't. If you can't even protect your own students, how do I know you will be able to protect mine?"

The Magical Superior leaned on his staff. "Because I promise to keep them safe. That's why."

"Your promises are beginning to mean littler and littler to me every hour," said Yorak. "You said North Academy was safe. I used to believe that myself for years. But now ... now, I am not so sure that my students or I should be involved in this."

The Magical Superior bit his lower lip, thinking about what to say to that. Her words were far more rational than he liked to admit, but he had been so looking forward to fixing the rift that had grown between him and Yorak over the years. He had hoped that inviting her and her students to his school might be the first step in that direction, but now it looked like it would only deepen the divide that existed between the two schools.

Maybe Nijok was right, the Magical Superior thought, thinking of something that his deceased younger brother had said to him years ago, well before he became the Magical Superior of North Academy. *Maybe my actions will never match my intentions.*

But he rejected that thought outright. He was not going to let Nijok's words burrow into his brain and control him. Nijok was long dead. The Superior had other things to worry about, things far more important than what his former brother had once said to him offhandedly so many years ago.

Returning to the present, the Magical Superior said to

Yorak, "If you want to leave, you can. But I think you may be making a mistake. I am going to find out what is going on here and I will fix the problem and make the school safe once again."

"Another one of your promises," said Yorak with a bitter chuckle. "How many more are you going to make before one of my students—or one of your students—actually dies?"

The Magical Superior had no answer to that. He just said, "I will do my best, as I always have, and that will have to suffice."

"Your best has so far resulted in the destruction of one of your dorms and the near-fatal injuries of two of your students," said Yorak. "But what am I doing here, berating you for problems you've always had? I'm going to gather up all of my students and take them home. This chimera attack was the last straw."

Yorak looked at Auratus. Her pupil, as always, had been completely silent during the entire discussion, but as soon as Yorak looked at her, Auratus stood ramrod straight. She looked more like a soldier than a mage, which was appropriate, the Magical Superior thought, because Yorak had been a commander in the East Yudran army prior to becoming the head of the Undersea Institute.

"Auratus, get the other students and tell them that we will be leaving within the hour," said Yorak. "Tell them to gather at the *Soaring Sea* and that we'll leave as soon as everyone is on board. Do you understand?"

Auratus nodded.

"Then go," said Yorak, gesturing in the direction of the

Institute students who were still listening to Kuroshio's story. "And make sure that *everyone* is ready to go. I want no dilly-dallying, no unnecessary delays. Understood?"

Once again, Auratus nodded. Then she left, running toward the group of Institute students with more grace than the average aquarian showed on land. The Magical Superior almost called her back, but he restrained himself. Even if he did call her, she would not have listened. Auratus listened only to Yorak, her master and teacher.

"I need to tell the pilot to get the engine running," said Yorak, turning in the direction of the sports field, where their airship was still landed. "He's still on the ship, if I'm not mistaken, and no doubt wondering what is going on here and what we are going to do next."

The Magical Superior held out a hand. "But Yorak, could you please reconsider? I want both of our schools to get to know each other better. Isn't that better than remaining separate, as we have for so many years?"

He did not expect her to listen to that, but much to his surprise, Yorak did look a little hesitant, as if she was second-guessing herself. Of course, the Magical Superior was one of the few mortals who could ever pierce her confidence like that, although he did not push the point, knowing as he did that Yorak did not appreciate that kind of pushing.

Yorak's small whale eyes closed for a moment before she opened them again. This time, she looked as firm as she always did, the way she did the first day the Magical Superior had met her so many decades ago.

"I, too, would like for our schools to get closer," Yorak admitted. "But I am not willing to risk the wrath of the gods —and the lives of my students—by getting in the way of some god's strange plan. I have a feeling that, whoever this god is, he will not hesitate to snuff us out if we prove a threat to him."

"Not unless I can find out who he is and what he is up to before he succeeds in it," said the Magical Superior. "I know how you feel about getting in the way of the gods, but I believe it is of utmost importance that you stay. We might need your help."

"Help with what?" said Yorak. She gestured at the Arcanium. "Help with getting your students in the medical wing? Help with angering the gods? I suppose you must be getting senile, Chen, because you don't seem to remember Auratus."

The Magical Superior had not heard his full name uttered by anyone in years. Even his deceased younger brother, Nijok, had not called him Chen Wirm when they had met for the very last time thirty years ago. He blinked once or twice, wondering if he had misheard, but when Yorak did not correct herself, his shoulders slumped.

"Yorak, you know I don't go by that name anymore," said the Magical Superior. "I am the Magical Superior of North Academy. I abandoned that name long ago, after I devoted my life fully and completely to the service of the gods."

"Maybe so," said Yorak. "But I still think of you as Chen Wirm. Besides, if you had truly devoted yourself to the gods, you would do as I am doing and get out of this god's way."

Before the Magical Superior could respond, Jenur Takren appeared, like she had teleported, in front of him and Yorak. She looked harried, with her curly dark hair smelling like smoke and soot. Her robes were stained with ash, which told the Magical Superior that she must have just gotten back from the ruins of the Third Dorm.

Panting, her hands on her knees, Jenur took a moment to catch her breath before she looked up at the Magical Superior and asked, "Darek. I was told Darek is hurt. Where is Darek?"

She must have heard about his battle with the chimera, the Magical Superior thought, but aloud, he said, "In the medical wing of the Arcanium, where Eyurna is looking after him."

Jenur let out a powerful sigh of relief. "Oh, that's good. I thought he might be … but never mind. I am going to go see him now."

"I hope your son recovers," said Yorak, who looked a little annoyed at how Jenur had ignored her. "What he did was foolish yet brave. Let him know I am thankful that he stopped the chimera before it caused more trouble or harmed any of my students."

"Why?" said Jenur. "Can't you tell him yourself? It's not like he's going anywhere."

"I will be leaving soon," said Yorak. "I and all of my students. We're going back to the Institute. Today, most likely within the next hour."

Jenur stood up, a look of confusion on her face. "But … why?"

"Because this school is dangerous," said Yorak. "First, one of your dormitories blows up, leading to the injury of one student. Then two katabans destroy your Guardian machine. And then this chimera attacks and almost succeeds in killing another student."

"None of that is our fault, though," said Jenur. "It's ... well, I don't know whose fault it is, but it's not ours. Why not stick around a little while longer until we get this all figured out?"

"I already had this discussion with the Superior," said Yorak, gesturing at him. "I already made my points to him and I do not wish to rehash them for an arrogant, disrespectful teacher like you."

"Arrogant? Disrespectful?" said Jenur, her eyes widening in anger.

"Jenur, please calm down," said the Magical Superior, holding up one hand. "Yorak is very stressed out at the moment, as we all are. She did not mean to insult you."

"I only spoke the truth," said Yorak. She spread her arms, as if to encompass the whole school. "And the truth is, North Academy is right in the middle of something far worse and far deeper than I care to find out about. And even worse, this situation may result in the deaths of my own students if we stay here but a moment longer than we have to."

Jenur opened her mouth, most likely to make the same arguments that the Magical Superior had already made. The Superior did not want her to waste her time, however, or to anger Yorak further, as he did not want to destroy all ties between North Academy and the Undersea Institute.

So he said, "Jenur, I see you must have just returned from the ruins of the Third Dorm. How is the investigation going?"

Jenur turned her attention to the Superior as she dusted some ash out of her hair. "About as well as you'd expect. So far, we haven't found any clues as to the identity of the attacker ... well, except for this."

Jenur pulled something small and round from out of her robes' pocket. She held out her hand toward the Magical Superior and opened it. The Superior leaned forward to get a better look at the clue. He heard Yorak leaning forward, too, but he did not look at her because his eyes were focused entirely on the object in Jenur's hand.

Lying in the palm of her hand was a stone that was blackened on one side, but blood red on the other. It was perfectly round, like the beads crafted by the Divine Carvers, but the Magical Superior at first did not know what it was.

"It's a blood tear," said Jenur, though neither the Superior nor Yorak had asked. "A magical item that's usually associated with Mica, the Goddess of Stone and Ink. It was found in the wreckage of Darek and Jiku's room, hidden under the remains of their bunk bed."

"What is so impressive about this?" said Yorak. "Do either of them own blood tears?"

"That's the thing," said Jenur. "Neither Darek nor Jiku have ever owned a blood tear. We think it was left by the attacker."

Pulling back, Yorak said, "Surely you must know which one of your students owns a blood tear, shouldn't you? After all, this is your school, isn't it, Superior?"

The Magical Superior also pulled back. He stroked his chin, deep in thought. "I do not keep track of every little physical possession that my students own or bring with them from the outside world. It could belong to one of the Micans, but that's unlikely because all of the Mican students were gathered to greet the Institute mages earlier."

"So the only clue you have to the identity of the attacker, and it is completely useless," said Yorak. She rubbed her large nose. "That's it. If even the only clue we have is useless, then that must be a sign from the gods that I and my students must go."

Yorak walked past the Magical Superior, brushing against him roughly. He did not turn to watch her go, because he was still looking at the blood tear, trying to think of who could be its owner. He heard Jenur make a noise of disgust at Yorak's leaving, but that was all she did.

Blood tears are very rare, the Magical Superior thought. *Whoever dropped theirs must have been in a hurry. They had somewhere they needed to be, somewhere they could not afford to be late to. Otherwise, the suspicions of every person in the school would fall on their shoulders, thus ruining their schemes.*

Although the Magical Superior had one of the most brilliant minds in the world—there was no point in being modest about it, it was a fact that had been confirmed again and again in his lifetime—this mystery stumped it as easily as if it were one of the dumbest.

And then, without warning, an explosion erupted behind him. Whirling around, the Magical Superior saw Yorak standing there, frozen in fear and shock, staring up at the massive pillar of fire shooting into the air hundreds of feet away from them, the flames showing over the top of the First Dorm.

It took the Magical Superior's brilliant mind another moment to realize that the explosion was coming from the sports field. In the exact spot where the *Soaring Sea* had landed.

Chapter Eight

Darek's dreams were strange, to say the least, although he supposed that dreams were always strange. Still, these dreams were even stranger than normal. Whereas in most dreams he was not aware that he was in a dream, in this one, he was. That may very well have been the strangest part of this whole affair.

He was standing in the Arcanium's lobby, looking up at the Wall of Mastery, a wall that was normally covered with gold-framed pictures of the greatest students to graduate from the school. In real life, the Wall of Mastery normally held paintings of hundreds of past students, all of which looked as new as the day they had been painted. This in spite of the fact that many of those paintings had been painted centuries ago, although it made more sense when you considered that the paintings had been made using a special type of paint that did not age.

But today, the Wall of Mastery was completely black, with no sign of the paintings to be seen. It was an inky, purplish, ugly black, like the skin of a snake. Not only that, but it moved and groaned, like it was a living thing. Morbid curiosity compelled him to touch it and find out what it would do, but Darek's deeper instincts told him to stay as far away from the strange, seemingly organic wall as he possibly could.

Because Darek was not the adventurous type, he decided to stand at a distance and look at it. He had no idea what he was looking at, in all honesty, but as long as it didn't try to attack him, he knew he would be okay.

Besides, Darek thought, *this is just a dream. Even if it was hostile, who cares? I'll be fine either way.*

I wouldn't be so confident in yourself, young mortal.

Darek froze. Unless his ears were playing tricks on him—always a possibility in his dreams—that voice had sounded like it was coming directly from the 'wall' in front of him, like the 'wall' had spoken.

That's ridiculous, even for a dream, Darek thought, shaking his head. *I am alone here in the Arcanium's lobby. I must be going crazy.*

Then the voice spoke again, immediately wiping away all of Darek's lingering doubts about its true origin. *Alone? I would question the usefulness of such a concept. No one is ever truly alone, even at the end of the world. We are always surrounded by someone or something, even if that someone or something refuses to acknowledge us or share its presence with us. You are not alone, Darek Takren, adopted son of Jenur Takren.*

Darek felt his heart beat increase. *What are you talking about? Who are you? Why are you in my dreams?*

A wave of anger crashed over Darek, like the waves of the ocean. Only, it was not his anger, but someone else's.

Who am I? the voice said. *You ask who I am? I should not be here. You should not be here. We should not even be talking. By becoming aware of my existence, you are jeopardizing my entire plan, the plan that will restore the world to the way it once was.*

I didn't come looking for you, whoever you are, Darek said, feeling somewhat annoyed. *Actually, I was hoping for a dream-less sleep. I nearly froze my hands off earlier, you know.*

I am quite aware of what you did, Darek Takren, said the voice, which was now clearly coming from the wall. *It was I, after all, who had sent the chimera. I did not think it would do much good, and I was correct, but it lasted long enough to allow my servants to escape. That's all I really wanted in the end.*

So you're the one behind the chimera, Darek said. *Are you also behind the explosion at the Third Dorm? Just who are you, anyway?*

A superior being like myself does not need to answer such silly questions like that, the voice said. *I am trying to figure out how we even managed to cross paths like this. Far more importantly, I am trying to figure out how to break this connection between us.*

No, Darek said, pointing at the wall. *You're going to tell me who you are and what you are trying to do. Otherwise, I'll—*

You'll what? the voice jeered. *This is a dream, after all. Even if it wasn't, you are still far beneath me in terms of sheer power. The power I command is the kind that your kind only ever dreams of. I am the first, the one who existed before all of this infernal, ugly creation. You are an* ant *whose life will be snuffed out shortly if you continue to get in my way like this.*

The one who existed before creation? Darek repeated. *Are you some kind of god? Or maybe one of the Powers?*

Nice try, the voice said with a sneer. *I am not going to let you know who I am. If—no, when—my plan succeeds, then all of the world, including you, will know who I am, will know and tremble before my might.*

Darek didn't like the sound of that one bit, so he decided to do something about it. Remembering his oneiromancy lessons with Noharf Ximin, Darek held out his hand and willed his old wand into existence. It popped into his hand like it had always been there and began to glow with suppressed energy as he held it out in front of the wall.

Your wand? said the voice, sounding not at all afraid of it. *Do you honestly believe that that little piece of wood will help you in the slightest? This is a dream, after all, and in dreams, you cannot actually hurt anyone.*

I know, said Darek. *I remember what Noharf always taught me. But I'm not going to hurt or even kill you. I'm going to expel you from my mind.*

You mean you don't want to know what I am going to do? the voice asked. *You aren't going to ask about my plans?*

You've already made it clear that you aren't going to tell me a thing, Darek replied. *Therefore, why waste my time talking to you when I could spend it waking up and finding out what's going on in the physical world?*

The voice seemed genuinely shocked by that, but it said,

You are pragmatic. I like that in individuals, even in inferior individuals like yourself.

A cold wind blew from the voice, making Darek shiver, even though it was just a dream. It was like standing bare naked in the Great Berg on a cold winter day, almost causing Darek to drop his wand.

But Darek managed to gather the strength necessary to keep holding his wand. He said to the voice, *I don't care what you like in people. The point is, I don't want you in my mind infecting my dreams anymore.*

Infecting? I am doing no such thing, said the voice. *I am still not even sure how we became tied like this. If I had to guess, I would say you must have fallen unconscious at the exact same time I was contacting one of my pawns. Perhaps it was the excess magical power you used that caused your mind to link with me, at least temporarily.*

That theory seemed reasonable to Darek. It was similar to something that Noharf had once taught him ages ago. Occasionally, it was possible for two mages who fell asleep at the same time to enter each other's dreams, especially if one or both of them were oneiromancers. It was an extremely rare phenomenon, not very well understood even by the best oneiromancers, but it was known to happen and when it did, it often linked the two mages for a long time, sometimes for life.

Because Darek did not want to be linked with this voice for life, he aimed his wand at the wall again, ignoring the cold wind that continued to blow from it. *Your theory might be correct, but I'm not going to stand around here and find out.*

With a practiced twist of his wrist, Darek fired a blast of fiery energy at the wall. It was a spell Noharf had taught him, which, if used correctly, would expel unwanted visitors from his dreams. Darek had used this spell only a couple of times before, during his classes and training sessions with Noharf, but he remembered the basics of it well enough to understand how to use it.

The blast of fiery energy slammed into the wall, causing the voice to scream in pain as the flames enveloped him. Of course, the voice was not actually being burned alive, but the spell was supposed to emulate that feeling in order to get the intruders out of one's dream.

The dream fire sparked and crackled, but it was silent in comparison to the voice's screams. Darek had to put his hands over his ears to save them from getting hurt, although it was mostly out of instinct he did it because he was in no danger of permanently losing his hearing in a dream.

And then, without warning, Darek awoke.

Gasping for breath, Darek did not understand where he was at first. He felt soft sheets, saw a bright yellow light reflecting off the white walls of the room he was in, and could barely feel his hands. His senses were completely disoriented, yet for some reason, he felt as cold as if he had been sitting outside in the snow all day.

It took him a few moments to gather his senses back into something halfway coherent. Even so, his memories of the dream—and the voice—were already rapidly fading, like memories of dreams always do whenever you awake, and he had no way to write them down so he could recall them later. Even if he did have a pen and paper on hand, his hands felt so uncooperative that he didn't think he'd be able to write for a long time.

When his senses finally began to work again, Darek looked down at his body. He was lying underneath a thick white blanket and he could feel a soft mattress underneath his body. He realized that he was lying down in one of the beds in the medical wing.

Why am I in the medical wing? Darek thought, looking up at the high ceiling directly above him. *How did I get in here? Why can't I remember?*

One thing Darek did remember—albeit vaguely, as the memory had taken place a while ago and he had not thought about it in a long time—was that dreams like that almost always left the memories of the dreamer muddled and confused. Noharf had taught him that even memories of what happened before the dream were often affected, although the damage was rarely permanent.

It will all come back to me, probably, Darek thought. *That's pretty usual for people who suffer from temporary amnesia like me. Any … minute … now.*

Right on cue, his memories of the battle against the chimera came roaring back. Because they all returned at once, they were muddled and confused, even more so than they had been previously. But in a minute, the memories coalesced into something coherent and they became easier to understand.

That's right, Darek thought. *The chimera attacked us out of nowhere. I took it on alone. The others tried to help, but somehow the chimera stopped them from doing so. What a strange, random thing to happen.*

With a jolt, he remembered his hands freezing themselves off and he pulled them out from under his blankets. His hands were still there, as whole as ever, but they were so cold that he could barely feel them. It reminded Darek of the time a potential student, a Carnagian boot maker who had been convinced that he was destined for greatness, had fallen through the ice of the Great Berg and drowned. When they had fished out his body just ten minutes later, it had been completely blue.

Now Darek's hands did not look quite as blue as the boot maker's body. He did not know how much time had passed since he had fallen unconscious, but it must have been quite some time because his hands were a lighter shade of blue than he remembered them looking at first. Nonetheless, he still couldn't feel them, although he could move the tips of his fingers slightly.

Then Darek heard someone start nearby and he looked to his left. Aorja was standing above Jiku's bed, looking startled. She held one of her hands behind her back, like she was hiding something, although Darek didn't focus too much on that.

"Darek?" said Aorja. A scowl flickered across her face briefly before being replaced by a smile. "Oh, Darek. I'm so glad to see you're getting better. How do your energy reserves feel?"

Darek closed his eyes and felt his energy levels. As soon as he did, his limbs became astonishingly weak, as if all of his muscles had turned into mush.

Opening his eyes again, Darek said, "I feel like all of my bones are gone. I just need to rest, I think, and let my body recover from the excessive amount of magic I used."

"Of course," said Aorja. "I honestly didn't expect you to wake up so soon. You looked like you were out for the count."

Darek shrugged. "I'm still not entirely well. I only woke up because I had the strangest dream, which I can't remember very well at the moment."

"Strange dreams do that sometimes," said Aorja, still smiling, although to Darek the smile didn't look very sincere. "But you do sound tired. I thought you were whispering at first, but I can see now that it's because you are still weak from your fight with the chimera."

Darek hadn't noticed any difference in his voice, but when he spoke again, he did notice how quietly he was speaking.

"The chimera," said Darek. "What happened to it?"

"Transported to the catacombs," said Aorja. "The biomancy students are going to dissect it to find out who created it. Kind of disgusting if you ask me, but hey, if it will help us figure out who is behind all of this stuff, then I guess it will be worth it."

The sincerity in her words matched the sincerity in her smile, which was to say, she sounded quite insincere. It was as if she was trying to hide her true feelings on the subject, although why she would, Darek didn't know.

And right now, he didn't need to know. He just needed to find out what else had happened since he had gone unconscious. Knowing how quickly things happened at this school, he bet he had missed quite a bit.

"How is everyone else?" said Darek. "Kuroshio and Auratus?"

"They're fine," said Aorja. "But Yorak is really pissed. She doesn't like how North Academy has become about as safe as Rock Isle, so she's taking her students and leaving as soon as they get a new airship."

"What?" said Darek. "A new airship? But doesn't their old one still work?"

"Someone blew it up," said Aorja. She spread her arms like she was pantomiming an explosion. "Big fiery column of death. The pilot of their ship was still in there when it happened, so as you can guess, he was completely vaporized."

"That's horrible," said Darek. "Do we know who did it?"

Aorja shrugged like it was no big deal. "Nope. The Institute mages are still investigating the wreckage, but to be completely honest, I don't think they'll find much in the way of evidence."

"Why wouldn't they?" said Darek. "Granted, I don't know how good they are at investigating explosions, but I think it would be hard for an attacker to cover his tracks with so many mages investigating his work."

"Because I think that whoever is behind these attacks is quite the clever little devil," said Aorja. "He's probably hiding among the students even as we speak, I reckon, keeping a low profile and doing his best to seem as frightened and scared and ignorant of what is happening as anyone else."

Aorja said this with an admiring tone of voice, although Darek didn't see any reason to admire such an obviously deranged person. Of course, Darek could have been misinterpreting her tone, seeing as he was still washed out from the fight with the chimera.

So Darek said, "The Third Dorm. How's the investigation for that going?"

"About as well as you'd expect," said Aorja. "Which is to say, they've had no luck in finding any clues as to the attacker's identity, last I heard. It's a shame, but like I said, I think this guy has to be pretty smart. After all, he's managed to hide his identity from the Magical Superior *and* Yorak, easily two of the smartest mages in the world. That's not easy."

Darek sank deeper into the pillow his head rested on, staring up at the ceiling. "You make a good point. Maybe this guy has already left. After all, everyone is on high alert now. Any suspicious behavior on his part is bound to be noticed by everyone, after all."

"Quite true," said Aorja, scratching her arm. "But I don't think he's run. I think he's still around here, probably keeping an eye on things in case he needs to cause another explosion somehow."

"If I were him, I'd definitely run," said Darek. "Not that I am him, obviously. I'm just saying that as a hypothetical."

"I understand," said Aorja. "I would never think of you as the attacker, Darek. I mean, you're smart and all, but not smart enough to fool both the Magical Superior and Yorak."

"Thanks a lot," Darek muttered. Then he said, in a louder voice, "How is Jiku doing? Has he awoken yet?"

"Not yet," said Aorja, shaking her head. "He's still resting from the attack on the Third Dorm. It's sad because I was really hoping to speak with him, but I guess I won't be able to do that until tomorrow at the earliest."

She sighed, but her sigh was more relieved than wistful. It was as if she was happy that Jiku was not yet awake, which made no sense to Darek at all.

"Well, you can talk with me instead," said Darek, giving her a weak smile. "But at least Jiku is going to be all right. He was in bad shape when I rescued him from the flames of the Third Dorm like that. I didn't think he'd recover at all, but I guess Yorak really is a great mage, huh?"

"Yep," said Aorja. "That's why they call her the Grand Magus, after all. It's not exactly a title the aquarian mages bestow upon any old mage."

"Yeah," said Darek. Then he looked around and frowned. "By the way, has Mom come by to see me yet?"

"Nope," said Aorja. "I think she's helping the Institute mages investigate the destruction of their airship, to be honest. You know how your mom gets. She seems to be attracted to explosions."

"Mom's helpful, that's what she is," said Darek. "She likes to help people, even people she doesn't know very well. It's what I've always admired in her."

"She's also a very strict teacher," said Aorja. "I mean, all of the teachers are strict, obviously, but Jenur really pushes us, doesn't she?"

Darek nodded. Mom had a reputation among the students for her no-nonsense attitude and intolerance towards laziness and irresponsibility. Even he wasn't immune from her sometimes harsh diatribes in which she would push him to his limits, and he was her son.

If anything, I think she's always treated me harsher than the others, Darek thought. *Probably to avoid being accused of favoritism, I bet.*

"Honestly, though, I think it's good we're both alone together here," said Aorja. "It's only been a couple of hours, but it feels like it's been days since you, me, and Jiku here were all together like this."

"Yeah," said Darek. "Hopefully we'll figure this out soon enough. Then maybe everything can go back to normal. Like how it was in the old days."

"Yep," said Aorja. "So, Darek, why don't you just go back to sleep? You really do need your rest. I can see it in the bags under your eyes. You look like a zombie."

Darek didn't have a mirror on hand to check that claim, but he was feeling tired and sleepy. The feeling in his hands was slowly returning, but he doubted it would completely return for a few more hours at least.

Nonetheless, his attention returned to Aorja's other arm, the one she was hiding behind her back. He tilted his head to the side and asked, "What have you got behind your back there? Your blood tear?'

Aorja laughed, although it was a hollow laugh. "Of course not. You know I never carry that with me anywhere. It's back in my room in the Third Dorm."

"Oh," said Darek. "Right. I keep forgetting that. I guess I just think that if I had a magical object like that, I would take it with me everywhere I go."

"It's not all that special," said Aorja. "Besides, I'm not much a geomancer, so it couldn't really help me even if I did carry it around."

"Okay, but that still doesn't explain what you have got behind your back," said Darek. "Is it a present for Jiku? Or for me?"

"Where would I get a present for either of you?" said Aorja. "It's not like there's a gift shop in the Arcanium's lobby or anything."

"I know," said Darek. "But I'm just curious because you've held your arm like that for a while now and I was wondering what it was."

"It's nothing," said Aorja. "Just go to sleep, Darek. You need it."

"Not until I find out what that is," said Darek, craning his neck in an attempt to look around her body. "Is it a new wand for me?"

Aorja turned her body to keep Darek from being able to look around at it. "No. It's just not something you need to see, okay?"

"But I want to see it," said Darek as he craned his neck even further. "You do realize that your hiding it only makes me want to see it more, don't you?"

"I know," said Aorja, still turning her body to block his view of whatever she was hiding. "It's just not anything you need to see. Is respecting my privacy really that difficult for you to do?"

"If that privacy is right in front of me and you keep trying to hide it, then yes, it is," said Darek. His neck started to hurt, so he stopped craning it. "Come on. You were going to give it to Jiku, weren't you? What were you going to show Jiku that you can't show me?"

"It's nothing," said Aorja. "It's not really a present or anything."

"If it's nothing, then it shouldn't hurt to show me what it is, right?" said Darek. "Come on. Just show it to me already."

Aorja was starting to look annoyed, even angry, but before she could respond again, Jiku moaned.

Both Aorja and Darek looked at Jiku. He was still lying in his bed in between them, but now he was beginning to stir. His eyes flickered several times before finally remaining open.

Darek could hardly believe his eyes. He watched with excitement as Jiku blinked several times and looked around with a dazed, confused look in his eyes.

"Jiku's awake," said Darek with a laugh. "Oh, Jiku, it's great to see you're doing well, old buddy. How—"

Darek's question was cut off when Jiku took one look at Aorja and pointed at her accusingly. "You! What are you doing—"

Moving faster than Darek had ever seen her move

before, Aorja whipped out her wand from behind her back and pointed it point blank at Jiku's face. Jiku immediately shut up, his eyes screwing up as he looked down Aorja's wand, which was softly glowing with suppressed power.

"What in the name of Skimif, the Northern Pantheon, and the Southern Pantheon is going on here?" said Darek, looking from Aorja to Jiku and back again. "Why are you two acting like mortal enemies? Aren't we all friends around here?"

Without taking his eyes off Aorja's wand, Jiku slowly shook his head. "I thought we were, but—"

"Shut up, old man," Aorja snarled, her voice losing even the fake kindness it had originally. "Or I will finish the job I started in the Third Dorm."

"Wait, what?" said Darek. His eyes widened as her words sank in like a stone. "Impossible. Aorja, *you* were the one who blew up the Third Dorm?"

"I guess there's no hiding it anymore," said Aorja with a sigh, although her wand never wavered from Jiku's face. "Yes, I, Aorja Kitano, created the explosive spell that almost completely destroyed the entire Third Dorm. It was *supposed* to kill Jiku, too, but then you just had to play the hero, didn't you, Darek?"

Darek opened his mouth, but no sound came from it. He felt like he had completely lost the ability to speak. Nothing Aorja said made any sense. It was like someone had revealed to him that Martir was perched on the back of a turtle and he wasn't sure whether they were joking or being dead serious.

126

"This was all supposed to work out how I planned it," Aorja said, her voice angry. "It was a simple plan, but you messed it up, Darek. Jiku also messed it up by acting like an idiot."

"Trying to stop you from killing everyone here is what you call acting like an idiot?" said Jiku, although his voice was weak. "That's an odd definition of the word."

"Aorja was planning to kill everyone?" said Darek. "But why?"

"Jiku's getting senile," said Aorja. "I'm not some kind of crazy mass murderer. I was simply trying to create a distraction."

"A distraction?" said Darek. "Who were you trying to distract? And why?"

Aorja shot such an annoyed look at Darek that he thought she was going to shoot daggers from her eyes. "Are you really that dense? I was trying to distract *you* and every other mage in this school. By blowing up one of the Dorms, I thought I would successfully distract you from what my allies were doing."

"Who are you allies?" Darek asked. "And who do you even work for? How long have you been this way?"

"My 'allies' are a couple of idiotic katabans who got captured anyway," said Aorja. "Sometimes I wonder about Master's choice of servants, I really do, whenever I think about those two stooges."

"Hold on," said Darek, raising his hands, which were still quite blue. "Back up. What is going on here? Why are you betraying us? Why did you try to kill Jiku? And who is this

'Master' you spoke of?"

"Well, considering neither of you are going to be alive for much longer, I suppose I can tell you a thing or two about me and my Master," said Aorja. "Not much, obviously, because it won't be long before the Magical Superior and everyone else figures out I did it. So I'll keep it short and to the point."

She grabbed the collar of her robes with her free hand and pulled it down. Darek grimaced when he saw the thick, scythe-shaped scar at the base of her neck. It looked old, like it had been there for a while, but Darek could not recall ever seeing that scar on her neck before.

"See this?" said Aorja, stroking the scar with one finger. "This is the symbol of the Ghostly God. It's a symbol he carves into the flesh of every servant who agrees to work for him. The scar symbolizes his power, the kind of power that he could use to utterly destroy us if he wanted to."

"It's an ugly scar," said Jiku, whose eyes were still focused on Aorja's wand. "Why would you ruin your skin with such an ugly thing?"

"Because the Ghostly God demanded it," said Aorja. "When I went to work for him, he carved it into my flesh. When you work for the Ghostly God, you generally work for him for life. And, if the rumors are true, beyond life."

"The Ghostly God," said Darek. "I don't think I've ever heard of him. Is he a southern god?"

Aorja nodded as she pulled her collar back up over her neck scar. "Of course. He lives in the southern seas, well away from human or aquarian civilization. He's not very active, preferring to rule his little island in solitude, but he's like the rest of the gods in that he always has some kind of plan going at some point or another, plans even I am not always aware of."

"Why would you ever work for a southern god?" said Jiku. "The southern gods like to eat mortals. I know all gods are worthy of respect and honor, but the southern gods rarely hesitate to kill mortals who cross their path."

For a moment, fear seemed to flash in Aorja's eyes, like she had seen something horrible.

But then she shook her head and said, "The Ghostly God doesn't like to eat human or aquarian flesh. He doesn't really eat at all. Besides, he likes having me here, acting as his spy, sending him information about the happenings in the north. It helps him plan more effectively."

"He'll eat you one of these days," Jiku warned. "When he decides that he no longer needs you, he will devour you whole."

"Shut up," Aorja snapped. "You don't know him. Besides, if he ever tries to pull a stunt like that, I can protect myself."

"That's a very arrogant thing to say," said Jiku, "considering you are just a student still in school and the Ghostly God is a deity who is thousands of years old."

"The point is, I serve him," said Aorja. "And it is a great job, albeit one where I have to be very careful about who I talk to and what I share with people."

Darek blinked. "But ... why? You still haven't explained why you work for the Ghostly God. What did he promise to give you in exchange for your service?"

"What he promised me is none of your business," Aorja said, although the abruptness with which she said that made Darek think he had hit a nerve. "All you need to know is that Master finally gave me orders to act. That's why I blew up the Third Dorm. Master is finally putting his plan into action, and to do so, he needs the mages here disoriented and distracted."

"You've certainly done a good job of that," said Jiku. "A little too good, to be honest. Your master must be proud."

"You shut up," said Aorja. "Or I will blow your face off. Actually, I should probably do that anyway. You know too much."

"I'm still confused," said Darek. "Jiku, what part do you play in all of this?"

"Nothing special," said Jiku. "Prior to the arrival of the Institute mages, I had returned to our room to grab something I forgot. When I arrived, I found Aorja casting some kind of spell. When she saw me, we briefly struggled before she knocked me out, though the explosion briefly awoke me."

"He was easy to subdue," said Aorja. "He still thought I was his friend. Made it easy for me to take him out before he even realized what hit him."

"I ..." Darek struggled to process everything Aorja had just said. "So you were never really our friend? You never really liked us?"

"At first, I did like you two," said Aorja. "I did consider you both good friends. I came to this school under the mistaken belief that it was my destiny to become a master mage, but then it got boring."

"Boring?" said Darek. "How can you call North Academy *boring*? Every day is an adventure here."

"Every day? Hardly," said Aorja. She gestured at the ceiling. "Every damn day, it's the same old grind. We wake up, the teachers put us through all kinds of 'tests' to teach some some obscure, useless spell or aspect of magic, have meals at predetermined times of day (always the same awful food), and then we go to bed and repeat the whole process again the next day. If you think that's an 'adventure,' then I'm afraid you're even dumber than I thought."

"You're the one who makes it sound boring," said Darek. "And even if it was as you said it was, does that mean that you must put the lives of innocent people at risk, just so you can satisfy your own desire for excitement?"

"It's not my fault you guys are boring as hell," said Aorja. "Master was right. You don't understand."

"Don't understand what?" said Darek. Then he shook his head. "It doesn't matter. What is your Master planning? Tell me that, at least."

"I don't know," said Aorja. "Master doesn't tell me everything just because I work for him. He's the kind of leader who only lets his servants know what they need to know in order to complete their individual jobs. His two katabans servants don't even know I work for him, much less that I've been helping the bumbling buffoons along without their knowledge."

She must be referring to the intruders that Junaz

caught, Darek thought

Aloud, he said, "Well, why didn't your Master have you do whatever he is planning? You were here the whole time. Seems like a waste to send two other people to do a job you could do yourself."

Aorja shook her head. "How am I supposed to do their job when I am a student here? The point of this plan was to make sure that no one knew I was working for him, but that all clearly went down the drain, now didn't it?"

Aorja's wand hand shook, but it was still aimed squarely at Jiku. "It was supposed to be *simple*. While I distracted you idiots, Durima and Gujak were supposed to sneak in and out. But I forgot about that idiotic Guardian, which put us in the same mess that we're in now."

"It's not quite as bleak as you think," said Jiku in a surprisingly calm voice. "After all, that little hitch in your 'brilliant' plan showed us your true colors."

"What did I say about you talking?" said Aorja.

Jiku did not respond, but he no longer looked quite as frightened as he had before.

"Jiku has a good point," said Darek. "It's over, Aorja. You shouldn't have chosen this moment to reveal your plan to us. Sooner or later Eyurna or someone else will come in and stop you."

"Don't be so certain about that," said Aorja in a singsong voice. "You see, I sealed all of the doors and windows out of here. I also sent Eyurna out by telling her that there is a student in the First Dorm who is sick to her stomach. So it's just the three of us in here and it will continue to be just the three of us for quite some time."

Darek reached for his wand before remembering that he had lost it while rescuing Jiku earlier. Jiku, too, had made movements like he was reaching for his wand, but like Darek, he apparently did not have his wand anymore, either.

"This is just perfect," said Aorja, her eyes glinting malevolently. "The only two people in the school who could stop me are unarmed and as weak as twigs. The rest of Master's plan may not go correctly, but I can at least take joy in the knowledge that a couple of idiots died thanks to my efforts."

As Aorja's wand glowed brighter and brighter, Darek closed his eyes and prayed. He prayed to Skimif, to Xocion, and to any other god or goddess who he thought would listen to him, even though he did not know if any of the gods would come to his aid.

The only god he did not try to pray to, however, was the Ghostly God. That would have been the same as asking Aorja for mercy.

Chapter Nine

The Magical Superior closed the door to his study, turned around, and sighed. His old age was finally catching up with him. His bones grew weaker and weaker, his joints and back ached in places he had never felt before, and he became more and more tired with each passing year. He had managed to use magic to counteract the worst aspects of old age, but even magic couldn't hide the effects of aging forever.

Every mortal life has to end at some point, the Magical Superior thought grimly. *I am no different in that regard, despite my unusually long lifespan.*

His old age seemed especially apparent every time one of his students' life was in danger. Just a few minutes ago, he, Yorak, and many of the other teachers had arrived at the campus courtyard to find Darek Takren fighting a chimera. Darek had succeeded in killing the beast, but Darek himself was currently lying asleep in bed in the medical wing due to the fact that he had nearly frozen his hands off by using magic without a wand.

And then, not long after that, the explosion had happened. It had appeared out of nowhere, without even the slightest warning, unlike the explosion that had demolished the Third Dorm. When the Magical Superior,

Yorak, and Jenur—along with all of the Institute students—went to the sports field to see it, they had discovered that the *Soaring Sea* was little more than burnt scrap and its pilot dead meat. The Institute students themselves were investigating this one, but it seemed unlikely to the Superior that they would find any actual clues.

After that, Yorak had said that she was going to gather up all of her students and leave tomorrow. The only reason they weren't leaving right away was because their airship was no more. She was going to send a gray ghost to the Institute tonight requesting another airship be sent (apparently, the Institute had several, which the Magical Superior found odd, considering how that school had been built underwater). They were not going to teleport because most of the students Yorak had brought with her were not very good at it and Yorak did not think she had the energy to teleport so many students at once over such a vast distance. Nonetheless, they *were* leaving, which was a basic fact that Yorak had made crystal clear to the Superior earlier, and there was nothing the Superior could do about it.

And in all honesty, the Magical Superior understood her fears. He himself was becoming more and more worried for his own students' safety, even though no one had died yet. He tried to convince himself that the rest of the school was going to be fine, but it was hard to believe that when he had no idea whether another attack was coming or not.

That was why he was back here in his study. He was going to speak to a god, the only god who could possibly know what was going on here, and he was going to do it alone. Yorak had demanded to come with him so she could find out what was going on as well (the destruction of the *Soaring Sea* seemed to have given her new motivation to find out who was behind the recent explosions at the school), but the Magical Superior had explained to her, as patiently as he could, that only the current bearer of the title of Magical Superior could speak to the gods in his study. Otherwise, he said, none of the gods would speak to him.

Of course, Yorak had not been at all happy about that. She seemed to think that the Magical Superior was trying to hide something from her, even though she knew about that rule already. He had had to explain to her that he was not hiding even one scrap of information from her. Even then, the gods didn't always honor his requests. More than once over the Magical Superior's career, he had gone into his study to speak to the gods only to spend hours waiting for a god who chose not to show up. Sometimes a completely different god would show up instead, which always put a wrench in the Magical Superior's plans.

Today, the Magical Superior did not know if the god he wished to speak with would come. This god in particular was busy, busier than the rest of the gods even, and for good reason. Still, this god was also a lot more reasonable and kind than the others and was far more likely to agree to a meeting with him. After all, Skimif, the God of Martir and the god who the Magical Superior wanted to talk to today, had once been a mortal himself.

The Magical Superior's study was a dome-shaped room,

with tall, slanting walls that carried dozens of thick tomes within them. The room's walls had the colors of magic: Red, green, blue, and yellow. The walls had been painted such in order to help facilitate the magical powers for the Superior who lived there, because for some reason those four colors were more conducive to a magical environment than others.

In the center of the room was a large, round wooden table, upon which were gathered together hundreds and hundreds of tiny stone figurines. The table had been expanded ever since the Magical Superior had learned about the southern gods thirty years ago, forcing him to hire one of the Divine Carvers to create another several hundred or so statues to go along with the statues of the northern gods. Even then, the Magical Superior was not sure that all of the southern gods were represented, as most southern gods shunned contact with humans, even now years after they had become common knowledge to the peoples of the Northern Isles. He suspected that several southern gods had not yet announced their presence to the mortals, although he did not know for sure.

Today, however, the Magical Superior was not going to talk to any of the southern gods. Instead, he walked up to the table and picked out the statue of Skimif, which was in the very front of the group due to Skimif's status as the leader and ruler of the gods. It was right in front of the statue of the Ghostly God, which the Magical Superior ignored as he picked up Skimif's statue.

Hefting the stone figurine, the Magical Superior walked to the back of his study. Thick curtains in the same colors as the walls separated the back wall of his study from the rest, but it was a simple matter to push them away, revealing piles of soft pillows sitting inside the curtains. Upon the pillows were about half a dozen books, in various stages of completion, that the Magical Superior had been reading. His eyes fell briefly on his copy of Hanyu's *Prophecies*, but he did not linger on any of them because he was not here to read (much to his regret).

Walking over the pillows—if using magic to allow his feet to float an inch above the pillows counted as 'walking,' as he had no intention of climbing over their uneven surface in his old, weakened state—the Magical Superior went to the back wall itself. He made sure to close the curtains first, even though there was no one else in the room except for himself. Still, with everything that had happened recently, he felt justified in taking these protective measures, no matter how silly they may have seemed.

Then he turned his attention back to the back wall. It looked as plain and unremarkable as any wall, but that was because it had been designed that way years ago by the founder of North Academy. It was supposed to look that way to keep out potential intruders in the incredibly unlikely event someone managed to break into the Magical Superior's study. Whether it worked out that way in practice, the Magical Superior didn't know, seeing as no one had yet succeeded in breaking into his study (aside from the time his deceased younger brother had broken in years ago, although even then, his younger brother had not known about the secret passageway and therefore had not tried to look for it).

The Magical Superior placed his hand against the smooth back wall and pushed. He heard the clicking of gears and several locks being undone; the next moment, the wall swung inwards like a door, revealing a dark spiral staircase that went down well out of his sight.

He had walked down this staircase countless times over the years. He was as familiar with each step as he was with the back of his hand. He didn't even need a light to see where he was going because he knew the staircase so well.

Descending the staircase, the Magical Superior made sure to close the door behind him as he entered. Again, he was not concerned that someone would enter his study and follow him, but just to be absolutely certain, he had to close it. It was just habit at this point.

The staircase was now completely black, with no light at all to guide his feet. He relied solely on memory, going down each step carefully, until in just a few minutes he reached the bottom of the stairs, where he found himself standing before a thick, ancient stone door that he had opened as many times as he had walked down these stairs over the years.

The door opened easily enough. He simply knocked on it once and the door swung open, its bottom scraping across the floor. When the door opened completely, the Magical Superior stepped through. And when he stepped through, the lights activated.

Green lights running along the top of the room's walls shone down on the Superior, but they did not show much.

The Chamber, as he had always called it, was a tube-shaped room with no decorations, no paintings or windows or anything of interest. The only piece of furniture that existed in the Chamber was a stone podium with a slot that was the exact same shape and size as the base of the Skimif statue he held.

The Magical Superior walked up to the podium and placed the statue in the slot. He stepped back, knowing from experience that divine statues sometimes radiated divine energy that even he couldn't handle.

"O Skimif, God of Martir, Leader of the Gods, and Ruler of All," said the Magical Superior, bowing his head as he raised his staff above his head. "I, the Magical Superior of North Academy, request an audience with you today. I will understand if you do not wish to speak with me, but the matter that I am contacting you about is urgent and I wish to speak with you about it right away."

He raised his head, but the Skimif statue looked as normal as always. He didn't sense any magical energy from it, not even so much as one spark. It was as if Skimif was ignoring him, even though he knew that the God of Martir had to be listening.

The divine statues, as they were known, were not just any normal statues. They were tied to whichever god they represented. How that worked, exactly, the Magical Superior didn't know, because he had hired one of the Divine Carvers to carve this one and the Divine Carvers did not reveal their trade secrets to the general public.

Nonetheless, the Magical Superior understood that

when the statue was placed in the podium, the god it was based on could hear him no matter where he or she was at the time. That did not mean the god or goddess in question would actually answer his summons, but they knew he was summoning them, at least.

The Magical Superior tried not to feel too disappointed. He hadn't expected Skimif to listen to him. Skimif, as the God of Martir, had more responsibility than any of the other gods combined. He not only maintained Martir itself, but also had to keep an eye on the gods to make sure none of them were up to anything they shouldn't be. The gods had a bad habit of doing things they shouldn't, things that usually caused a lot of trouble and danger for everyone involved.

That was exactly why the Magical Superior had tried to contact him. Skimif, more than any other god, would know who the 'Master' of those two katabans was. He might even know why this 'Master' had even sent those two here in the first place.

Yet the longer the Magical Superior stood there, the more time passed in which Skimif didn't appear. He began to wonder if waiting for Skimif was a fool's errand when the lives of his students and faculty were still at risk.

Just as the Magical Superior was about to take the Skimif statue and leave, he sensed a powerful magical presence—far above his own—flood the room like water from a bursting dam. He shivered with anticipation, watching as a light on the other side of the Chamber appeared from nowhere.

The glow grew brighter and brighter, becoming so bright

that the Magical Superior was forced to cover his eyes to avoid injuring them. Soon the bright glow had enveloped the entire Chamber, causing the Magical Superior to close his thin eyelids completely.

Then a familiar, yet somewhat detached, voice spoke from within the light. "Hello, Magical Superior of North Academy. How are you today?"

As the voice spoke, the light rapidly faded until the Magical Superior could tell through his eyelids that the light was gone. He opened his eyes and looked over the statue of Skimif to see the newcomer.

Standing on the other side of the Skimif statue was a being who resembled the statue almost exactly. A cursory glance showed that Skimif resembled an aquarian, as he had indeed been during his past life. He had the head of a hammerhead shark and the skin of a fish that glistened in the green lights running along the top of the Chamber.

But a more thorough observation showed that Skimif was no mere aquarian. His muscles were thicker and bigger than any aquarian's, he wore white robes that were as bright as the sun's rays reflecting off the snow of the Great Berg, and he carried a scepter in his right hand that was pure gold from top to bottom. He even smelled divine, a scent which reminded the Magical Superior of roses mixed with cream.

Although the Magical Superior had met many gods over his lifetime, none of them were quite like Skimif. The God of Martir radiated a power and authority that put him a step above the other gods, and this in spite of the fact that he had only been the God of Martir for thirty years. The Magical

Superior had often speculated how strong Skimif would be in a hundred years or a thousand years, although he knew he would not live long enough to see that.

"I am not doing well, Lord Skimif," said the Magical Superior. "And neither is my school or the visitors from the Undersea Institute. You are aware of what has recently been happening here, haven't you?"

Skimif nodded. "How can I not be? And please, simply call me 'Skimif.' 'Lord' is too formal."

The Magical Superior felt uncomfortable with that request, but he had made it a personal policy to follow the gods' request and commands, so he decided to go along with it. "So you understand what I have been through over the last couple of hours."

"Of course," said Skimif. "The gods have always paid special attention to North Academy, and I am no exception to that rule. I am quite aware of most of what has happened here."

"Then you know that it is one of the gods who is behind it," said the Magical Superior. "I don't know which god, but we have captured two katabans servants who have confirmed that they are serving a god."

Skimif folded his arms across his chest. His face was a difficult read, even for the Magical Superior, who had many years of experience deciphering unusual godly facial expressions, many of whom did not have normal human or even aquarian faces.

"That is the problem, Magical Superior," said Skimif. "Although I have been keeping careful track of the situation,

I don't know which of the many, many gods are behind this."

The Magical Superior leaned forward slightly; always a dangerous move in his old age, as he never knew when he would simply topple forward. "But you are the God of Martir. There is nothing in this world that happens without your notice."

Skimif sighed. "In comparison to some gods, I am still quite new and still figuring out the full extent of my abilities. My omniscience, for example, is imperfect. I can only really know what is going on in any one particular location at any one time. I can't focus on everywhere at once. Believe me, I tried, and it almost drove me insane."

"Do you have any theories about this 'Master's' identity?" said the Magical Superior. "Could it be Hollech? This seems like his doing."

"No," said Skimif. "I banished Hollech beyond the Void years ago. He hasn't been seen since. And he couldn't return, anyway, because I sealed the Void from his side to prevent him from coming back."

"Oh," said the Magical Superior. "But how can you not know which god it is? Haven't you been searching?"

"I have," said Skimif. "But it's not easy. Aside from the fact that there are hundreds of gods in both the Northern and Southern Pantheons—many of which are still unhappy with my rule—there's been some presence obstructing my own senses."

"A presence?" the Magical Superior said. "What do you mean by that?"

Skimif unfolded his arms. "Ever since the end of the Katabans War, I have noticed a powerful presence emerging deep from underneath the surface of Martir. At first, I dismissed it as nothing more than the collective magical energy of the gods collecting in Martir's core. That happens sometimes because the gods produce so much magical energy that not all of it is used by you mages and so it will usually end up collecting somewhere until it is used up."

That was the first time the Magical Superior had ever heard about something like that before. That made him wonder just how much the other gods had hid from him over the years.

Another reason I like talking to Skimif, the Magical Superior thought. *Unlike the others, he has no great distrust of mortals like myself, so he feels freer to mention things like that to me.*

"But that energy is usually discovered and used up by a mage or group of mages at some point," said Skimif. "Often quickly. I am sure you are aware of those mages known in history as the arcanians?"

The Magical Superior nodded. "You mean the most powerful mages in Martirian history."

"Yes," said Skimif. "They got that way by stumbling upon these energy wells, as I tend to call them, and using their power to boost their own. It is an effective way for a mortal mage to push past his own limits and become stronger, although it is always temporary."

"Very interesting," said the Magical Superior. "But it is irrelevant to the discussion. Tell me more about this presence."

"It's hard to tell you anything about it because sometimes I am not even sure it's real," said Skimif, glancing at the floor. "Like I said, I first noticed it after the end of the Katabans War, although I have a feeling that it is much older than that. In times of crisis it is more noticeable, but every time I try to focus on it, it goes away and becomes impossible to find again. It acts like a real, living being, but I don't know what it is or where it came from."

"That is disturbing indeed," said the Magical Superior. "Is it friendly or unfriendly?"

"I have no idea," said Skimif. "As I said, every time I try to focus on it, it will draw into itself. I have spoken with some of the older gods about it—Nimiko and the Mechanical Goddess, among others—and even they have no idea what it is. They've promised to keep an eye open for it, but I doubt they'll be able to find it."

"I don't understand what this presence has to do with our current situation," said the Magical Superior. "Do you think it has something to do with this 'Master' fellow that the two katabans mentioned?"

"I think this presence is hiding him from me," said Skimif. "I don't know why, but I usually feel this presence at its strongest whenever I search for the identity of the one known as 'Master.' I suspect that the presence is either an ally or a manipulator of this god, whoever he is, but why, I don't know."

"This is all far too disturbing for my tastes," said the

Magical Superior. "I don't like it."

"Neither do I," said Skimif. "It's disturbed me so much that I've even tried to talk to the Mysterious One about this and see what he knows. But he seems to have vanished from Martir; at least, none of the other gods have been able to tell me where he might be and Bleak Rock is practically a ghost island at this point."

That was another interesting revelation. The Mysterious One was one of the few gods that the Magical Superior did not have a divine statue of, for the simple fact that no one knew what he looked like or, for that matter, if he even existed. Legend said that the Mysterious One was the God of Mystery and Magic, but up until now the Magical Superior hadn't even believed that he was real.

"What's even worse is that this presence is powerful," said Skimif. "I only get occasional glimpses of its might every now and then, but I can tell that it is at least on my power level. It might be able to beat me in a fight if it wanted."

"Forgive me for my impudence, Skimif, but that is ridiculous," said the Magical Superior. "There is no one in Martir who even comes close to your might. The Powers made you the strongest being in the world, didn't they? Not even the other gods can match your might."

"I thought so, too, but apparently there exists someone who can match my power here," said Skimif, his voice troubled. "I don't know who he or she is, but if you want my theory, I think this presence is far older than Martir, maybe even older than the Powers themselves."

The Magical Superior had a hard time wrapping his head around that. Years ago, after Prince Malock and Skimif had succeed in convincing the Powers to spare Martir after their disappointment with its development, the Magical Superior had conducted a brief interview with Prince Malock to find out more about the Powers.

Malock had told the Magical Superior that the Powers had revealed to him that a world had existed before Martir, but that it had been in complete ruin when the Powers arrived. The Powers had then used the remains of that world to create Martir, according to Malock, which meant that Martir was literally built on the ruins of another world.

It was that thought that prompted the Magical Superior to ask, "Do you think it could be something left over from the world that existed before Martir?"

"I don't know," said Skimif. "I have been investigating the Old Ruins and—"

"The what?" said the Magical Superior. He immediately put a hand over his mouth when he saw Skimif's startled expression. "Oh, forgive me, Skimif, for interrupting you. I just had to ask that question, but if you do not want to answer it that is fine."

"No, no," said Skimif, shaking his head. "I was just taken aback. I should have explained what I meant."

Secretly, the Magical Superior was relieved. The gods hated it when mortals interrupted them, even for a good reason. It was a hard, painful lesson that the Magical Superior had learned decades ago when he first became the Magical Superior and it was not a lesson he intended to take again.

"The Old Ruins are a place no mortal has ever set foot in," said Skimif. He gestured at the floor. "They exist deep, deep beneath the surface of Martir, well out of the reach of even the most sophisticated mortal magic. The gods have known about them for years and it was one of the first things I was told about when I ascended to godhood."

"But what, exactly, *are* the Old Ruins?" said the Magical Superior, careful to keep his tone and words as respectful as possible.

Skimif shrugged. "From what the other gods have told me, and from what I've learned on my own, the Old Ruins are the only remnants of the world that existed before Martir. My theory is that the Powers left them because they did not know how to use them for Martir or maybe they finished Martir and the Old Ruins were what was leftover. Either way, they are an unusual sight to behold."

A million questions exploded in the Magical Superior's mind when he heard that, but for some reason he suspected Skimif was not interested in answering any of them at the moment.

So he asked, "What did you find in the Old Ruins?"

"Not much," said Skimif. "There's a lot of writing, but it's all in a language I can't read. The only god who has had any luck in translating it is Ranama, the God of Language, but even he hasn't been able to decipher much other than a few words. And trust me, he's been at it for thousands of years."

"No clue at all as to the identity of this presence or what it even wants?" said the Magical Superior.

"None at all," said Skimif. Then he frowned. "Well, I guess that's not entirely true. Ranama found this. He gave it to me for my own study, but I feel comfortable sharing it with you."

Skimif held out his hand. His hand glowed brilliantly bright, but it lasted only for a second. When the light faded, a square stone tablet lay grasped between his fingers.

He let go of the tablet, which floated across the Chamber to the Superior. The Magical Superior caught the tablet with his free hand and peered at it closely.

The stone tablet was ancient. That he could tell right away. It felt crumbly and weak in his hand, like it was about to fall apart any minute. It was probably even older than the Arcanium. And if it truly was from the world that existed before Martir, then it definitely was older than the Arcanium, older even than the gods themselves.

The tablet's surface was faded, but he felt tiny raised ridges running across it, like some type of ancient writing. It reminded him, oddly enough, of the raised ink used by the ancient Primordians to write their books. He suspected that whoever wrote this tablet must have used a form of geomancy to raise the ridges, but considering that this tablet existed well before the gods—and therefore, before magic—its writer must have used a different method to achieve that effect.

"What is it?" said the Magical Superior, looking up at Skimif, who had folded his arms across his chest. "I mean, what is it, exactly? A history? A poem? An essay? Or something else?"

"Not sure," said Skimif. "From what little Ranama has translated of it—and he hasn't translated much, even with all of the study and work he has put into it over the years—he thinks its a diary."

The Magical Superior frowned. "A diary? Written by whom?"

"That is another thing Ranama is unsure of," said Skimif. "According to him, the diary was written by someone chronicling the last days of the world that existed before this one. The writer's name is there, but it is the most faded and difficult-to-read part of the text, so Ranama calls him Diary-Writer."

"This is an amazing find," said the Magical Superior. He suddenly felt like he was holding pure gold. "It may be the rarest and most valuable object in all of Martir because it didn't even come from the Powers. In all my years, I never thought I'd get to so much as look at something not created by the Powers."

"You are indeed lucky," said Skimif, although his tone did not sound congratulatory. "But in the end, I don't care about the obvious academic value that tablet has to someone like yourself. I am interested in finding out if it is related to that presence I felt, the presence I think is up to no good."

"So you think it might say something about that?" said the Magical Superior.

Skimif shrugged. "Ranama said that the diary appears to chronicle some powerful presence destroying the world before Martir, the Prior World, if you need a name for it.

Based on what little he has translated, Ranama has concluded that the Diary-Writer was one of the final victims of the presence that destroyed his world."

"He learned all of that from this?" said the Magical Superior, holding up the tablet.

"It's his theory," said Skimif. "You've met Ranama before, no doubt, so you know how he tends to jump to all kinds of crazy theories given the slightest bit of evidence. Nonetheless, I think he may be onto something this time. He showed me his reasoning and I think it's pretty sound, although I admit that I'm no linguist."

"As interesting as this is, I wonder how relevant it is to our current situation," said the Magical Superior. "Do you think that the presence you sense today is the same presence that caused the destruction of the Prior World?"

The God of Martir shook his head hopelessly. "Maybe, maybe not. It might be something entirely different, but I doubt it. Whatever destroyed the Prior World is aiming to do the same thing with Martir. I'm sure of it."

"Why would it do that?" said the Magical Superior. "What does this presence have to gain from the deaths of so many millions of lives?"

"How am I supposed to know?" said Skimif, shrugging. "This presence, whatever it is, is still in the shadows. I'm only aware of it because it is starting to get confident. Just half an hour ago, I sensed it directly inside this very school."

The Magical Superior gasped. "How could it have entered without my knowledge? If the presence is as strong as you, I should have noticed it."

"Remember, it took me years to be certain it even existed and wasn't some strange magical anomaly," said Skimif. "I have a feeling this presence has been around much, much longer than the last twenty-four years."

The Magical Superior could not help but shudder at the thought. "Then does that mean that this presence is possibly manipulating this 'Master' fellow? Or do you think Master is knowingly working with the presence?"

"That's another question I don't have the answer to," said Skimif. "But I will say this: The gods hate submitting to any authority higher than them. That is the one trait the northern and southern gods share. Even though I've been their leader for a while now, I know for a fact that most of the gods still don't respect me or see me as legitimate. I doubt any of the gods would be willing to submit to this presence."

"If this presence offered to overthrow you, would that not be tempting to the gods?" said the Magical Superior.

The temperature in the room—which had been cool—suddenly rose high enough that the Magical Superior felt almost too warm in his robes. The temperature increase had to have come from Skimif, who was now scowling.

"The gods aren't stupid," said Skimif. "They remember what I did to Hollech all those years ago. They would never even think of standing against me, not unless they wish to be stripped of their powers and thrown beyond the Void as well."

For the first time since he had gotten to know Skimif, the Magical Superior felt a tinge of fear. Most of the time,

Skimif acted like a normal mortal, despite being almighty and powerful. Prior to becoming the God of Martir, Skimif had been a simple seaweed farmer, as honest and truthful as they came, with a strong belief in the brotherhood of all mortals, human and aquarian alike.

At least, that was what the Magical Superior had learned while doing research on Skimif shortly after the farmer's ascension to godhood. Right now, however, he was starting to understand that, whatever Skimif may have been in his mortal days, he was slowly becoming more and more godlike.

Thankfully, the Magical Superior had decades of experience interacting with various gods, so he knew how to speak in a way that would not ignite Skimif's temper.

Lowering the tablet, the Magical Superior said, "Skimif, I did not mean to anger you. I was simply offering an idea that may not have occurred to you yet."

"Magical Superior." Skimif said those two words as authoritatively as any god. "I know what you were trying to do. I was just angry that that is clearly not the answer. If it was, it would be very simple for me to banish this Master guy beyond the Void. Alas, it is not so."

The Magical Superior still sensed an undercurrent of intense hostility in Skimif's words, a hostility that he had never heard in the god's voice before. It made him wonder just what kind of toll Skimif's ascension into godhood had taken on him, but the Magical Superior knew better than to ask. Skimif did not seem to be in the mood to answer such personal questions.

Before the Magical Superior could ask another question, a gray ghost flew through the ceiling and landed in front of him. It took the Magical Superior a moment to recognize the gray, slightly transparent, smoke-like being was Junaz's gray ghost, because it looked exactly like the ex-airship mechanic, simply without any color.

"Magical Superior, sir," said Junaz's gray ghost, his voice echoing from the ghost's mouth. "Urgent news. The two katabans intruders from before were discovered to be missing from their cells. But don't worry, we know where they are, because one of them was captured by the traps I set up at the graveyard's entrance. I and several other mages, including the Institute mages, are heading there right now to apprehend them once and for all.

"Additionally, Eyurna has discovered that the entrance to the medical wing has been completely sealed off. She said that the last people in there were Darek Takren, Aorja Kitano, and Jiku Nium, but she doesn't know why the door is sealed. Jenur Takren is working with her to open it, but so far they have had no luck. Jenur is looking for alternative means of entrance, as the medical wing has proven to prevent even teleportation into it."

"What?" said the Magical Superior, even though he knew that the gray ghost couldn't hear him.

"We are requesting your assistance to deal with these two problems," Junaz's gray ghost continued. "You do not have to reply to this gray ghost."

With that, the gray ghost dissipated into a thin, gray cloud of smoke that quickly evaporated into nothingness.

Skimif frowned. "I forgot how urgent mortals sound when dealing with what appear to us gods as minor crises."

"Skimif, I am sorry, but I must leave immediately," said the Magical Superior, turning to leave. "I trust that Jenur Takren has the medical wing situation under control, so I will go and help Junaz and the others re-capture the katabans."

"Good luck with that," said Skimif.

The Magical Superior stopped before he left. "Wait, you mean you aren't coming to help?"

Skimif shook his head. "I wish I could, but I have other things to attend to. I think you mages are perfectly capable of handling whatever is going on here by yourselves."

The Magical Superior was about to ask Skimif what other things the god needed to attend to when Skimif suddenly burst into a bright shining ball of light. Like before, the Magical Superior was forced to cover his eyes, this time using the ancient tablet, in order to protect them.

When the light faded, the Magical Superior lowered the stone tablet and looked at where Skimif had stood previously. The God of Martir was gone, almost as if he had never been there at all.

It doesn't matter, the Magical Superior thought. *Skimif is probably right. Whatever is going on right now, we will simply have to handle it on our own.*

Before he left the Chamber, however, the Magical Superior placed the old stone tablet on the floor in front of the podium. He felt it would be safe here until he had enough time to study it further. Then he walked out the door and up the stairs.

As the Magical Superior ascended the staircase leading up to his study as fast as he could, he found himself wishing that Skimif had stayed and helped. He had the feeling that whatever was about to happen next would require all the help that he and his students and faculty could get.

Chapter Ten

"**O**h dear," said Gujak, who was still hopping from foot to foot, succeeding only in making Durima more nervous. "You're trapped. You're caught. We're dead."

"We're not *dead*," said Durima in an annoyed voice. "Not yet. There's still a chance we could recover from this."

Having gotten off the fence, Durima now stood on the floor of the cage. She was right up against the cage's bars, her claws wrapped around them tightly. Although they were covered in dirt and smelled like it, the bars stood as strong as the bars in the catacombs had, if not stronger. They looked newer than the bars of her cell, like they had only been installed in the ground recently.

"We're still dead," said Gujak. "Dead, dead, dead."

"Would you shut up?" said Durima. "The mages don't even know we triggered their trap yet. We still have plenty of time to—"

She stopped speaking when she saw that Gujak had gone perfectly still. His large yellow eyes were focused on something behind her, his mouth open with dread, his whole body shaking. It was like he had seen a ghost.

"What are you staring at?" said Durima. She twisted her head over her shoulder to see if she could spot it. "Did you see Master or ... damn it ..."

A whole crowd of mages—comprised of human and aquarians—was running down from the Arcanium to the graveyard. There had to be at least two dozen of them, divided half and half between the two species, but for once, the humans and aquarians were not fighting amongst themselves. Instead, they were united in their purpose, and their purpose was obvious.

"They're going to kill us!" Gujak moaned, his hands clinging to his face. "This is it. Good bye, cruel world."

Durima shook her head and returned her attention to the cage. She was looking for a weak spot, any weak spot, that she could try to break. Unfortunately, her lack of familiarity with cages in general meant that she could not spot any part that looked easily breakable.

The only thing she noticed was a large lock on the door. Neither she nor Gujak had a key to unlock it, but she was tempted to summon a massive stone fist from the ground to smash it. She didn't do it, however, because the cage was so small that even if she succeeded in smashing it open, she would probably end up crushing herself in the process.

She glanced over her shoulder again. The mages were drawing ever closer, their wands waving, glowing with suppressed energy. The Institute mages were not waving their wands around (if they even had any), but one look at the sheer hatred in their eyes and Durima knew that they were going to be just as merciless as the humans, if not more so.

Durima turned back to look at the lock. Then an idea

occurred to her, one she hadn't considered before. She didn't know if it would work, but she was willing to try anything at this point, no matter how crazy it may have seemed.

"Gujak," said Durima, grabbing the bars and looking at her partner straight in the eyes. "Can you turn your index finger into a key shape and use it to unlock this lock?"

Gujak stopped dancing around, but he still looked as nervous as a frightened baba raga. "I-I don't know. I've never tried that before. I'm not a locksmith and I don't know if I can concentrate long enough to even try it."

"Just do it," said Durima, glancing over her shoulder at the advancing crowd of murderous mages. "It's not like we have anything to lose at this point."

"Except our lives," said Gujak, but he was already walking up to the cage anyway, holding up his right index finger, which was starting to transform into a generic key.

When Gujak reached the lock, the transformation of his index finger was complete. He inserted his finger key into the lock and turned.

Durima honestly didn't expect it to work, despite having originally suggested the idea. So when she heard a tiny but audible *click* and saw the lock come undone, she could hardly believe her eyes.

But Durima, being a practical katabans, recovered from her shock in less than five seconds. Gujak pulled his finger out of the lock, looking just as disbelieving as she felt, and Durima slammed her shoulder into the cage door.

Immediately, the lock snapped and the door flew open.

Durima tumbled out of the cage into the dirt, almost crashing into Gujak, but he jumped out of the way just in time. Rubbing the top of her head, Durima got up to her feet and said to Gujak, "What are you staring at? We have to find that grave now before the mages get here."

As Durima took off in a random direction, Gujak followed, saying as he did so, "But how can we find Braim Kotogs' grave if we don't even know where to look? I mean, there's a mob of crazy mages who want us dead! How is that going to give us time to—"

Gujak was cut off when a figure suddenly appeared directly in their path, like a ghost materializing from thin air. Durima and Gujak were forced to come to a screeching halt when the figure appeared, not because they wanted to, but because they both recognized him instantly and knew there was no way they could get past this particular mortal.

Standing in their way was the Magical Superior himself. He leaned on his staff like an old man, but the magical encrgy he radiated was just as powerful as before. If anything, he seemed stronger, although that may have been because Durima was feeling weaker than usual at the moment.

"Hello," said the Magical Superior in a tone that was far too friendly for Durima's tastes. "I see you two have escaped from the catacombs. I don't understand how you did that, but it doesn't really matter."

Durima looked over her shoulder again. The crowd of angry mages was closer to the graveyard now, so close she could practically see the whites of their eyes. It didn't make her very comfortable, to put it lightly.

"G-Get out of our way," said Gujak, pointing at the Magical Superior in what he clearly thought was a threatening gesture, but his arm shook so badly that it just made him look pathetic. "Or we'll cut you down where you stand, old man."

"Cut me down? Without a sword or other type of bladed weapon?" said the Magical Superior in an amused voice. "Of course, I see at least one of you has claws, but you know how powerful I am. Fighting me would be one of the worst decisions you could ever make in your life, or at any rate one of the most painful."

"He's not bluffing," said Durima, putting one hand on Gujak's shoulder. "You sense his might as well as I, don't you? He's no god, but if we tried to fight him, he'd probably kill us before we even realized we're dead."

"I am not seeking to kill either of you," said the Magical Superior. His eyes flicked over their shoulders. "Although to be perfectly honest, I can't say the same about my students, who look more like an undisciplined horde of lynchers than a group of thoughtful, intellectual scholars."

Again, Durima looked over her shoulder. At this point, the mages in the front of the crowd had reached the graveyard's walls. They were kept out thanks to Gujak's tree and the walls themselves. That gave Durima and Gujak maybe another minute or two, if even that much, before the mob got inside.

"But I can offer you protection," said the Magical Superior, holding out a hand, "and freedom, if you would but only tell me why you are here and who your Master is. My students will listen to me because I am their leader. If I tell them to leave you alone, they will, even if they don't want to."

"We'll never tell you anything," Durima said. She bared her teeth. "Our loyalty belongs to Master, and to Master alone. We swore an oath never to betray Master under any circumstances."

"Yeah," said Gujak, nodding. "We'll never tell you that Master sent us here to find the grave of Braim Kotogs. We're not stupid."

The Magical Superior smirked. "Collectively, you may not be dumb, but individually, I am afraid that is not the case, if the fact that you just revealed your reason for being here is a reliable indication of your general intelligence."

Durima punched Gujak in the shoulder. "Idiot! When will you learn that everything you say usually backfires and that I am the one who should do most, if not all, of the talking in these kinds of situations?"

Gujak rubbed his shoulder, looking quite ashamed of himself. "I didn't mean to—"

"Why do you want to find the grave of Braim?" said the Magical Superior, interrupting him like Gujak hadn't been speaking at all. "What is so special about his grave that you have to cause so much trouble for us?"

Durima, of course, did not know why Master had told her and Gujak to find this grave, but she wasn't about to let this mortal know that.

She said, "We aren't going to say even one more word

about Master or our mission. You don't deserve to know."

"Perhaps," said the Magical Superior. "But I can see that my students are already making progress in getting past the fcw obstacles that lie between them and the graveyard."

Alarmed, Durima looked over her shoulder for the umpteenth time today. The Magical Superior was right. One of the students, maybe a botamancer, was waving his wand at the tree. Gujak's tree was starting to pull its roots out of the ground, while Junaz, the fox-masked mage, was levitating the cage out of their path.

"I have no doubt that they will make it into here within the next minute," said the Magical Superior. "The offer still stands. Tell me everything you know about your Master and his plans and I will allow both of you to leave unharmed and with all of your freedoms intact."

As much as Durima hated to admit it, the Magical Superior's offer was very tempting. While the students and teachers trying to get into the graveyard were not even close to being on the same power level as the Magical Superior, collectively she did not think that she and Gujak could stop them. There were too many of them, especially if they had the Magical Superior on their side.

On the other hand, Durima knew that she and Gujak were in big trouble already. Master probably already knew about their capture and how they had just spilled the beans to the Magical Superior. If they told the Magical Superior everything else, it wouldn't matter if he freed them or not, because either way, today was not going to end well for Durima and Gujak.

Master will punish us no matter what, Durima thought. *But maybe he will punish us less if we abort the mission now.*

The only question was, how to escape? If they tried to run, the students and teachers would get them. Yet neither Durima nor Gujak were very good teleporters, which left them with only one option, an option she wasn't sure would work but she would have to try anyway.

"I am not kidding when I said that the offer still stands," said the Magical Superior. "I truly, honestly will protect you if you agree to tell me everything you know."

"That may be true," said Durima as she took a step back. "But Master has a strict policy about how to deal with traitors and I, for one, do not want to trespass it."

As fast as she could, Durima grabbed Gujak's arm, wrapping her claws around it as tightly as she could, and jerked backwards. The whole world seemed to melt and morph around her and Gujak as they left the mortal plane and entered the ethereal. As they did so, Durima heard the Magical Superior shouting at them to come back, but she felt comfortable ignoring his calls.

For a brief moment, Durima's world went black. Then she and Gujak landed on a bright, sparkling white road that stretched on in both directions for as far as the eye could see. Durima landed on her back, allowing her to see the stars that shone in the black sky above them. With a gasp, Durima floated up and looked at the portal she and Gujak had just fallen out of. Through the portal, she could see the shocked expression of the Magical Superior, but only for a brief moment, because in the next minute, the portal closed with a small *pop* and she could see him no more.

Panting from the effort, Durima looked down at her body. As always in the ethereal, Durima looked more like a ghost than a living being. Her upper body was as large and bearlike as ever, but her legs had disappeared, replaced with only a wispy, ghostlike tail that was strange to look at.

She looked at Gujak. Like her, his legs had disappeared, replaced by a wispy tail that was slightly greenish, in contrast to her reddish ghost tail. He looked at her with wide, frightened eyes, as if he did not understand what was going on.

"We made it out alive," said Durima, even though she knew that was a useless thing to say. "Though we can't enter the school via the ethereal, I guess we can exit using the ethereal, at least."

Gujak floated upright, frowning like Durima had just killed his favorite pet. "You know Master is going to punish us for this, right?"

Durima nodded. "Yes. I am more than aware of what Master does to servants who abort their missions. I just thought that we might at least be able to tell him that we didn't tell those mages everything. Maybe he will not punish us as severely as he would otherwise."

"Even if he does give us a lighter punishment, it'll still be painful," said Gujak. "I mean, we had to abort the entire mission. It was a complete fiasco. There's no way Master will be happy about it."

Durima shrugged. "What other choice do we have, but to

return to Master and report our loss? Better to do it now rather than later."

"Yeah, I guess you're right," said Gujak. "But aren't you the least bit afraid of Master? I can't even begin to imagine how angry he is going to be with us once he finds out we failed. Horribly."

Durima briefly flashbacked to an old memory, of the first time that Master had punished her for failing to complete a mission. She shoved the memory out of her mind, however, before she could dwell on it for too long because she did not want to relive that particular memory.

"I know exactly how angry Master will be," said Durima. "I've served him for twenty-four years now. I would be a fool not to know."

Gujak floated back and forth uncertainly. "Then what do we do?"

Durima looked down the shining white road they floated upon. She could not see the end of it—it was too long, and besides, it didn't even have an end, considering it was actually one giant circle—but she knew that somewhere down that way was Master's island, where he was no doubt patiently awaiting their return.

"We go back to Master's island," said Durima. "We tell him everything that has happened, including our own failure, and prepare ourselves for whatever punishment he will dish out on us. It's the only thing we can do."

Chapter Eleven

Darek first expected to hear Jiku cry out in pain when Aorja killed him. Jiku was a strong man, but even the strongest of men were afraid of death.

Then Darek expected to be killed next. He didn't know what kind of spell Aorja would use on him, but he fully expected it to be painful. Aorja was not much of a fighter, but considering how she had managed to blow up the Third Dorm, he had no doubt that she knew far more dangerous spells than she originally let on.

Though I do wonder how her magic even works, Darek thought, even though this was not the most appropriate thought for this moment. *She's a mousimancer. That means she swore fealty to Yaona, the Goddess of Music. I wonder how Yaona feels about Aorja working for the Ghostly God instead.*

Not that any of that really mattered. Soon, Jiku and he would be dead and Aorja would escape. He doubted that anyone would even realize what had happened until well after Aorja was gone, which of course was part of her plan.

But rather than hearing a burst of energy and Jiku crying out in pain, Darek instead heard the sound of glass shattering and Aorja cursing in surprise. He opened his eyes to see who had broken in, because he had also heard a pair of heavy boots land on the marble floor of the medical wing like boulders dropped from the sky.

To his shock—but delight—Mom stood opposite Aorja amidst shattered glass scattered on the floor underneath. Behind Mom, one of the windows was completely broken, like someone had tossed a rock through it. It was somewhat sad because the windows in the medical wing of the Arcanium were beautiful works of art in themselves, but he forgot all about how beautiful the window was when he realized that he and Jiku were saved.

Or were going to be saved, anyway. Aorja had whirled around and was aiming her wand directly at Mom. Mom had drawn out her own wand, however, and was pointing it at Aorja like a gun.

"Aorja?" said Mom, her wand arm steadier than her voice. "What ... what is going on here?"

"Nothing you need to know about," said Aorja. "Now, Miss Takren, why don't you put your wand down? I'll spare your son and his best friend if you do."

Seeing an opportunity, Darek shouted, "Don't listen to her, Mom! She's trying to disarm you so she can kill you."

"I know that, Darek," said Mom, her eyes focused completely on Aorja's wand. "I'm no amateur. I've run into far worse than a silly, scared little girl with a glowing stick before."

"Silly, scared little girl?" said Aorja with a laugh. "That would perhaps better describe *you*. Although, seeing as you are not quite so young anymore, maybe you would be better described as a silly, scared old hag."

"Really? Old hag?" said Mom with a chuckle. "Is that the best insult you can come up with? I've been called far worse before. Your insults aren't the most creative."

"So what if they aren't?" said Aorja. "Let's cut the crap. If you don't drop your wand and stand down, I will kill Darek and Jiku. Actually murder them in their beds."

"How do you plan to do that?" said Mom. "Your wand is aimed at me and if you take it off me for even one second, I will take you out."

"I am quite aware of that," said Aorja. "That's why I made sure to do this."

Aorja shook her other arm and another wand fell out of her sleeve into her hand. Without even looking, she pointed the other wand in Jiku and Darek's general direction. The second wand began to glow even more brightly than the first.

"Hold on," said Mom, her eyes widening. "*Two* wands? Mages are only supposed to have one wand each. Where did you get another?"

"This was Jiku's wand, actually," said Aorja. "Stole it when I tried to kill him." Then she addressed Jiku without looking at him. "See, Jiku? You didn't lose *everything* in the explosion. Just most of your things."

"Give me back my wand," said Jiku, holding out one of his hands. "Now."

"Why should I?" said Aorja. "Then I'd have *two* armed opponents, and I think one is more than enough, in my humble opinion. And if you try to get up and take it, you'll be dead before you even realize it."

Jiku lowered his hand, but he clearly wasn't happy with the situation. Darek wished he still had his own wand, but right now it was probably little more than burnt wood, if not ash, amidst the ruins of the Third Dorm. His hands were still blue and he could barely feel them, so he couldn't even use his hands to channel his magic again.

"All right, Miss Takren, I hope you see the situation that you're in," said Aorja. She cracked her neck. "If you attack me, you might—*might*—succeed in taking me down. But you might not be fast enough to stop me before I kill Jiku and Darek."

"Of course I'm fast enough to stop you," said Mom. "Back in my younger days, I was one of the fastest Dark Tigers in the Guild."

"But you aren't quite so young anymore, are you, old hag?" said Aorja. "No, of course you're not. Your joints are getting stiffer and stiffer every year. Would you really risk the lives of your son and his best friend like that?"

"You'll kill them either way," said Mom. "And if I drop my wand and surrender, you'll kill me as well. There's no way to win if I listen to you."

"Of course there isn't a way to win," said Aorja. "Because I made sure to set up this situation so that *I* would win. Even if the Magical Superior himself were here, I'd still have the upper hand over him. He may be the most powerful mage in the world, but he's also a sentimental old fool who can't bring himself to sacrifice his students or anything else for the greater good."

Darek slammed his hands on his lap. "Shut up! The

Magical Superior is a thousand times better than you will ever be. Just because he's not a traitorous psychopath like you doesn't mean—"

A flame bolt shot out from Aorja's second wand and flew past Darek's head. The heat scorched his eyebrows, causing him to sit back in his bed instinctively. The flame bolt struck the bed next to Darek's, sitting it on fire, although it was not a large fire, thankfully enough.

"Be quiet," said Aorja. "I don't need any of your moralizing bull. I'm going to kill all three of you and get out of here before that idiot Superior or anyone else manages to break the seal."

"Shouldn't be long now," said Mom. She gestured at the broken window behind her with her head. "The window is open. Now the others aren't as nimble as me, but I think it's only a matter of time before Eyurna tells everyone and sends them this way."

"By which time Jiku and Darek will be corpses and you will be a pile of ash on the floor," said Aorja. "And I will be long gone from this dumb, boring school."

"What are you waiting for, then?" said Mom. "Why don't you attack us? Do you lack faith in your own speed or are you just bluffing?"

Aorja's hands shook, but she didn't run or let her guard down. "Neither. I'm just ... I was hoping you would make it easy by dropping your wand, but I can see that's not how it's going to work today. Fine. I can kill you regardless of whether you have one wand or one hundred."

"Don't do it, Aorja," Mom warned. "Remember, I am one

of your teachers. I have a far better understanding of your own weaknesses and strengths than you do."

"No, you don't," Aorja said, although her voice trembled. "Stop trying to throw me off. It won't work."

Mom shook her head, although she didn't move her wand arm at all, even though several minutes had already passed. "No, I do. That's one of the things I've had to learn about being a teacher ever since I got this job ten years ago. Each individual student has their own strengths and weaknesses that they don't share with anyone else."

"No," said Aorja. "You don't know me. Not the real me. I've been hiding my true colors for years. You only know what I chose to show you."

Mom tilted her head to the side. "Really? You aren't a Hollechian. You think you're clever, but while you managed to fool even the Magical Superior into thinking you were innocent, that doesn't change the fact that your strength and weaknesses have been on display for me and the other teachers to see for years."

"Does it matter?" said Aorja, although she tripped over the words in her hurry to get them out. "I'm the one with the power here. Two wands over your one and over Jiku and Darek's none."

"Do you really have any power?" said Mom. "Think about it. I am a professional mage with three decades of experience. You have almost nine. I may be older and a bit slower, but I have a deep knowledge of you, both as a person and as a mage. And I am confident when I say that I can beat you, even without backup from the others."

"Stop lying," said Aorja. "You're lying. You can't beat me. You're old and slow, like you said."

Mom's eyes briefly met Darek's. It was a very brief glance in his direction, so brief that he at first thought he must have imagined it. After all, why would Mom risk taking her eyes off Aorja's wand for even a second?

Unless Mom was trying to tell me something, Darek thought. *Which isn't an entirely illogical conclusion, now that I think about it.*

Over the years, Mom and Darek had developed their own ways of speaking to each other without actually saying a word. It wasn't telepathy or some other form of magic. They had simply become so good at reading each other's body language that sometimes they could communicate without saying a word.

The look Mom gave Darek just then ... he was sure it hadn't been some kind of fluke. No, she had been trying to tell him something. He might have missed it under other circumstances, but now he understood what she had been trying to communicate to him.

She's going to attack Aorja, Darek thought. *And she wants me to help, somehow.*

At first, he was at a loss for how to help. He was still too worn out from his fight with the chimera. Not to mention his hands, while slowly warming up, were still basically useless. His wand was gone and he did not have access to another.

How does Mom expect me to help when I can't really use my magic at all? Darek thought. *Has she forgotten*

174

why I'm in the medical wing in the first place?

But then he realized he was looking at the situation all wrong. He didn't need magic to help Mom. In fact, Aorja was probably expecting a magical attack. Granted, she most likely expected the attack to come from Mom, but she was probably ready to kill anyone who even tried to attack her with magic, including Darek.

Therefore, Darek needed something he could use to hit her with that she wouldn't see coming. He needed to throw something at her. His fingers had recovered enough feeling by now that he felt confident he could pick up and throw something. The only question was, what?

Then it hit him like a ton of bricks.

Darek slowly reached for his white, fluffy pillow behind him as Aorja and Mom's stare down continued.

"Ran out of clever comebacks?" said Aorja. "Good. I was getting tired of listening to your stupid old voice anyway. I always liked you better silent."

"I'm just waiting for the best opening in which to attack," said Mom. "Should be any minute now, I think."

"Takren, you must be getting senile early if you think that you'll ever get an opening," said Aorja, seemingly unaware of Darek, who was now holding his pillow in front of his chest. "Do everyone a favor and stop trying to play the hero. It won't—"

In one smooth motion (or as smooth as he could be, considering how tired he was), Darek aimed and hurled his pillow at the back of Aorja's head. Aorja's head whipped around to see the pillow coming, but it didn't even get halfway to her before she raised Jiku's wand and unleashed another fire blast that completely incinerated the pillow in midair.

As the ashes that had once been Darek's pillow fell to the floor, Mom acted immediately. She jabbed her wand in Aorja's direction, sending an electrical burst from her wand that flew through the air like a throwing disk.

Although the pillow had only distracted Aorja for perhaps three seconds at most, it was more than enough time for the electrical burst to strike the traitor directly in the chest. Aorja gasped and dropped both of her wands as she fell face forward onto the marble floor with a loud *thump*. She did not rise again.

Mom approached their beds, keeping her wand trained on Aorja the entire time. She flicked her wand to the right and both of Aorja's wands flew up into her hands. Another flick and thick ropes appeared out of thin air and wrapped themselves securely around Aorja's unconscious body.

"There we go," said Mom. Then she looked up at Jiku and Darek. "Are either of you hurt?"

Jiku shook his head slowly. "No, teacher. Just ... betrayed."

He said that while staring at the unconscious Aorja, who lay at the foot of his bed.

"Good," said Mom. "I was worried for a moment there that she might have hurt you two."

"Don't worry," said Jiku. "She wouldn't have done it. Right? That was your whole game. You were betting that Aorja was a scared and frightened little girl, like you said she was."

Mom nodded. "Exactly. I wasn't lying when I said I know Aorja better than she knows herself. While she is magically gifted, she's not very brave or much of a fighter. She isn't even faster than me. The only reason I relied on Darek attacking her is because I needed to be sure that I could outrun her."

"Looks like your plan worked out after all," said Jiku. "Teacher Takren, I've always respected you, but I think that my respect for you has just increased tenfold today."

"Same here," said Darek. Then he frowned. "But what are we going to do about Aorja now?"

Mom glanced down at Aorja. "The Magical Superior will have to know about her betrayal. He'll be the one who decides her ultimate fate."

"She deserves to be kicked out of the school," said Jiku, his tone firm. He put a hand on his chest. "She betrayed us. She tried to kill us. She's a threat to everyone here. She does not deserve to learn along with the rest of us."

Mom scowled, but it didn't seem to be because of what Jiku had said. She looked like she was remembering something that had happened a long time ago. "I understand the feeling. I once knew someone who I thought I could trust, who everyone thought we could trust. Turned out to be a psycho who deserved what he got coming to him."

Darek didn't know who Mom was talking about, but he didn't ask, either. Based on how angry she looked, Aorja's betrayal was bringing back memories she hadn't thought about in a long time and was in no mood to be questioned about, despite having been the one to bring it up in the first place.

"You guys will need to fill us in on the details later," said Mom. "Why did Aorja betray us? What did she think she was doing? Is she working for someone or is she on her own?"

"I can answer all three of those questions right away," said Jiku. "She was bored, she was following orders, and she's working for the Ghostly God."

"The Ghostly God?" said Mom. She groaned. "By the Powers, it just had to be one of the southern gods, didn't it? Oh, never mind. I'll go undo the seal she put on the door and tell the Superior what happened. You two stay put."

Darek was about to say that he and Jiku weren't going anywhere, but he didn't get a chance because Mom was already making her way down to the door. Outside the broken window Mom had used to enter, Darek heard the sounds of the students and teachers gathering outside, which made him feel safer, knowing that the others were close enough to help should Aorja somehow wake and free herself.

Then he looked down at Aorja. She was so still that she might have been dead. Tiny, barely visible wisps of smoke rose off her body, most likely from the burst of electricity that Mom had hit her with. She obviously wasn't dead—Mom wasn't a killer—but Darek doubted she would awake for a very long time.

He then looked at Jiku. His old friend was lying back in

his bed now, looking worn out from the excitement of the past ten or fifteen minutes.

"Well, what do you think?" said Darek.

Jiku didn't look at him. "I think Aorja should be punished to the fullest extent of the Academy's law. In other words, what I just said a few minutes ago."

Darek nodded, but somehow he found it hard to agree with. The pain of Aorja's betrayal did not seem to have hit him yet, at least not in the same way that Jiku had been hit. That wasn't very strange, as over the years, Darek had learned that he did not seem to handle trauma the same way as everyone else.

"What do you think?" said Jiku, looking at Darek. "Do you think she deserves to be expelled for good? Or better yet, shipped off to some miserable prison somewhere to rot for the rest of her sorry life?"

Darek bit his lower lip. "I think ... I will leave that up to the Magical Superior and the teachers."

Jiku sighed. He looked much older now than he had before. "You're right. Still, as a Grinfian, I can't just sit by and let this kind of injustice be swept under the rug."

"It won't be," Darek said. "The Magical Superior is a fair but just headmaster. He won't let Aorja get away with this."

"Let us hope so, Darek," said Jiku. "Now if you will excuse me, I must rest. All of the tension has worn me out, not including the fact that I'm still recovering from the explosion."

Darek yawned. "I would like to join you, but someone has to keep an eye on Aorja until the rest of the teachers get here."

"Very well," said Jiku. "We can talk more later, after I've rested up a bit."

With that, Jiku closed his eyes and sank deeper into his pillow and mattress. Darek wished he still had his pillow, but all that was left of it was a small pile of ashes on the floor near his bed and he certainly couldn't rest his head on that.

So he kept his eyes on Aorja, looking at her prone body until he heard Mom succeed in opening the door. Then he looked away as Eyurna, Noharf, Junaz, and the rest of the North Academy faculty entered and took Aorja away. He would rest like Jiku and then, later on, if he was feeling better, he would try to see Aorja one last time before her sentence was handed to her, whatever it was going to be.

Chapter Twelve

Durima had never liked Zamis, the Ghostly God's island. It was partly due to the bad memories she associated with the place, as the Ghostly God had punished her here many times, but it was also due to the strange nature of the island itself.

Zamis—which was located somewhere in the southern seas, but where, Durima didn't know, as its location seemed to change every day—was not very large. It only seemed big because of the thick jungle that towered over her. The jungle reminded her of the jungle on Ikadori Island, the domain of the Loner God, which she had only visited once but which had left a strong impression on her due to its eerie silence.

But unlike Ikadori Island, the jungle here was never silent. There was always the sound of animals rustling in the trees, insects buzzing in the air, and the wind blowing through the leaves. Sometimes it would rain heavily for days on end and then abruptly stop, leaving the jungle even stickier than normal.

Exactly what kind of creatures lived on Zamis, Durima didn't know. She had never taken the opportunity to explore it, mostly because the Ghostly God kept her too busy to even think about doing that kind of exploration. Nonetheless, whenever she came back to visit, Durima would sometimes catch glimpses of yellow monkey-like creatures in the treetops, but they always vanished the moment she tried to focus on them.

There wasn't much in the way of what mortals might call 'civilization' here. A rough path—largely cut out by Durima and Gujak to make it easier for them to reach the beach— led from the southern beach to the center of the island, but beyond that, it was obvious that no mortal had ever set foot here, or would ever set foot here. The island was ruled by the Ghostly God, but only in theory. In practice, nature ruled with an iron fist.

Now there was a reason Durima was thinking about all of this, even though none of it was new information to her. She and Gujak had arrived on Zamis about ten minutes ago, landing in the wide clearing in the middle of the jungle where the Ghostly God lived. She was thinking about this in order to distract her mind from thinking about what the Ghostly God was going to do to her and Gujak once he found out about their failure.

Of course, it was harder to distract her mind from such gloomy thoughts when she and Gujak now stood on the front porch of the Ghostly God's mansion. It was a two-story building, with a broken window on the first floor next to the front door. The roof was missing several shingles and the front door was kept closed only by a simple, rusted lock that never really worked anyway.

The mansion was perhaps the strangest feature on Zamis. How old it was, who built it, and why, Durima didn't know. It certainly didn't look like something built by a katabans or a god. It reminded Durima of the massive mansions in the Northern Isles, the ones some mortals lived in, but why a building either built by or based on something mortals had made existed in the southern seas, of all places, she didn't know.

Master never thought it important to tell us about that, Durima thought, watching as Gujak undid the latch on the front door. *He never tells us anything unless it's directly relevant to whatever job he's given us.*

A flash of blue light appeared out of the corner of Durima's eye. She looked up and saw that the westernmost window on the second story was glowing. That was the Ghostly God's room, which meant that he was indeed here and not anywhere else.

Of course Master is here, Durima thought with a scowl as Gujak opened the front door and walked inside. *Master is hardly what I'd call a socialite. He doesn't even socialize with his fellow gods.*

Durima followed Gujak into the mansion, but only reluctantly. While the outside was warm and muggy, inside the mansion, it was freezing and crisp, like the Great Berg, although not quite as cold.

The foyer they had entered looked much as it always had. Torn, graying curtains hung on the windows, while a moth-eaten carpet was spread out on the floor before them. Empty painting frames hung on the walls, while an equally empty stone podium stood in the center. There must have been a statue on it at some point, but what happened to the statue was another mystery Durima did not have the answer to.

Durima continued following Gujak, who was now climbing up the steep staircase that led to the second floor. The steps creaked and groaned under their feet, a familiar sound that Durima had heard many times over the years. Sometimes she thought she heard the steps actually whispering under her feet, but she dismissed it as her fear making her hear things that weren't there.

When they reached the top of the steps, they turned to the left and began walking down the long hallway all the way to the end. A door, looking as withered and beaten as the front door, stood at the end of the hall. Flashes of blue light shone underneath it, making Durima briefly wonder what the Ghostly God was up to until she realized that that was none of her business.

Besides, whatever it is, it is probably gruesome and nightmarish, Durima thought as Gujak fumbled with this door's latch, just like with the front door.

That may have seemed harsh, but it was true. The Ghostly God spent much of his time studying the spirits of the far gone. Although he was the God of Ghosts and Mist, he always said that what lay beyond the veil of death was a mystery even to him. Hence why he spent so much time studying ghosts and spirits and the concept of the afterlife in general. For whatever reason, he wanted to know what lay beyond death.

In that respect, I guess he's no different from the rest of us, Durima thought. *Maybe that's why he wanted us to find*

Braim Kotogs' grave. Perhaps he thought it might hold the answers he is looking for.

Her thoughts were interrupted when Gujak said, "Okay. Got it," and opened the door. Bracing herself for the Ghostly God's inevitable burst of anger at their failure, Durima went in after Gujak, her mind racing as she struggled to come up with any excuse to help mitigate Master's anger.

The room they had stepped into was very plain, although not entirely so. Coffins ran along the walls, almost like bookshelves, and like bookshelves, these coffins were packed tightly together. Those coffins usually contained the bodies of recently deceased mortals and katabans, a fact Durima had learned a while ago when she had seen the Ghostly God open one of them.

But that was not what had grabbed her attention. Instead, her attention was drawn to the hulking figure in the center of the room. He sat with his back to them, his head down like he was reading some kind of book. He didn't even seem to have heard them enter, but of course, he must have, as they hadn't been exactly silent.

"Durima, Gujak," said the Ghostly God, his voice very quiet, though Durima and Gujak jumped to attention anyway. "You have returned later than I expected."

Durima kept the trembling out of her voice as best as she could. "We apologize for our lateness, Master. We faced several unexpected issues at North Academy, including an automaton guardian."

"Automaton?" said the Ghostly God, still without turning to face them. The sound of a book slamming shut followed that word. "Is my sister giving out her children to mortals now? I wonder what happened to the Mechanical Goddess I once knew, the one who would lure mortals into her body and then allow her siblings to feast on them? I suppose she must have died when she met that mortal prince from the north. Weakling."

Durima was used to hearing the Ghostly God badmouth his siblings. He usually criticized his northern siblings due to their love of mortals, but he had choice words for his southern siblings as well. That made Durima wonder if the reason he was often alone had less to do with his disinterest in socializing and more to do with his rudeness towards the other gods.

"Not that it matters, one way or the other," said the Ghostly God. "I don't care what my siblings do, as long as they do not get in my way. Did any of my siblings get in your way?"

"N-No, sir," said Gujak, shaking his head. "We didn't face any opposition from any of the gods, whether northern or southern. It was mostly the mortal mages who got in our way. They didn't appreciate our breaking into their school and causing so much trouble."

"Of course they wouldn't," said the Ghostly God. "Anyway, I clearly should not ask if they captured you because Uron told me that they did. You two are very good at failing spectacularly at whatever I ask you to do."

Durima bit her lower lip. The Ghostly God was always saying things like that. She didn't think he actually meant it, seeing as he hadn't fired them yet, but he always focused on their failures. In fact, Durima couldn't even remember the last time the Ghostly God had actually congratulated or thanked her or Gujak for doing a job well done.

"I assume you did not tell the mages anything of importance?" said the Ghostly God. "Uron tells me that you managed to avoid revealing my identity to the enemy."

Durima could not help but feel a little proud about that. "Yes. We withstood their harsh interrogation techniques and—"

"It doesn't matter," said the Ghostly God, waving one hand to silence her. "They caught my other servant, my spy within the school. She is a weakling who will probably tell them everything. Mortals tend to put self-preservation above everything else, which is why I rarely employ them."

"Hold on a minute," said Gujak. "Excuse me, Master, but I didn't know you had another servant in the school. I thought it was just me and Durima."

The Ghostly God sighed. "Did you forget the part where I said that you two always fail? I had to employ a third servant to deal with any problems that might arise while you were trying to break in. Clearly, however, I made a mistake in trusting her, as she obviously did not deal with every possible problem that could affect your mission."

"What does this mean, then, sir?" said Durima. She hastily added, "If I may ask."

"It means that I will have to avoid hiring mortals again," said the Ghostly God. "And it means that Skimif will likely be paying me a visit sometime soon. He will undoubtedly want to make sure I am not up to no good, as though I am a little child who needs to be looked after."

The Ghostly God's words had a venomous tinge to them, which didn't surprise Durima. Any time Durima heard the gods talking about Skimif, they never sounded happy about him at all. Even if they didn't actually insult him, the tone they used was usually enough for Durima to guess how they felt about him.

"Are you still going to punish us?" Gujak asked in a breathless voice, like he was trying to get all of it out quickly. "Because Uron gave us a note you wrote that said you were going to punish us even if we succeeded, uh, sir."

The Ghostly God did not move for a minute. "No. Not today."

Gujak let out a huge sigh of relief. Durima wanted to join him, but she sensed that the Ghostly God was not happy about that, so she didn't.

"I cannot afford to have cripples working under me, not in this situation," said the Ghostly God. "With that silly mortal woman out of the picture, I now only have you two buffoons and Uron. I must therefore be careful with how I treat you, lest I end up with no servants at all."

Durima was so relieved that they were not going to be punished that she almost felt like jumping for joy. Then she remembered that the Ghostly God was putting off their punishment until later, which dampened her happiness somewhat.

"Speaking of Uron, sir," said Gujak, whose voice shook with a kind of repressed happiness, like he also realized that the Ghostly God would not appreciate any overt displays of joy in his presence, "where is he? I thought for sure that he would be here when we returned."

A low hiss behind them caused Durima to jump. She didn't even get a chance to look over her shoulder because a moment later Uron slithered past her, a large, purplish-black snake at least as long as a fully-grown oak. Uron didn't look at either her or Gujak as it went over to the Ghostly God, where it curled up neatly by his side, looking almost like an obedient dog rather than a disgusting reptile.

"He is right here," said the Ghostly God, a hint of sarcasm in his voice. He lifted his hand and patted Uron on the head. "Unlike you two, Uron is always at my side, ready to do what I ask efficiently and without complaint."

Although Uron did not flinch or pull away when the Ghostly God patted his head, Durima thought that the snake looked a little put off by being touched in that way. It might have just been her imagination, of course, as snakes did not have easy-to-read facial expressions.

"So what are we going to do now, Master?" said Gujak. "If Skimif is going to come and put an end to your plans, does that mean that we are going to give up?"

The Ghostly God's hand froze on Uron's head. "Give up? Of course not. It is a setback, a minor one at that, and nothing more. I still have an important mission for you two to take. A very important mission."

"We'll complete it to the best of our ability, sir," said Gujak. "Just tell us what it is and we'll get on it."

Yet the Ghostly God did not respond to Gujak immediately. He tilted his head to the side, toward Uron, almost as if he was listening to the snake talk. That was ridiculous, obviously, seeing as Uron was not even hissing at the moment.

But in some ways, it was not that strange. Ever since the Ghostly God had taken on Uron as his pet/servant, he had behaved this way every time he sent Durima and Gujak on some mission. At times, the Ghostly God's eyes would glaze over, as if he was not himself. He only ever acted that way whenever Uron was around. When the snake was nowhere to be seen, he usually acted like his normal self.

There's something not right about that snake, Durima thought, looking at Uron carefully. *But for the life of me, I can't figure out what.*

Then the Ghostly God's head snapped up straight. "All right. Your mission is simple. I want you two to go to Bleak Rock, a tiny spit of land hundreds of miles to the east of here, and retrieve an important object hidden there. It is a gauntlet."

Durima knew what Bleak Rock was. It was an island that was allegedly home to the Mysterious One, the so-called God of Mystery and Magic, who may or may not actually exist. The island was generally avoided by everyone, even by the gods themselves, because of its strange, eerie aura, in which magic generally did not work the way it was supposed to.

Durima herself had never been to Bleak Rock. She was not superstitious, but she was wary of anything she couldn't explain rationally. She had heard plenty of stories about it from other katabans, though, including one story where a katabans explorer had entered it, only to never return.

"Bleak Rock, sir?" said Gujak. "What kind of gauntlet is hidden there?"

"You do not need to know," said the Ghostly God. "Uron says ... I mean, it is important to my plans. It shouldn't be hard to find."

"Sir," said Gujak, "while I am in no way, shape, or form afraid of Bleak Rock, rumor says that it's the home of the Mysterious One."

Durima rolled her eyes. The Mysterious One was a myth and a legend. She thought everyone knew that. She supposed it made sense that Gujak would believe in that story because Gujak was as naïve as a young child.

"And?" said the Ghostly God. "What difference does that make?"

"Well, I was just thinking that the other gods don't like it when the servants of their fellow gods enter their domain without their permission," said Gujak. "I mean, of course, sir, you are free to do what you like and as your loyal servants we must obey you no matter what, but I was just wondering if you had already spoken with the Mysterious One about it."

The Ghostly God growled. "The Mysterious One is a myth designed by my siblings to explain something we can't. Bleak Rock is under the domain of no god or goddess. Anyone is free to take the island for their own purposes, if they want it, but the rest of my siblings are too superstitious to claim it. Which will make your mission that much easier, although knowing you two, you will probably find a way to mess it up even then."

"We will do our best, sir," said Gujak, saluting the Ghostly God. "We'll go to Bleak Rock, find that gauntlet, and return without delay."

Perhaps Gujak thought that by saying that he was going to win the Ghostly God's favor. Durima knew better than that. No matter how this next mission worked out, the Ghostly God would still punish them for their failing the last mission. Acting like a sycophant would do nothing except possibly make the Ghostly God like them even less.

The Ghostly God continued to stroke Uron's head. "Then what are you two still doing here? Leave me at once. I don't want either of you here when Skimif shows up to question me."

Durima turned to leave without saying another word, as she didn't want to aggravate the Ghostly God anymore than they already had.

Then she noticed Gujak was still standing there. He looked like he was about to ask a question. What question that was, Durima didn't know, but she had a feeling it was going to be stupid, so she reached out to grab his arm and drag her along behind him so they could leave for Bleak Rock.

But then Gujak asked, in a hurried voice, "But what about your servant back in North Academy? The one you said was captured by the mages?"

"What about her?" said the Ghostly God. "Do you think I am going to send someone to rescue her? Of course not. If she is weak enough to be captured like that, then I want nothing to do with her anymore. I do not waste time with fools like her."

"Oh, of course," said Gujak, rubbing his hands together nervously. "But while I would never, ever think to question your orders, what about the grave of Braim Kotogs? I mean, we failed to reach it. Don't you still want us to get it for you?"

"Don't worry about it," said the Ghostly God. "One of the rules I live by is that you should never send a katabans to do a job for a god. And clearly, this is a job for a god like myself."

His voice sounded distorted for just a moment, almost like someone was talking through him, but then his voice returned to normal. Durima concluded that she was probably just hearing things. Not surprising, considering her age.

Then the Ghostly God stood up. At his full height, his head almost scraped against the ceiling, and as he turned around to face them, Durima could not help but gaze upon their Master's face and body, even though she had seen both many times before.

The Ghostly God wore pale white armor, nearly as thick as the trunks of the trees that grew in the jungle outside of the mansion. His face was vaguely humanoid, with two glowing green eyes and a mouth full of crooked teeth, but his skin was so pale that she could almost see the veins under his body. His fingers appeared to be made out of metal, like they had been constructed by a blacksmith. A slim book was grasped between the fingers of his right hand, but Durima did not know what the book's title or author was.

"Now," said the Ghostly God, looking down on them like they were ants beneath his feet, "do either of you have any other dumb questions to ask or will you finally start to follow my orders wholeheartedly and without question, like good katabans?"

Gujak's jaw trembled as he said, "W-We'll go right away."

"Then leave," said the Ghostly God, pointing with one of his massive fingers over their heads and at the door behind them. "Now."

They didn't even hesitate. Durima and Gujak ran out of the room, but even as they did so, Durima glanced over her shoulder to see the Ghostly God sitting down again, his back to the door and his head bowed like he had returned to reading his book. Uron still sat next to him, and unless Durima's eyes were playing tricks on her, she thought that the snake looked about as annoyed by recent events as its owner.

But Durima turned her head away from the door. Master had given her and Gujak a job and they were going to complete it in as timely a manner as possible.

I must admit, though, that I feel sorry for the mortal mages at that school, Durima thought as she and Gujak walked down the stairs as fast as they could. *Because Master will not hesitate to snuff out their lives if they get in his way.*

Chapter Thirteen

One week later ...

The night was as dark as the catacombs beneath North Academy, not helped by the odd mist that had settled over the campus grounds, although the light shining from the moon and stars in the sky helped illuminate the area somewhat. At least Darek could see where he was going as he walked down the path that wound around the Arcanium down to the graveyard.

As he walked, he drew his mage's robes more tightly around his body, because a cold wind was blowing in tonight from the northern Walls. Granted, the heatstone that made up the school's buildings radiated enough heat to make the cold tolerable, but ever since nearly freezing his hands off trying to stop that chimera last week, Darek had been even more susceptible to cold than normal. It was getting so bad that he was starting to rethink his decision to become a pagomancer.

It's too late for that, I suppose, Darek thought as his shoes crunched lightly against the gravel path he walked upon. *I've spent nine years training as a pagomancer. I don't want to spend another ten learning to specialize in some other area of magic.*

Darek knew he should have been sleeping right now. It was midnight and everyone else in the school was soundly asleep in their dorms. Besides, he had a pyromancy class early in thc morning, right around dawn. Jiku, if he was awake, likely would have told Darek to go back to bed.

But as much as Darek wanted to, he couldn't sleep. It was probably because of that dream he had had a week ago, in which he spoke with that strange voice that had said so many odd things to him. The memories of that dream had faded from his mind since then, but he still recalled the strange, purplish-black wall and what it had said about itself.

Not only that, but Darek was thinking about Aorja as well. Just like he thought, the feelings of betrayal that Jiku had experienced were starting to affect him. Just thinking about Aorja now—without even thinking specifically about how she had betrayed him—was enough to make him want to smash something.

But Aorja was gone now. After the teachers had transported Aorja out of the medical wing, they had taken her to the Superior's study, where the Magical Superior had interrogated her for hours. The Superior had not revealed exactly what he learned from her, but he apparently learned quite a bit, because afterward, Aorja had been sent away.

'Sent away' was probably not the best word for what they did to her. According to Junaz, who had been there when the Magical Superior had made his decision about Aorja, Aorja had been sent to Rock Isle, an island far to the south of the Great Berg. Darek had never visited Rock Isle, but he

196

had heard plenty about it.

It's the most dangerous, worst prison in all of the Northern Isles, Jiku had told him after they learned about Aorja's fate. *Only the worst criminals are placed there. The Magical Superior must have been very angry with Aorja if he decided to send her there for her crimes.*

Jiku had sounded very happy about it. That made sense. Jiku was a follower of Grinf, the God of Justice. No doubt he saw this as perfectly just, although Darek had a hard time feeling happy about this when he thought about how awful Rock Isle was supposed to be. As much as he hated Aorja for what she did, he wasn't sure if she deserved that kind of punishment.

Darek didn't get a chance to say good bye to Aorja, either although looking back, he realized that was probably for the best. He had been so angry with Aorja that he likely would have attacked her if he'd seen her one last time. Part of him regretted that he would likely never see Aorja again, but another part of him thought *Good riddance.*

He suspected that Aorja's sentence had probably been influenced by Yorak and the Institute mages. He well remembered how Yorak, upon learning that Aorja had been the cause behind the destruction of the *Soaring Sea* and the Third Dorm, had demanded that Aorja be executed right here in the school in front of everyone. Only the Magical Superior's calm and collected reasoning had prevented that from becoming a reality, although Darek was under the impression that it had just barely worked.

Her sentence to Rock Isle was probably a compromise,

Darek thought. *This way, we get rid of a dangerous traitor and the Institute mages can rest safely knowing that someone who had tried to harm them is no longer a threat to their lives.*

Even though Aorja had been captured and sentenced to Rock Isle, the Institute mages had still left the next day when another airship—this one blue in color and possibly an older model than the last one, based on the loudness of its engine—flew in and landed in the sports field in almost the exact same spot where the *Soaring Sea* had landed the previous day. The Institute mages climbed inside without hesitation, left in three minutes, and hadn't been seen or heard from since.

Darek stopped for a moment on the path and looked up at the dark night sky, remembering how the Institute's new airship had looked as it zoomed through the sky over the Walls and out into the Great Berg. He didn't miss the Institute mages very much, mostly because he had barely gotten to know them, except for Auratus and Kuroshio.

And based on the conversations he had had with the other students, none of them missed their aquarian counterparts, either. If anything, the general consensus among the students seemed to be that the fewer aquarians in the school, the better. Apparently, some of the Institute mages had been incredibly rude and bigoted toward the Academy mages, made even worse by Yorak's display of blatant disrespect toward the Magical Superior.

Hence, Darek had not heard any of his fellow students wishing that the aquarians had stayed a little while longer.

Nor did he hear any talk of possibly inviting the Institute mages back again some other time, perhaps when things had settled down. Even the teachers did not seem to miss them much and he certainly hadn't heard anything about the Institute mages from the Magical Superior.

Maybe the Magical Superior's plan to bring the two schools together backfired, Darek thought, shaking his head as he continued walking down the gravel path. *Guess it doesn't really matter. Doesn't change the fact that I can't sleep.*

Granted, Darek could have used hypnomancy to put himself to sleep, but he was never a very good hypnomancer. Once, in a lesson on hypnomancy, he had been given the simple task of casting a basic sleep spell on one of his fellow students. Unfortunately, Darek had somehow messed it up and instead cast an insomnia spell on the student, which prevented the poor guy from sleeping for almost a full week before the teachers found the counter spell.

So Darek had decided that he would go out to the graveyard in the middle of the night and walk around until he got tired. Walking around a graveyard in the middle of the night certainly seemed like a foolish thing, but only if you were superstitious. There was nothing to fear about the school's graveyard. No spirits or ghosts lived there, despite some of the rumors he had heard from the other students.

It's just a normal graveyard, Darek thought. *Anyone who thinks otherwise clearly hasn't walked in it before.*

Another reason Darek decided to go to the graveyard

tonight was to see if he could find out why those two katabans intruders from earlier had come here. He had learned that the katabans had been searching for a particular grave, but whose and why, he didn't know.

So he decided that solving a good mystery would be enough to tire him out. He doubted he would find anything, but the thought that he might solve this puzzle that had stumped even the Magical Superior spurred him onwards. He liked having a goal better than aimlessly walking about, anyway.

In another minute, Darek reached the front gate of the graveyard. It looked as normal as it ever did to him, at least from what he could see of it in the darkness, mist, and moonlight. But according to Junaz, a large, strange-looking tree had sprouted in front of it a week ago, which the two katabans had tried to use to enter the graveyard. The tree had since been removed, its wood to be used for magical purposes, but Darek could see the plot of dirt where it had been growing.

Darek opened the gate without hesitation and entered. He was well aware of the various traps set up around the graveyard's perimeter by Junaz, but he did not think he would accidentally set them off. The traps, while mostly non-magical, did have very simple scanning spells cast on them that allowed them to tell the difference between invaders and mages who lived here. That was why Darek felt comfortable entering the graveyard through the gate.

The graveyard was quiet and cold tonight, as it usually was, the only significant difference being the thick mist that covered everything. What made the graveyard so strange in comparison to the rest of the Academy was that the tombstones were not made of heatstone. In fact, the oldest tombstones were made of marble, apparently imported from the south. The old stone path, too, was made of gravel, but why that was, Darek didn't know, as the graveyard was one of the oldest parts of the school and much of its history had been lost due to the lack of good record-keeping in the school's early years.

As Darek walked, looking at the various cracked and faded tombstones, he wished he knew what to look for. The two katabans probably did, but as far as he knew, only the Magical Superior knew what they were looking for, and he, in his usual secretive way, had not told anyone what they had said to him about it. Darek had considered speaking to the Magical Superior himself, but he rejected the idea because, as close as they were, he knew better than to ask the Magical Superior about topics that he refused to speak about. The Magical Superior usually had good reasons for keeping secrets, anyway, so Darek did not see any reason to badger him about it.

Besides, Darek didn't expect to find anything tonight, not really. Solving the mystery of what the katabans had came here for was merely a trick to help cure his temporary insomnia. As long as it did that, he didn't care if he solved a mystery or not.

That was when Darek realized that he wasn't alone. By now he had almost reached the back of the graveyard when he noticed, through a break in the mist, someone standing in front of one of the graves.

Darek stopped and stared at the figure, for a moment uncertain who it was. He thought at first that it might be one of the Diogian students, as they sometimes visited the graveyard at night in order to perform some basic rituals to Diog, the God of the Grave, and make sure that the graves were undisturbed.

But then he noticed the auburn robes and the staff and he realized who it was.

"Magical Superior, sir?" said Darek as he approached the old mage standing before the grave. "What are you doing up so late?"

The Magical Superior turned to face Darek. He looked tired, far more tired than Darek felt. His eyes had bags underneath them and he was leaning on his staff more heavily than usual. It was probably his age showing, although Darek didn't think that being up so late could be good for the Superior's health.

"I was about to ask you the same question, Darek," said the Magical Superior with a yawn. "Students are supposed to be in bed until morning."

"I couldn't sleep," said Darek. He tapped the side of his head. "Bad dreams and all that. Thought taking a walk through the graveyard might help some of that."

"That's an unusual way to cure insomnia," said the Magical Superior. Then he glanced over his shoulder. "Perhaps I should return to my study. I have a full day tomorrow and I need all the rest I can give my old bones."

Darek nodded, but he was still overcome with curiosity,

so he said, "That's probably a good idea, Superior sir, but you didn't answer my question. Why are you out so late?"

For a moment, the Magical Superior looked like he was going to avoid answering the question entirely. That would not have surprised Darek.

So Darek was surprised when the Magical Superior said, "I came to visit the grave of my deceased pupil, Braim Kotogs. You know who that is, of course."

"Oh, yeah," said Darek. "He was the guy who brought me and Mom here to the school when I was very young. I wish I could have gotten to know him better before he died, though. I didn't even get a chance to thank him."

"And I didn't get a chance to say good bye to him, even though I was there at his death," said the Magical Superior. "Nonetheless, we were able to give him a proper burial, which is ultimately the only thing we can do for those who passed away."

"Yeah," said Darek. "But why did you come out to visit Braim's grave? I mean, not that there's anything wrong with that. It just seems like an odd time to do that."

The Magical Superior rubbed the back of his neck, like he was thinking hard about what he wanted to say next. "I suppose I can tell you that. I trust you, Darek, so I must ask that you keep what I am about to tell you a secret, at least for now, okay?"

Darek nodded. "Does this have to do with what you learned from the katabans from last week?"

"Yes," said the Magical Superior. "It does. That is why I want you to promise me to keep this between the two of us for now."

"All right," said Darek. "I won't mention a word of this to anyone without your permission, then."

"Exccllent," said the Magical Superior with a tired smile. He stepped aside, allowing Darek a chance to see Braim's grave. "I will get straight to the point, seeing as I am tired and would like to return to my bed soon: The katabans invaders had been looking for the grave of Braim Kotogs."

Darek frowned. "Why?"

"I am not sure," said the Magical Superior. "I have been puzzling over it since last week. Even with Aorja's confession about her allegiance to the Ghostly God, I do not see any reason why they would want to find Braim's old grave."

Darek scratched his chin. The mist was getting thicker, but he decided not to mention it because he figured it was made by Junaz, who was also the school's katamancy teacher and was in charge of controlling the weather to make sure it didn't become unbearable.

"Did Braim know or worship the Ghostly God?" Darek asked. "Maybe the Ghostly God was trying to find the remains of one of his supporters?"

"No," said the Magical Superior flatly. "Braim did not worship any of the southern gods. He didn't even know about their existence until Skimif revealed them to everyone else. That's what puzzles me. What connection exists between the Ghostly God and Braim?"

Darek shrugged. "I wish I could help, but sadly, I'm in the same position as you."

"Maybe it's not worth worrying about," said the Magical Superior, looking at Braim's grave again. "There has been no activity from the Ghostly God or his servants since last week. Skimif told me that he was going to speak with the Ghostly God about his involvement in the matter, but I have not even heard from Skimif since then."

"Maybe the Ghostly God has given up whatever he was trying to do?" Darek suggested. "Skimif probably told him off, maybe punished him for causing so much trouble. I bet that was enough to make the Ghostly God give up."

A deep, bellowing laugh echoed from the mist just then, causing Darek to jump and the Magical Superior to look around in alarm, holding his staff more tightly as he did so.

"Foolish, naïve mortal," said a voice from within the mist. "You clearly do not know or understand us southern gods if you think a slap on the wrist from an upstart godling is enough to make us give up."

"The Ghostly God," said the Magical Superior, although there was no way he could have known that for sure. "Where are you? Show yourself."

"Amazing," said the Ghostly God. "You not only are willing to stand in the way of the plans of a god, but presumptuous enough to demand that I show myself to you? And here my northern siblings are always telling me that you mortals treat us gods with respect and reverence."

The Ghostly God's voice seemed to come from everywhere at once. The mist was too thick for Darek to see through, so for all he knew, the Ghostly God could be right next to him and he didn't know it.

"My loyalties lie first and foremost with my students," said the Magical Superior, his voice firm and clear. "And it was your servants who put the lives of two of my students in danger. If you think I will just ignore that, then you clearly do not know me."

"I do not care what you mortals think about me, anyway," said the Ghostly God. "You mortals never respected us southern gods, which is fine because we never wanted you to. I will admit, however, that I am surprised that you want me to show myself when I've been hiding in plain sight."

"What do you mean?" said Darek. "All I see is thick mist everywhere I look."

The Ghostly God's chuckle was right in Darek's ear. "I see you must not know what other domain I rule. I am not only the God of Ghosts, but the God of Mist as well, and right now, that means I *am* the mist."

Metal fingers—as cold as the mist—wrapped around Darek's neck just then. Darek choked and his hands flew to the fingers to pry them off, but the grip around his neck was as firm as a mountain.

"But I suppose it makes sense that you would show such startling ignorance," said the Ghostly God. "You mortals only barely understand us southern gods. It's not like I have a temple and religion that you could go to and find out all about me, like my northern siblings do."

The Magical Superior pointed his staff at the fingers around Darek's neck, but he did not fire anything from its tip.

"Trying to save your student?" said the Ghostly God. "Pathetic old man. You know you can't free him from my grasp without putting his very life at risk. I know how much you value the safety of your students, Magical Superior, so your bluff doesn't scare me in the slightest."

A brief glimpse into the Magical Superior's eyes was enough to tell Darek that the Ghostly God was correct. Lowering his staff, the Magical Superior said, "What do you have to gain from threatening the life of one of my students, Ghostly God? What did he do to deserve that?"

"I am looking to strike a deal with you, Magical Superior," said the Ghostly God. "A deal I did not think I would ever need to strike, but considering how my plans to open Braim's grave coincided with your need to find out what my idiotic servants were up to, I consider it a necessary deal."

"What kind of deal?" said the Magical Superior.

"A simple one," said the Ghostly God. "In exchange for letting your student here free, you will dig up Braim Kotogs' grave for me. That is all I ask of you."

"Why do you want me to dig up the grave of my deceased pupil?" the Magical Superior asked.

"That is none of your business," said the Ghostly God. "What matters is whether you accept the deal or not. Don't forget that I am more than willing to harm your student if you choose to reject the deal."

The Magical Superior looked from Darek and the grave and back again before saying, "Where is Skimif? He told me he was going to deal with you."

"Skimif doesn't even know I'm here," said the Ghostly God with a snort. "When he came to Zamis, my island, last week, I told him that I was sorry for causing so much trouble. The naïve idiot seemed to believe me because he left me alone after that and I haven't heard a word from him since."

"So you are a liar and a deceiver," said the Magical Superior. "Of course you are. I've heard all about the southern gods and their lack of decent morals. It is disgusting."

"I am beginning to rethink that all of the rumors I heard about your devotion to the gods were severely distorted," said the Ghostly God. "Disgusting ... you make us southern gods sound like rock slugs. But it doesn't matter. The point is, Skimif doesn't even realize I'm here. So I am waiting for you to agree to my deal."

"When did I say I would ever agree to that awful deal you offered me?" said the Magical Superior.

The Ghostly God's grip tightened around Darek's neck; not enough to cut off his air supply completely, but enough to make Darek gasp in pain. Darek reached for the deity's fingers again, but he was so weak now that he couldn't do more than pat the Ghostly God's fingers futilely before letting his arms fall to his sides.

"I will kill him," said the Ghostly God simply. "Without hesitation or mercy."

"But the Treaty says that you southern gods cannot kill mortals beyond the Dividing Line," said the Magical Superior. He pointed at the ground. "This is far above the

Dividing Line. Therefore, your threat is empty."

"Can you be so sure about that?" said the Ghostly God. "The Powers were creative geniuses of the highest order; however, they were not legal scholars. There are many loopholes in the Treaty that we gods, whether northern or southern, have learned to exploit over the years. No doubt I could find a loophole that allows us southern gods to kill mortals on the other side of the Dividing Line."

"*Could* is different from *can*, Ghostly God," said the Magical Superior. He pointed his staff at Darek. "Now let Darek go."

"Only after you open the grave," said the Ghostly God. "But I can see this is getting nowhere fast. The longer I stay here, the more likely it becomes that Skimif will notice I am here and come to stop me. Uron?"

At that moment, the sound of something long and heavy slithering across the ground entered Darek's ears. He at first could not see the snake (that was what he assumed it was, because what else slithered across the ground?), but then he felt something thick and powerful climbing up his body.

Looking down, Darek saw a snake—almost twice as long as his body—curling up around him. Its body felt icky and slimy, clinging to his torso as though it were covered in paste. Its skin was purplish-black, a familiar color, but Darek was too petrified to remember where he had seen that color before.

Soon the snake had wrapped its body around his completely, acting like a thick rope, making it impossible for Darek to move at all. He couldn't even reach for his new wand, which was in his left pocket.

The giant snake twisted its head so it was looking at Darek. Something flickered behind its sickly yellow eyes, something dark and intelligent, but the flickering was there for only a minute. In the next instant, the snake's eyes returned to normal, but that did not make them look any less frightening or intimidating.

Then Darek felt the Ghostly God's fingers leave his throat. Gasping for air, Darek breathed hard as the Ghostly God himself—a large titan of a deity—materialized into existence beside Darek. He began stroking the snake's head, a wicked smile on his face as he looked down at the Magical Superior.

"Meet Uron," said the Ghostly God, gesturing with his head at the snake. "My pet teleporter snake. He is a loyal servant, infinitely superior to my other servants in just about every way. He does whatever I ask of him, without question or comment, and always does it efficiently."

"I have never seen a teleporter snake that big before," said the Magical Superior, his old eyes focused on Uron's head. "Where did you find it?"

"That is none of your business," said the Ghostly God. "But allow me to give you a brief lesson about teleporter snake biology. The average teleporter snake is capable of crushing rocks into powder, making teleporter snakes one of the strongest species of snake in the animal kingdom. I know this only because my brother, the Loner God, once told me about them years ago."

"I don't understand," said the Magical Superior. "How is

that trivia relevant to—oh. I see."

The Ghostly God's pasty grin grew even larger. "Perhaps you are intelligent after all."

"What is going on?" said Darek. He was almost too frightened to speak, but he had to because he didn't like the way the Magical Superior's eyes had widened in horror. "I don't understand."

"But apparently, your student here has failed to take after you," said the Ghostly God with a sigh. "You see, student, I am incapable of killing any mortals beyond the Dividing Line, as your headmaster so accurately put it. But that says nothing about any of my servants who I may employ to kill mortals I do not like."

"Is that Uron's job?" said Darek, looking at the snake's face, which looked content being petted by the Ghostly God. "Is he going to—"

"He will," said the Ghostly God, without looking at Darek. "Unless the Magical Superior here agrees to my deal. I do not know, however, if he cares enough about you to want to save your life like this."

Darek returned his attention to the Magical Superior. He looked far more torn than Darek had ever seen him in his life. Under ordinary circumstances, the Magical Superior would probably keep resisting, but these were no ordinary circumstances. This was a god threatening to kill one of his students, a god who could easily carry out that threat no problem.

It was a hard choice to make. Even Darek had a hard time figuring out what the Magical Superior should choose to do. Darek didn't want to die, but he wasn't foolish enough to believe that the Ghostly God's plans for Braim's grave were benign.

Then the Magical Superior's shoulders slumped. "Fine, Ghostly God. I will dig up Braim's grave in exchange for Darek's safety."

"Excellent," said the Ghostly God. "You are a far more reasonable man than I thought. Good for you. Now get to work."

"Why don't you free Darek first?" said the Magical Superior. "That way, I know you will keep your end of the bargain."

"You mistake me for a businessman," said the Ghostly God. "And a very foolish one at that. I can see right through your tricks. You want me to let Darek go so you two can escape. I will not fall for it. Neither will Uron."

When the Ghostly God said that, Uron hissed at the Magical Superior. Its deep red tongue shot out of its mouth when it did so, the sound so loud to Darek that his ears ached.

"Get to work," said the Ghostly God. "Or I will order Uron to turn your student into little more than a fleshly sack of bone powder."

The Magical Superior looked like he was going to attack the Ghostly God, but then he let out a sigh of resignation and turned to face the grave. He pointed his staff at the grave, and for a moment, nothing happened.

Then the dirt began to rise out of the grave. It was like a giant, invisible hand was scooping up the earth. It rose slowly, but in a minute or two, the grave had been dug out. The giant clump of dirt, resembling a crude sphere, hovered in the air above it, bits of earth occasionally breaking off and falling into the open grave below.

Without a word, the Magical Superior moved the mound of earth over to the right of the grave. He placed it gently on the ground and then stepped back and looked at the Ghostly God.

"There," said the Magical Superior, gesturing at the now-open grave. He sounded close to tears. "The grave of Braim Kotogs, my former pupil and my nephew, is now open for your perusal."

The Ghostly God hovered past Uron and Darek, his eyes focused entirely on the open grave before him. Even Uron appeared eager to see what was inside, for his yellow snake eyes followed the Ghostly God's progress and his body tightened around Darek's.

As the Ghostly God drew closer to the grave, the Magical Superior stepped in his path. The God of Ghosts and Mist stopped and looked down on the Magical Superior, but it was impossible to see his facial expression with his back facing Darek.

"What are you doing, mortal?" said the Ghostly God. "Get out of my way."

"Not until you uphold your end of the deal and let Darek go," said the Magical Superior. "That was the deal."

The Magical Superior did not look even slightly afraid of the Ghostly God, despite the fact that the god was several feet taller than him and at least a foot thicker. That made

Darek admire the Superior even more than he already did, which was saying something, seeing as Darek already respected the Magical Superior more than anyone else at the school.

But his admiration turned to horror as the Ghostly God slapped the Magical Superior in the face. The blow sent the Magical Superior staggering to the right. He tripped over his robes and fell on his side, a stunned expression on his ancient features as the Ghostly God let out a sound of disgust.

"Superior!" Darek cried out, but Uron constricted more tightly around Darek's body, thus cutting him off before he could say anything else.

"As I said before, Magical Superior," said the Ghostly God, shaking his head. "I am not a businessman, especially not an honest one. As a god, I have no need to respect the pitiful agreements I may make with mortals, even if these mortals are allegedly faithful supports of the gods."

The Magical Superior groaned in pain, but he didn't say anything. Clearly, the Ghostly God's slap had been stronger than it looked if the Magical Superior was incapable of recovering from it. Darek was thankful the Superior wasn't dead, but he didn't look like he would be getting up anytime soon.

Then the Ghostly God pointed at the open grave. His hand balled into a fist and he jerked it upward.

At the same time, an old, boxy coffin rose out of the grave. It was almost too dark to see its features, but Darek could tell that its lid was cracked, almost in half, and that it was covered in dirt. He was surprised it was as whole as it was, seeing as the coffin had been in the earth for thirty years without being disturbed by anyone.

The Ghostly God directed the coffin over to the other side of the grave. When the coffin touched the ground, the Ghostly God pulled his arm back. A happy smile spread across the Ghostly God's face, the kind of smile that only someone who had succeeded in what they had longed to do could have.

"I am so close now to achieving what I want," said the Ghostly God, his voice low, but excited. "So close now."

He snapped his fingers. The coffin's lid exploded off, flying up into the mist and out of sight. A loud *thunk* was the only indication that it had landed somewhere, although Darek was too busy looking at the coffin in horror to care about where its lid had landed.

There's nothing I can do to stop him or avenge the Magical Superior, Darek thought. *Looks like it's over. He's won.*

So he thinks, young mortal. He may be a god, but that does not make him intelligent or clever.

Darek froze. That voice. He recognized it. It was the same voice that had spoken to him in his dream. He had not expected to hear it again. But where was it coming from?

Without really knowing why, Darek looked over to his left. Uron was staring at him, but his eyes no longer looked animalistic. An intelligence far above that of any teleporter snake gleamed within and Uron's snake-like mouth was twisted in a mockery of a smile.

That was when Darek put two and two together and realized just who the voice belonged to.

But before he could ask Uron just what—or who—he really was, the snake let go of his body. No longer constricted, Darek fell to his hands and knees, too weak to stand. The pressure that Uron had applied to his body had taken more out of him than he realized.

Nonetheless, he managed to look up in time to see Uron slithering toward Braim Kotogs' open casket. The Ghostly God must have noticed Uron making a mad scramble for the coffin as well because he shouted, "Uron! What do you think you're doing? Stop right this instant or—"

The Ghostly God did not get to finish his sentence. Uron slithered into the casket as fast as lightning. As soon as the tip of its tail disappeared into the coffin, a blindingly bright erupted from the coffin, so bright that it drowned out the whole world.

But although Darek was completely blinded by the light, his hearing worked just fine, and what he heard frightened him more than any sudden loss of sight:

A horrible, deep laugh ... the laugh that Darek had heard from his dream. And it was coming from Braim's open casket.

Chapter Fourteen

Stepping out of the ethereal and onto the island of Bleak Rock, Durima shuddered when a cold, biting wind blew through. Although her physical form gave her a thick fur coat which usually worked at blocking the cold, it was still imperfect (as all physical bodies were), which was why she shivered when she stepped onto Bleak Rock.

Gujak didn't even have fur. He had exited before her in order to scout ahead for any danger, but when Durima saw him, he was shivering like crazy. She wondered why he had not shivered so much back in the Great Berg, but decided that it was not a question worth thinking about right now, not when they had more important things to worry about.

"N-No enemies or traps," said Gujak, his teeth chattering. "At least none out here. Didn't go inside because I wanted to wait until you got here so we could go in t-together."

Durima nodded. She looked around at Bleak Rock, because this was the first time she had ever visited the island and so did not know what it looked like.

It was completely different from Zamis. It had no beach at all; instead, it had what appeared to be a high cliff with no railing to catch anyone who might fall off. They were hundreds of feet above sea level, which explained the strong gusts of wind that tore through like enraged baba raga.

The island itself was rather small, despite its height. There were no signs of wildlife, not even any seagulls searching for food. The waves that crashed against the base of the island below had smoothed out it to the point where the island's base was practically unclimbable. No wonder it was called Bleak Rock. Just standing here was enough to make Durima feel depressed.

"So how do we get inside?" said Durima.

Gujak jerked a thumb over his shoulder. "T-There's an entrance behind me, the only one I could find. Just like Master said there would be."

"Then what are we doing, standing around here getting our toes and fingers frozen off?" said Durima. "Let's go inside and find that gauntlet already."

Gujak nodded and turned, walking toward the gap in the rock that would take them deep into the island itself. That was another unusual thing about Bleak Rock. Whereas most islands were large enough to support their flora and fauna on their surface, Bleak Rock's surface was tiny, with little room even for the two of them. The island's actual terrain, where the object of their mission was supposed to be, was hidden underground. How far down it went and what was down there exactly, Durima didn't know, aside from a handful of vague, disturbing rumors she had heard over the years.

I sincerely doubt we'll find the bones of deceased gods down there, Durima thought. *Or anything else, for that matter. This island seems abandoned to me. No life here at all.*

Of course, she and Gujak *would* have came to Bleak Rock much earlier than they did, but the Ghostly God had given them specific instructions to wait one week before going. He had told them that he wanted to time their arrival on Bleak Rock with his own journey to North Academy. He had said that timing the two events so they would happen simultaneously was very important because it was the only way to keep Skimif from putting a stop to his plans before they came to fruition, as Skimif could not be in two places at once.

That made some sense to Durima, she thought as she watched Gujak pick up a rock and toss it into the gap in the rock to test for any traps they were unaware of. She remembered well how Master had told her about how Skimif had came to Zamis last week and threatened to punish the Ghostly God for what his servants had done, forcing Master to 'apologize' for what he did and to vow never to do that again.

It always amazed Durima how naïve Skimif was. He always seemed ready and willing to believe in the inherent goodness of other people, no matter how awful they acted. She had never spoken with the God of Martir himself, but she had seen and heard enough about him to understand that much.

Then again, godlings tend to be a lot more naïve than normal gods, Durima thought. *Perhaps he needs a few more centuries to grow up.*

"Okay," said Gujak. "L-Looks like the gap is safe to go through."

Durima looked at the gap more closely. It was a thin slit in the rock, wide enough for someone like Gujak to slip through without trouble, but she did not think that her bulk would fit. She would have to widen the gap.

"Stand back," Durima said to Gujak. "I'm going to use my geomancy to widen the entrance so I can enter. Shouldn't take more than a minute."

Gujak retreated as much as he could on the narrow cliff that was the exterior of Bleak Rock. Once he was safely out of the way, Durima walked up to the gap and grabbed it with both claws. The rock felt old and crumbly under her hands, but it clearly wasn't going anywhere without some effort on her part.

Concentrating hard, Durima channeled her geomancy through her hands and into the island itself. It shouldn't be a very difficult move. As she had said to Gujak, it should only take a minute. Durima had widened cracks in the ground before with her magic. It was one of the simplest tasks a geomancer could do, a task that even a bad geomancer could do without messing it up too badly.

Which was why she was shocked when she felt her geomancy rebound back into her body. It sent her staggering backwards from the gap as breathless as if she had been punched in the gut by a professional fighter. She put her hands on her knees, gasping in pain, as Gujak approached her with a worried look on his face.

"What happened?" said Gujak. "Why do you look so

tired?"

"Not … sure," said Durima. Her knees were wobbly and unstable, which was why she didn't dare take even one step forward. "My magic … rebounded into my body."

"See?" said Gujak. He gestured at the island all around them. "The rumors were true. Bleak Rock really is a place where magic doesn't work the way it's supposed to. I knew it."

Durima rolled her eyes. "Right. Well, whatever the reason for that, we still need to widen the gap. Otherwise, how will I get inside?"

"But how do we widen the gap without magic?" said Gujak, glancing at the entrance to the island's interior. "If it rejected your magic, it will probably do the same to mine if I try anything."

Feeling her strength slowly returning to her limbs, Durima said, "We'll have to do it the old fashioned way: With our hands."

It took Durima much longer to widen the gap with her bare hands and brute physical strength than it would have if her magic worked. Not to mention it required more effort, but there was no way around it, so she moved as fast as she could, her claws tearing through the crumbly rock like a badly formed pot of clay.

Ten minutes later, the gap was now wide enough for Durima and Gujak to pass through comfortably. Her fur covered in dust and her claws aching, Durima stepped back, panting as she looked at her handiwork.

"Wow, Durima," said Gujak, looking at the widened entrance with some respect. "Y-You did it after all."

"Of course," said Durima, kicking aside some of the rubble lying at her feet. "Now let's not waste time standing around here admiring my work. We have a mission to accomplish and we can't accomplish it by standing here doing nothing."

"I'll go first," said Gujak, holding up one hand to volunteer. "I can use my light to see what's in there. If it's safe to follow, I will let you know immediately."

Durima was in no mood, after her hard work of widening the entrance, to argue with that. She stepped aside as Gujak walked past her toward the entrance. He stopped in front of it and then held up his right hand, which began glowing like a torch.

He stuck his hand into the darkness of Bleak Rock's interior and leaned forward to get a better look. "Can't see much. It's really dark in there. But I do see what appears to be a natural stone slide that leads down."

"Down where?" Durima asked.

"Not sure," said Gujak. "Maybe it leads down to the bottom or maybe it will lead us into a pit full of poisonous snakes."

"You're still going in," said Durima. "You volunteered. If you try to go back on your word now—"

"I didn't say I wasn't going in," said Gujak in a somewhat annoyed voice. "I was just saying that I have no idea what is in there."

"Then why don't you stop your yammering and just go in

there and find out?" said Durima. "And if you get bitten by a hundred poisonous snakes and die, well, I'll at least try to get your body so we can give you a proper burial."

Gujak grimaced at that, but he didn't reply. He just grabbed the top of the entrance and then shoved himself forward. He rapidly vanished into the darkness, even with his hand still glowing. Soon he was gone completely, with not even one hint to suggest that he had been standing there moments ago.

Not more than a minute later, however, and Gujak's voice called up from the island's interior, "It's okay! The slide ends at a wall. No poisonous snakes or anything. But it is really, really cold down here, much colder than it was up there."

Another shockingly cold gust of wind cut through Durima just then, causing her to shout back, "I'm coming down, so you'd better get out of the way so I don't slide into you!"

Durima walked up to the entrance and launched herself into it the same way Gujak had. She soon found herself sliding down rapidly through the darkness, completely unable to see even one inch in front of her. The stone slide was smooth but slimy and damp, which made the ride far less comfortable than it could have been.

Thankfully, the slide was not very long. Soon she saw Gujak's light, the only beacon in the thick darkness, and thanks to his small light saw a tall, solid-looking rock wall waiting for her at the bottom of the slide. Unsure how to slow down, Durima put her arms in front of her face just as she slammed into the rock wall full force.

The blow was dizzying, but not the worst blow she had ever received in her life when she considered how an enemy soldier had once beaten her brutally during the Katabans War.

Durima stood up, her head spinning, as Gujak said, "You all right?"

Durima shook her head, trying to clear her thoughts. "Yeah. Just slightly dizzy is all. I'll be fine in a few seconds."

"That's good," said Gujak. "Anyway, I've found only one way to head down deeper into the island's interior."

"Only one way?" said Durima, looking at Gujak in confusion. "Are you sure there aren't anymore?"

"Absolutely," said Gujak. "I did a thorough check and found only one hallway. Whoever carved out the interior of this island didn't care about giving room for anyone to breathe."

Durima nodded. Now that her senses were returning, she, too, felt claustrophobic down here. Whether it was because of the heavy darkness that even Gujak's light only barely managed to penetrate or whether it was due to being inside an island, Durima felt like she was trapped in a cage. And she wanted out.

It's just a feeling, Durima thought. *You've felt this way before. Remember the pit in the War? You didn't come all this way just to run away. Especially when running away would guarantee your punishment by Master.*

"Then what are we waiting for?" said Durima. "Let's keep going. Master told us not to dilly-dally, and we won't."

Gujak nodded and walked to the left. Durima followed and in a minute they were inside a narrow hallway that made Durima feel even more claustrophobic. The ceiling was low, the walls on either side felt like the compactor of the Mechanical Goddess. It didn't help that it was indeed very cold, just as Gujak had said, even colder than the outside.

But their progress was sadly cut short when they came upon a large pile of debris—perhaps fallen from the ceiling —blocking their path. The pile of rock chunks blocked the passage completely, leaving not even one inch for them to crawl through. The pile looked like it had been here a very long time, perhaps for a decade or more, although Gujak's small light did not show enough detail for Durima to know for certain.

"Uh oh," said Gujak. "What happened here? Earthquake?"

"Probably," said Durima. "Either that, or Mica came through here and decided to block off the rest of this island from intruders."

"But this island isn't under Mica's domain," said Gujak, looking over his shoulder at Durima. "The Mysterious One is probably responsible for it."

Durima punched Gujak's shoulder. "Didn't you hear what Master said earlier? The Mysterious One is a myth. None of the gods rule this island. Myths can't block off underground tunnels."

"I know, I know," said Gujak, rubbing his shoulder where Durima had hit it. "But ... well, sometimes Master isn't always right. I mean, no one has ever disproved the Mysterious One exists, right?"

"No one has ever proved he exists, either," said Durima, "but that doesn't mean it's rational or intelligent to believe in him."

"But don't you remember what Messenger-and-Punisher said to us once?" said Gujak. "Back when the Powers were going to destroy the world? He said that a god named the Mysterious One had ordered him to help rescue a bunch of mortals stuck on the sea floor."

"Messenger-and-Punisher isn't exactly the most reliable source of information on the gods," said Durima, shaking her head. "Remember when he said that Master wasn't looking for any servants when we asked him if he knew of any gods who needed servants?"

"Yeah, but—"

Gujak's sentence was cut off by a sudden shaking of the island around them. Without thinking, Durima pulled herself close to the floor, a habit she had developed during her stay on the Volcanic Isles during the Katabans War, where quakes like this one—and worse—were very common. Gujak just ended up stumbling against the right wall, clinging to it like it was his mother.

"W-What's going on here?" said Gujak, his teeth chattering as the island continued to shake. "Is the island sinking into the sea or—"

Once more, Gujak was interrupted, this time by the sound of a rock wall collapsing nearby. Durima looked to the left and saw, by the dim light of Gujak's shining hand, that the wall to her left had completely collapsed, revealing a gaping hole large enough for both of them to go through.

As soon as the last of the wall had fallen, the island ceased shaking. Neither Durima nor Gujak moved right away, however, as both were waiting to see if this was only a pause and if Bleak Rock would continue shaking.

The seconds ticked by until it finally became clear that Bleak Rock was not going to be shaking again anytime soon. That was good. Because Durima had worried for a moment that she and Gujak would be trapped underneath tons and tons of rock or maybe even drown, if the island had sunk into the ocean like Gujak feared.

"I-I don't understand," said Gujak, his voice trembling. "Why did the island shake?"

"This area must be home to natural earthquakes," said Durima. She gestured at the debris blocking off the hallway. "That's probably what caused that, not some silly myth."

"Where does that way lead?" said Gujak, pointing at the area behind the collapsed wall. "To the gauntlet?"

"I don't know," Durima admitted. "But since I doubt we could move this debris in a timely manner, why not go down there and see for ourselves? Maybe it's a short cut."

Gujak shuddered. "Or maybe it's a trap."

"Aside from that tremor, we haven't faced any actual problems down here yet," said Durima. "Honestly, Gujak, I know what a dangerous place feels like and, while Bleak Rock is certainly, well, bleak, it's hardly what I'd call dangerous. We just need to be careful where we walk, that's all."

"If you say so," said Gujak. "I just keep expecting something really bad to happen at some point. I mean, this all seems way too easy. Surely we should have run into some kind of real problem at some point, right?"

"For once, I agree with you," said Durima. "Normally, I'd be as paranoid as you, maybe even more so. But right now, I say we should take advantage of every opportunity we get. Remember what Master said about timing this with his mission."

"All right," said Gujak, although the way he glanced back the way they came told Durima all she needed to know about how he actually felt. "I'll lead the way, I guess, since I'm the one with the light and all."

Gujak pushed away from the still-intact wall and entered the darkness beyond the collapsed one. Durima followed, keeping her eyes and ears wide open in case there was indeed something dangerous awaiting them below.

As it turned out, behind the collapsed wall was a spiral stone staircase that went down deep into Bleak Rock's interior. It was impossible to tell who had carved this staircase, and when, but based on how old it looked, Durima guessed that it had been here for years.

Despite its age, the staircase held their weight. The steps, however, were slightly slippery due to moisture in the air settling on them, forcing Durima and Gujak to walk down much more slowly than they otherwise would. This made Durima impatient because she remembered Master's emphasis on completing the mission quickly.

This gave Durima time to think, which she did not want to do (she felt it prudent to remain aware of her surroundings at all times, even if there was nothing much to remain aware of), but which she did anyway due to their frustratingly slow pace.

She wondered how Master was doing. No doubt he was already at North Academy, maybe had even dug up the grave of that Braim Kotogs mortal. She hoped that he had run into some unexpected complications; not because she wanted to see him fail (although she thought failure might humble him a little) but because she and Gujak had not yet found the gauntlet and she wanted to make sure that she got it to him on time.

That made her wonder exactly what this 'gauntlet' was. It had to be special and important. If it was any old gauntlet, Master could have easily stolen one from a mortal or gone and bought one from one of the merchants on World's End. It probably had something to do with Master's overarching grand plan, the details of which were still fuzzy to Durima, even after she had thought about it deeply.

I wonder what Master will do to us when his plan succeeds, Durima thought. *Will he reward us for our help? Or will he ignore us because of our many failures?*

Either way, Durima did not see her or Gujak's life changing much after all of this was through. They would continue to serve Master or, if he decided he didn't need their help anymore, would serve some other god or goddess who needed their help. Durima didn't know which of the many gods in both Pantheons would need their help, but she figured she would worry about that later.

Maybe Skimif himself will hire us, Durima thought. Then she chuckled to herself, low enough that Gujak could not hear it. *What am I saying? Skimif never hires katabans. He does all his work himself because he's just that kind of god. Most likely we'll end up working for someone like Kano, or worse, the Loner God.*

Her thoughts ran along this track until she and Gujak reached the bottom of the staircase. The claustrophobia down here was even worse than it had been in the hallway from before, making Durima wish that this gauntlet had been hidden on some wide open tropical island somewhere further down south.

Gujak stopped. "I stepped in something."

Durima grimaced. "Did I need to know that?"

"Not like that," said Gujak, shaking his head as he lowered his glowing hand closer to the floor. "It's ... webbing?"

Durima looked at the floor. A thick wad of spider web, glistening in the soft glow of Gujak's hand, was wrapped around Gujak's foot. He tugged at it and managed to pull his foot out of the sticky stuff, but his foot was still covered in it.

"Ew," said Durima. "Why is there spider web down here?"

"Better question," said Gujak, who based on his tone of voice was already on the edge of panic, "why is it so huge?"

Durima shook her head dismissively. "So what? We can deal with giant spiders. We just squash them like smaller ones."

"Durima, I don't think you understand, but this is really, really bad," said Gujak. "Spider web usually dissolves in a few hours if the spider in question doesn't recycle it. But this is fresh, which means that whatever made this web is probably still close by."

Durima looked around the area, but it was too dark to see much. "Well, maybe it's napping right now because I don't hear it and definitely don't see it. Anyway, not like we can just go back, not when Master is expecting us to get that gauntlet."

"You're right," said Gujak, although the way he stumbled over the word 'right' did not inspire confidence in Durima. "I bet that the gauntlet is just around the corner now. And if we do run into some kind of giant spider, well, we can handle it like you said."

It was painfully obvious to Durima that Gujak did not believe even half of what he said. Knowing him, Gujak was probably imagining her and him getting wrapped up in thick web cocoons and being fed to the giant spider's babies bit by bit. Gujak almost always let his imagination get the best of him, especially when he was scared out of his mind like he was now.

Still, Gujak did advance, heading deeper into the island's interior at the same pace he had walked down the staircase. Durima once more followed, but this time keeping her eyes and ears open for any skittering sounds. Despite what she said earlier, she didn't think that the giant spider was actually sleeping. Their luck was never that good.

This time, they found themselves walking down some

kind of wide open tunnel/hallway. Thick webbing hung from the ceiling, which slowed their progress considerably. This webbing didn't seem as fresh as the chunk that Gujak had stepped in and in fact went down easily when Durima cut it with her claws. Still, it was an ominous sign that whatever was down here had clearly made this island its territory. And Durima knew quite well what animals did to creatures that invaded their territory, even unintentionally.

But despite the mess of webbing they found, there was no other sign of the spider. It was almost like the spider had made the webbing and left; an odd thought, to be sure. Whether that was normal spider behavior or not, Durima didn't know, and she wasn't sure she wanted to find out.

The tunnel/hallway must have been much shorter than it seemed, however, because after only a few minutes of cutting through the webbing, Durima and Gujak emerged into a wide-open chamber that was a breath of fresh air after being in such a confined space for so long.

This chamber was designed oddly, though. It had no floor; instead, there was an open pool in the center, with dark seawater inside it as still as stone. The seawater must have been the source of the salty, ocean-like smell that permeated the room, reminding Durima of the beach on Zamis.

The pool was ringed by a stone walkway that offered little room for movement and no railing to keep anyone from falling into the water below. Durima had to be careful not to lean forward too much, otherwise she would fall into the water, which did not look friendly or safe to her.

A long, narrow stone bridge jutted out over the water, but it only went about halfway across. It wasn't the stone bridge that caught Durima's attention, however. It was the glint of silver at the end of it, which reflected the light of Gujak's hand as brilliantly as a mirror.

"What's that?" said Durima, pointing at the glinting silver object.

Gujak raised his hand and his light grew brighter. As it did so, the rays washed over the silver object, giving them a much better look at its appearance.

The object resembled a gauntlet designed for a human hand. It looked perfectly preserved, as if whoever had put it down here had made sure to come back and clean it regularly. It was still too far away to make out its finer details, but that didn't matter because Durima knew that they had hit the jackpot.

"There it is," said Durima, pointing at the gauntlet. "The gauntlet that Master wanted us to get."

"Are you sure?" said Gujak, looking around the place as if he expected to see an identical gauntlet nearby.

"How can I not be sure?" said Durima. "Master said there is only one gauntlet on Bleak Rock. That object looks exactly like a gauntlet; therefore, it *is* the gauntlet."

"I guess you're right," said Gujak. "Well, I'll go and grab it. It doesn't look like it's protected by anything, so hopefully we'll be out of here very soon."

Durima wanted to be the one to get it, but when she saw how narrow and unstable the stone bridge looked, she decided that it made more sense to stand back and let Gujak do it. She watched, scratching her arm, as Gujak walked carefully across the stone bridge, which held him with no trouble.

As Gujak walked, his light casting his shadow across the still waters below, Durima fully expected something bad to happen to him. Maybe a sea monster would shoot out of the water and bite his head off. Or maybe the stone bridge would fall into the water. Possibly, the gauntlet itself was rigged with some kind of magical trap, although Durima could not sense anything unusual about this gauntlet.

All she knew was that she was relieved when Gujak reached the end of the stone bridge and picked up the gauntlet. He turned around, the smile on his face evident even from a distance, as he held up the gauntlet and said, "I got the gauntlet, so that means we can go back to Master now! Maybe he'll be so pleased by our speediness that he'll waive our punishment."

"Great," said Durima. She gestured at Gujak with her right hand. "Now come on. No need to keep Master waiting any longer than he needs to, right?"

Gujak nodded, but then his smile contorted into an expression of pure, undisguised horror. He pointed over Durima's head and said, "Durima, behind you!"

Durima would have turned around to see what Gujak saw, but then she felt something sharp and burning bite her back. Her body went rigid as a board, causing her to fall flat on her face. As soon as she hit the floor, she lost all consciousness.

Chapter Fifteen

The light that exploded from Braim's casket rapidly faded away. The night returned to take back its domain, but Darek's eyes continued to see the light burned in his retinas as if it was still there. He rubbed his eyes furiously, trying to get them to work properly again even as that same horrible laugh from before became louder and louder. It sounded like a snake laughing, an awful sound that sent chills up Darek's spine.

When his vision finally returned to normal, Darek looked back up at the casket and was shocked by what he saw.

The casket was still wide open, but now there was someone standing in it. The being who stood in the casket was not the Ghostly God, nor was it the Magical Superior. The being had purplish-black skin, a color that made Darek's stomach churn, and the skin itself resembled smooth snake skin. He wore the white funeral robes that all Academy mages who died in the school were given; at least, at one point they were white, but now they looked faded and dirty from spending so many years beneath the earth, with a handful of holes in them here and there. His face was a combination of snake and human, with gleaming yellow eyes that spoke of an intelligence far above that of any mortal.

The being, who had ceased laughing, raised his arms and looked at his hands, which were wide and flat. Flexing his fingers, the being laughed again, as if the sight of his oddly long fingers amused him greatly.

Then he looked down at his thighs and legs. He lifted his right leg and almost lost his balance before putting his foot down on the ground and steadying himself. Even that seemed to amuse him, however, because he was smiling like a little kid who had just made an amazing new discovery.

"Oh, how many years has it been since I last had a *proper* body to walk around in," said the being. He then made an odd rattling noise that Darek belatedly realized was him inhaling air. "Oh, how many years has it been since I last breathed in fresh air. This is not the air of my world, but it is air nonetheless, as pure and clean as the rivers of Elda."

Darek shook his head and looked around. The Magical Superior still lay on the ground, but he no longer looked quite as stunned as he had before. Still, Darek didn't think the Magical Superior would be getting up anytime soon, so he began looking for the Ghostly God.

He found the Ghostly God soon enough. The God of Ghosts and Mist was lying flat on his back on the ground. He looked like he had been knocked out by a professional fighter and for a moment Darek didn't know if the deity was even still alive.

Then he saw the Ghostly God's chest heaving up and down, and Darek knew, with disgust, that the god was going to be okay.

The being apparently lost interest in his physical body, for he lowered his arms and began looking around at his surroundings. "My, how different the world looks from two legs. I have been in that accursed snake form for so long that I forgot what being two-legged was like."

Darek's teeth chattered, even though it wasn't very cold out. His senses were starting to return to normal and he was sensing that this being, whoever he was, was absurdly powerful. Far more powerful than the Magical Superior, dwarfing even the Ghostly God, this being seemed to be on a level all his own. He was definitely not a god, but what he was, exactly, Darek didn't know.

But what he said about that 'accursed snake form' ... Darek thought. *Could he be—?*

"Yes, Darek Takren," said the being, who was now looking directly at Darek. "It is indeed I, Uron the teleporter snake. Or at least, that's the identity I chose until I could get a new and better body. Obviously, I am not and never was a real teleporter snake."

Darek's eyes widened and his hands shook underneath him. "Then what are you? What is going on here? Where did you even come from?"

"You have many questions," said Uron. "I probably should not answer them, but you and the whole world will know my name soon enough. Perhaps you can become my herald who will tell the entire world about me."

"I won't be your herald," said Darek. "I swore an oath to the gods, not to ... whatever you are."

"Why would you ever swear loyalty to idiots like them?" said Uron, gesturing at the Ghostly God. "They are pompous, arrogant, and foolish, not to mention easily manipulated. I do not even want to get into their pathetic jealousies or vendettas against each other, nor how their constant scheming against themselves and their ruler are more irritating than amusing."

"Even so, I'm not your servant and I never will be," said Darek. He was finding it hard to talk, but with both the Magical Superior and the Ghostly God out for the count, he knew he had to keep it up until he could come up with some kind of plan to stop Uron. "I'd rather die than serve you."

Uron shrugged. "I haven't even told you who I am and you are already saying such silly things. I know you mortals tend to jump to conclusions based on very little information, but this is another thing entirely."

"You can still tell me all about you," said Darek. "Just because I won't serve you doesn't mean I don't want my questions answered."

"Very well," said Uron. He stretched his arms. "I need to give myself a few minutes to stretch out the kinks in my bones anyway. This body hasn't move an inch since it was buried all thirty years ago. I am lucky it hadn't turned into dust."

"Then start," said Darek. "Begin at the beginning."

"The very beginning?" said Uron as he put his hands on his back and pushed it inwards. "That is a very, very long time ago, well before the gods, well before Martir, even before the Powers. But very well. The beginning it is."

Uron went silent for a moment, as if he was thinking about how to start. Darek kept glancing at the Magical Superior, but the headmaster didn't seem likely to wake up anytime soon.

"All right," said Uron. He gestured at himself. "Do you know about the world that existed before Martir?"

Darek snapped his attention back to Uron. "What?"

Uron sighed. "Of course you don't. The world that existed before Martir is unknown to the vast, vast majority of mortals who live in this world. The gods know of it, of course, but even they don't know everything about it. They know only what little the Powers shared with them about it, but even the Powers only knew about the ruins they found."

"What does that world have to do with anything?" said Darek. "If you're telling the truth, it is long gone. It's not relevant."

"Only the ignorant say that history is not relevant," said Uron, rubbing his face as if he had never done it before. "You see, Darek Takren, I am *from* that world. It is where I was born, raised, and yes, where I died. And it is a world I intend to bring back."

Darek blinked. "Died? But you're still here. How can you say that you died when I am talking to you? I'm not dead, am I?"

"No, of course not," said Uron. "And I suppose I technically didn't 'die,' but it certainly felt that way."

"I still don't see how you could possibly be from some other world that existed prior to this one," said Darek. "You can't be telling the truth."

"Allow me to finish my story before you make any judgments," said Uron. "Now, you see, my world was once a beautiful and majestic place. It made Martir look like the cobbled-together mess that it is. My people, after eons of hardship and war, were a prosperous and advanced society, constantly improving and innovating in every way. It was not the kind of world you ever expected to end, especially when our fearless leaders kept reassuring us that nothing was wrong no matter what anyone said."

Then Uron's face made a very obvious scowl. "But it was all a sham. A sham built on lies and deceit. For you see, Darek Takren, on that world, I was what you called a scientist. I studied nature and the world in an attempt to learn how best to use it to advance my race. It was a noble profession, one in which the truth was revered above all else ... except when that truth contradicted the truth taught by our leaders, of course."

Uron cracked his neck. "You see, during my studies of the world, I discovered that my world was dying. It was not dying due to anything my people did. My world was simply reaching its natural end, its core slowly cooling. I tried to warn my people of this because there was still a chance we could survive, even save the planet itself, if we acted immediately."

Uron spoke of it like it happened yesterday. To Darek, this all sounded like the ramblings of a mad man, but as this was a very powerful mad man, he knew better than to interrupt.

Uron squatted and stood up again. "My leaders did not

like that. They started a campaign to slander my name. They called me a liar, a deceiver, and a charlatan even as the cooling of our world's core began to cause devastating natural disasters everywhere. Millions of people died, and by the time my leaders finally began to listen to my plans, it was too late. Our world was dead, and we who had survived the previous natural disasters went with it. Including all of our art, history, technology, and discoveries."

He said that with such heartbroken-ness and bitterness that Darek, strangely enough, felt moved by this story. He still didn't know if it was true, but Uron seemed to believe it at any rate.

"But I survived," said Uron. He put his hands on his chest. "Prior to the final day of our world, I placed my soul into the core of our world, where I went into a deep, self-induced sleep. My plan was to awaken at some point, get a new body, and begin the process of rebuilding my world and saving my people. A noble goal, wouldn't you agree?"

"But your world is gone," said Darek. "And your people are dead. How do you intend to do that?"

"I am not finished telling my story," said Uron in a tone as sharp as a knife. "Or do you want me to skip to the part where I kill you in cold blood?"

"Continue," said Darek. "I'm listening."

"Good," said Uron. Then he stroked his chin. "Now where was I? Oh, yes. After I sealed my soul, the Powers came. They saw the remains of my world, believed no one to be using them because they saw no life there. They took the remains and, along with some of their own materials, began building a new world that would one day bear the name of Martir.”

His hands balled into fists. *“Martir* ... what an ugly word. Do you know it's etymology, Darek Takren? It is from an ancient Divina word meaning 'a new creation.' Perhaps an appropriate name, but the word has a positive connotation to it, a connotation I cannot agree with.”

Darek already knew about Martir's etymology. It had been part of his early education as a North Academy mage, one of the very first things he had been taught. Hearing Uron attack it made Darek want to punch him out.

Uron lifted up his hands. “I awoke shortly after the Powers finished building Martir. I was confused at first. I thought that maybe my world had survived, that its end had been a terrible dream, and that my people still existed. Sadly, a deeper look showed me that my thoughts were wrong. Martir was—and still is—nothing like my world. Nor will it ever be.”

“It doesn't have to be like your world,” said Darek. His strength was returning to his limbs, but he was still too weak to get up. “Martir is its own world.”

“And that is the problem,” said Uron. “Who gave the Powers permission to use the remains of my world to build one of their petty creations? Nonetheless, in the beginning, there was very little I could do about it. I had no physical body, for one. For another, I did not know how strong the gods were. I was afraid that if I revealed myself right away, the gods would defeat me. The gods were one at that point, not divided like they are now, which is why it will be so much easier for me to do what I need to do today than it was so many eons ago.

"It was then that the Godly War started, which I watched with interest. I thought that the Powers' beloved creation, the world that should not exist, was going to destroy itself. I planned to begin the rebuilding of my world after the gods had torn each other apart, but then the Powers returned and ended the conflict."

Uron shook his head, but it seemed to be more because he was still getting used to his body rather than communicating his disapproval. A quick glance in the direction of the Magical Superior told Darek that the headmaster was still out.

Although even if he wasn't, would he be strong enough to defeat Uron? Darek thought.

He was so lost in his thoughts that he almost missed the next part of Uron's speech/story.

"They divided the gods and forced them to sign a Treaty," said Uron. "As you can imagine, I was disappointed. I had hoped that the gods would do all of the hard work for me. That is just further proof of what happens to those who rely on others to do everything for them, in my opinion."

Darek didn't really care about Uron's opinions, but at the moment there was little he could do about them. Not when he wasn't even sure he would live long enough to see the sun rise in the morning.

"So what did you do after that?" said Darek. "The Godly War was thousands of years ago. Why did you only choose to act now?"

Uron flexed his muscles. "Do you honestly think this is the first time I've tried to do this? Many times over the eons, I've awoken long enough to try to put my plan into action. Each time, events I did not foresee forced me to abort it to avoid detection by the gods. My last attempt was a mere 50 years ago, when my botched attempt to get a new body for myself ended thanks to the death of the mortal man I was manipulating at the time."

"Why do you need a humanoid body?" said Darek. He tightened his fist around a clump of dirt. "Your snake body seemed just as effective as a humanoid one."

"It was weak and pathetic," said Uron. He gestured at his muscular body. "If I had revealed my true identity before, I likely would have been crushed by the Ghostly God. I needed a stronger body, and you mortal mages have very strong bodies, despite not being nearly as powerful as gods."

"Why Braim's?" said Darek. His eyes glanced at the coffin. "What makes Braim Kotogs so special? Why couldn't you just find the grave of some other mage? There are plenty of other magical graveyards in the world, after all, that are less well-protected than this one."

Uron stroked his chin. "I see you weren't listening. I needed a *stronger* body capable of holding all of my power. North Academy is well known for producing mages of the highest caliber. Therefore, it was reasonable for me to assume that their deceased were of a better quality than the deceased mages from other lands. Braim Kotogs, as I understand it, was the personal pupil of the Magical

Superior himself, after all, which puts him head and shoulders above even the other students at the school. He was the logical candidate, if somewhat of a hassle to get."

That made some sense, although Darek wondered if Uron would have done just as well with the corpse of a slightly less powerful mage from some other school or part of the world. Certainly, it would have been much simpler, at any rate.

"And I couldn't have taken the body of an already living mage, either," said Uron. "That's not how it works. I could only possess a deceased corpse. And seeing as Braim Kotogs has been dead for thirty years, I felt his remains were the perfect candidate to house my spirit."

Darek glanced at the Ghostly God. It was disturbing to see a god lying in the dirt like a beaten animal. Granted, Darek didn't particularly like the Ghostly God, but he had always been taught that the gods were the highest powers in the world.

Just what kind of power am I dealing with here? Darek thought. *If he can knock out a god in one hit—*

"Concerned about the Ghostly God?" Uron said, interrupting Darek's thoughts. "Don't be. He's not dead, although he will be very soon, I imagine, along with the rest of his accursed siblings."

"What do you mean?" said Darek.

"You will find out soon enough," said Uron. "Because before the night is over, both the Northern and Southern Pantheons—along with Skimif himself—will be trembling at the mere mention of my name."

He said that with relish, like he was thinking about how delicious it would be to terrorize the gods. His eyes dilated and he rubbed his hands together eagerly.

"So did the Ghostly God even know that you were manipulating him?" said Darek. "Or was he ignorant about you the entire time?"

"Your second guess is correct," said Uron. He tossed an annoyed look at the Ghostly God. "He thinks he is smarter than his siblings, but he was easy enough to fool. He never once suspected that his loyal pet snake was manipulating his every move and thought. He truly believed, right up until the moment I knocked him out, that this whole plan was a concoction of his sad, strange little mind. The fool."

"But why the Ghostly God?" said Darek. He could feel his energy returning more rapidly now, but he still didn't risk getting up and trying anything. "There are hundreds of other gods in the world you could have manipulated. Why him?"

"Because he's arrogant," said Uron. "And arrogant fools are always the easiest kind to manipulate. They believe themselves too smart to fall for even the most complicated schemes, which causes them to let their defenses down. All I did was take advantage of his obvious weakness and control him as easily as an obedient puppy."

"What about Aorja?" said Darek. "Did she know about you?"

"You mean the human woman who acted as the Ghostly God's spy?" said Uron. "She is just as ignorant of my existence as the Ghostly God himself. She is irrelevant to this discussion anyway. I could not care less about her life."

"All of this," said Darek, his breathing hard, "the destruction of the Third Dorm, the chimera, the destruction of the *Soaring Sea*, and everything else ... it was all just so you could get a new body?"

"More or less," said Uron. "Ideally, I should have gotten my new body a week ago, but those two idiot katabans messed everything up. No matter. I have a new body now, and with it, I will lay waste to Martir and rebuild my home and my people, just as I promised to do so many years ago."

Uron raised his hand. Thick, ugly black tendrils emerged from his fingertips, looking like little more than sludge given life. The tendrils swirled around each other until they formed a large, black sphere the same color as Uron's skin.

"It's your lucky day, Darek Takren," said Uron, a disturbing, terrifying smile crossing his lips. "You will be the very first mortal to die at my hands. This is an honor no one else will be able to claim; in fact, even you won't be able to truly claim it, because once I toss this sphere at you ... you won't live long enough to claim it."

Chapter Sixteen

Durima's head throbbed. So did her back. She didn't know why. Her memory was fuzzy, and growing fuzzier by the minute. Not to mention her arms ached, like she had been holding them in one position for too long.

She wanted to go back to sleep, and she almost did, but then she felt someone poking her and heard a familiar voice whisper, "Durima. Hey, Durima. Wake up. Are you okay? Durima, please wake up. I'm scared."

Even that soft whisper was enough to make her head hurt. She rubbed the back of her head, but that mostly out of habit than out of conscious thought.

"You're awake," said the familiar voice, which belonged to Gujak, who sounded somewhere close by. "Or are you just moving in your sleep again?"

Durima forced her eyes to open. It was much harder than it normally was. It felt like someone had glued her eyelids shut, but soon enough her eyes were wide open and she could see again.

Blinking hard, Durima looked to her right and saw Gujak. That in itself was not strange. What was strange was how he was hanging upside down, his arms hanging beneath him, and how Durima was eye level with him.

Startled, Durima looked up. Her short legs were tied together by a thick, grayish white webbing that hung from the ceiling. Gujak was also hanging from the webbing with a look of resignation on his face.

"Wh-Where are we?" said Durima. Her voice was alarmingly weak. "How long have we been out? What happened?"

Gujak gave her a weak smile. "Look down."

Durima did as he said. At least two dozen feet below them was an empty pit, which was covered with several thick layers of web. Though the webbing was the same grayish white as the webbing that held Durima and Gujak, a glowing purple liquid could be dimly seen pulsating through the web, like blood flowing through the veins of a mortal. Directly opposite them was a cavernous opening that appeared to be the only way in—or out—of this cave.

She saw all of this thanks to a row of green lights running along the top of the walls. They were not very strong lights, but they were bright enough to allow her to see a good deal of the chamber they were in, although everything had a slightly greenish tinge as a result.

"Webbing?" said Durima. "Have we been caught by some kind of giant spider?"

"Not sure," said Gujak with an awkward shrug. "It all happened so fast that I barely had time to put the gauntlet on my hand."

"What?" said Durima.

Gujak held up his right hand. A shiny silver gauntlet completely covered his hand up to his wrist. Durima noticed tiny writing on the knuckles, but it was too small and indistinct for her to read, especially while hanging upside down in a dimly lit chamber.

Durima shoved Gujak in the chest. "Idiot! Master didn't say to *wear* the gauntlet. He said we're supposed to get the gauntlet and bring it to *him*."

Gujak swung backwards from his webbing and almost slammed back into Durima, but she caught him with her claws before he could do that. After steadying him, she let go of Gujak and looked at him hard, wondering what his excuse was going to be.

"I know," said Gujak, sounding apologetic (as he should). "But I just didn't want to lose the gauntlet. I saw the thing coming and I wanted to at least make sure I had the gauntlet with me. So I slipped it on my hand and now ... now I can't get it off."

Durima raised an eyebrow. "Can't get it off?"

"It's stuck to my hand," said Gujak, extending his gauntlet-covered hand and shaking it. "I can't do anything about it. It's like the gauntlet wanted me to wear it and no one else."

"That is the most ridiculous thing I have heard in a while," said Durima. "You must have jammed it onto your arm too tightly or maybe some web fluid somehow got into it. Either way, it will have to come off once we get out of here and return to Master."

"If you say so," said Gujak. "How do we get out?"

Durima clicked her claws together. "Easy. I cut away our webbing and we fall onto the web below. We crawl across it to that exit over there, find out where the heck we are, and then retrace our steps until we're on Bleak Rock's exterior again."

Durima aimed her claws at Gujak's webbing, but then Gujak grabbed her hand. She looked at him in annoyance, but was astonished to see he had a grim expression on his face.

"Don't do it," said Gujak. "Falling on that web below is probably not the smartest move we can make."

"What do you mean?" said Durima. "That web looks thick enough to catch us."

"I don't doubt it will hold even if we fell on it at full speed," said Gujak. "But that purplish liquid ... I've seen it somewhere before, but on a much smaller scale."

Durima glanced at the webbing below them. The glowing purple liquid was as eerie as ever, but she didn't see anything dangerous about it.

"There's this type of spider back on World's End called a lethal widow," said Gujak. "It's not really common and generally hangs out in abandoned buildings or underneath bridges and the like. What makes it different from other spiders is that it embeds its poison directly into its webbing. That way, if something flies or crawls onto its webbing, the victim dies almost instantly."

"Almost?" said Durima in alarm, looking up at the webbing that they hung from.

"Don't worry about this," said Gujak. "If it was poisoned, we'd be dead already, though I imagine that won't matter if you went through with your plan to cut us free. That poison below looks like lethal widow poison, so we'd probably die if we fell on it."

Durima cursed. "What kind of spider produces poisonous and nonpoisonous webbing? It makes no sense."

"That's what I wanted to tell you," said Gujak. "See, this giant spider came out of nowhere and knocked you out with one bite. I tried to fight it, but it was big and fast. One touch from its barbs and I was down for the count."

Durima shuddered. "Where is it now?"

"No idea," said Gujak. "When I woke up, I was hanging here and the spider was nowhere to be seen. Maybe it went looking to see if we had brought any friends with us."

Durima gulped. "Then we don't have much time before it returns, probably. Which means we have to act fast if we're going to get out of here alive."

"Alive?" said a feminine, slightly insectoid voice from within the cave opening before them. "You must be a blind optimist of the worst kind if you think you will be escaping my web alive."

Durima turned her head toward the only exit in the cave. She heard the sound of large, powerful legs walking across the earth, drawing closer and closer to them with each step until the creature emerged from within the darkness of the cave.

The creature was a giant spider. It had eight hairy long legs that looked capable of smashing boulders into pieces, with a behind as large as said boulders. Its fangs glistened in the green lighting, while its dozen eyes looked far too intelligent to be the eyes of a mere arachnid.

"That's it," said Gujak, pointing at the giant spider. "That's the one that attacked us and brought us in here."

"Did it just talk?" said Durima, tilting her head to the side. "How can a mere spider, even a giant one, talk?"

The giant spider made a strange clicking noise which might have meant that it was offended. "A mere spider? I am no mere spider, katabans. I am the Spider Goddess, Goddess of Spiders and Sleet. And you two have invaded my domain because you are apparently suicidal or my brother hates you."

"By the gods," said Gujak, who was now shaking uncontrollably. "We are so, so sorry for invading your domain, great Spider Goddess. We were told no one lived here and that none of the other gods had claimed this island as theirs."

"Did my brother tell you that?" said the Spider Goddess in a sharp tone. "He was always an uninformed shut-in, brother was. I see he hasn't changed a bit since I last spoke with him what was it, three hundred years ago, maybe? I find time hard to keep track of these days."

"How do you know we work for the Ghostly God?" said Durima. "We didn't say that."

"Because I smelled his scent on you two," said the Spider Goddess, gesturing at them with one of her thick legs. "Oh, it's not something you katabans can smell, so don't even try. But we gods can smell each other right away."

Gujak had been about to sniff his armpit, but then he stopped immediately and tried to look nonchalant, although the look of fear on his face ruined the attempt for Durima.

"I took over Bleak Rock about a year ago," the Spider Goddess continued. "I didn't tell anyone, obviously, because I value my privacy and did not want any of the other gods coming here to bug me about this or that. I expected to run into the so-called 'Mysterious One,' but I haven't seen even one hint of his existence since I've been here. Either he left and will never return or he never existed at all. Either way, this island is now mine."

Durima gulped. "So what are you going to do to us, Spider Goddess? Will you let us go? Gujak and I did not mean to invade your domain. We were only looking for that gauntlet Gujak is wearing."

She gestured at Gujak's gauntlet-covered hand. "As you can see, we got it. So if you would only let us down, we will leave immediately and never come back to bother you ever again."

The Spider Goddess clicked her fangs together. "A nice offer ... too bad I won't take it."

"What?" said Durima. "But we're not trying to trick you or anything. We honestly only came here for the gauntlet and nothing else."

"That useless piece of junk?" said the Spider Goddess, her twelve eyes flickering toward the gauntlet before returning to focus on Durima. "It doesn't do anything. That's why I left it where it was when I got here. I don't know who or what put it down here—maybe it was the Mysterious One—but I can't even wear it in my current form. I don't even want to know why my idiot brother wants it."

"Master—the Ghostly God—said he wanted it as a part of his plan," said Durima. All her blood was in her head, making it harder to think, but she had to keep speaking because it was the only way she and Gujak could get out of this situation alive.

"Oh, great," said the Spider Goddess, rolling her spidery eyes. "Another one of my brother's great plans. How many has he done over the centuries? Honestly, he's the only one of us southern gods who spends more time acting like one of our northern siblings than ruling his domain. What a fool."

"Why won't you let us go?" said Durima. "The Ghostly God made it very clear that we needed to get the gauntlet to him right away. If we delay the delivery, it will mess up his plans and he will be angry with you."

"You think I care whether my brother is angry with me or not," said the Spider Goddess with a strange clicking sound that Durima realized was a laugh. "I don't. We've never gotten along. Even during the Godly War, when we fought on the same side, we didn't work well together. If he gets angry at me now, so what?"

"What are you going to do to us?" said Gujak with a gulp.

"Eat you, of course," said the Spider Goddess. "You two will be a warning to any of the other gods who are thinking of sending their servants to Bleak Rock. If they think they will lose their servants, then that will give them yet another reason to avoid this island and everything associated with it."

"I didn't know gods ate katabans," said Gujak. "I thought

they only ate humans and aquarians."

"We usually don't eat katabans," said the Spider Goddess. "But today, I think I will make an exception. I haven't had much to eat today, so between the two of you, I think I will have enough to tide me over until tomorrow."

"Please, Spider Goddess," said Gujak, putting his hands together pleadingly. "Don't kill us. We'll do whatever you want if you'll just let us live."

The Spider Goddess paused. "Well, I suppose there is one thing I'd like for you two to do for me."

"What's that?" said Gujak, looking both eager and relieved to find out that they might live after all.

Then the Spider Goddess made a dangerous clicking sound with her teeth. "Stay still and let me eat you without a lot of fuss."

Without further ado, the Spider Goddess took off across the webbing below. Despite her size and bulk, she crawled across the net-like web below with the speed and grace of a seasoned runner. Durima realized that the Spider Goddess was heading for the back wall, the one she and Gujak were closest to, and there was nothing she could do about it.

"Oh my god, oh my god, oh my god," said Gujak in between deep, shuddering breaths. "We're gonna die, Durima, we're gonna die."

Durima wanted to moan and whine with Gujak, but with the Spider Goddess almost at the back wall, she knew she didn't have time for such luxuries. She reached out with her geomancy, trying to form a pillar of stone from the back wall, but then her magic rebounded into her again and she pulled her arms back to her body.

"Ow," said Durima under her breath. "Forgot about that."

"Now we're *really* gonna die!" said Gujak, putting his hands on his face. "This is it. There's nothing we can do. Our lives are over and I didn't even get to do everything I wanted to do before I died. Good bye, cruel world."

By now, the Spider Goddess had reached the base of the back wall. The Goddess of Spiders and Sleet was only seconds away from them, which meant that they had only seconds to live, seconds to figure out how to survive.

Durima looked around at their surroundings, trying to spot anything she could use to help them escape. All she saw was webbing everywhere she looked, useless, stupid webbing that wouldn't help them in the slightest.

Then her eyes fell on the gauntlet on Gujak's hand. The gauntlet looked as boring and useless as ever, yet there had to be something valuable about it if Master had ordered them to get it. It had to do something, probably something amazing, but it didn't seem like they could use its powers, whatever they might be.

Not like we have any other choice, Durima thought, glancing below, seeing the Spider Goddess rapidly climbing up the wall toward them.

Durima grabbed Gujak's arm and pulled his gauntlet toward her face. Gujak immediately stopped going on about how they were all going to die and looked at her in shock.

"Durima, what are you doing?" said Gujak in a panicky voice. He kept looking between her and the approaching

Spider Goddess. "Have you lost your mind? The Spider Goddess is going to kill us and you're admiring my gauntlet?"

"I'm not admiring it, idiot," said Durima, twisting and turning Gujak's arm to see the gauntlet from as many angles as possible. "I'm trying to figure out how to use it."

"Use it?" said Gujak. "How do you know it will be able to save us?"

"I don't, but do you have any better ideas?" said Durima. She squinted at the text carved into the knuckles, but in the dim green light it was impossible to read. "Whatever it does can't possibly be as bad as what the Spider Goddess will do to us."

"But what if Master finds out and gets angry?" said Gujak. "He didn't say we're supposed to use it!"

Durima quickly glanced down again. The Spider Goddess was only a few feet away now, which meant it was now or never.

"Then I'll take full responsibility for whatever happens next," said Durima. "Now shut up and help me figure out how to—"

The clicking of the Spider Goddess's fangs—which were far too close for comfort—made Durima look around Gujak. The Spider Goddess was now clinging to the wall behind them, so close that Durima could literally smell her horrible, unwashed body odor. The goddess smelled like a mixture between seawater and webbing, a scent that assaulted Durima's nose like a battering ram.

"She's here!" Gujak said. He looked at Durima with pure

despair in his eyes. "We're dead for real!"

"You speak too early," said the Spider Goddess, the anticipation in her voice so evident that Durima could practically see it. "You still have a few more seconds to live, after all."

Even though it was probably useless at this point, Durima kept looking over Gujak's gauntlet. No matter how hard she looked, she didn't see anything to indicate exactly what the gauntlet did. As far as she could tell, it was nothing more than an unusually shiny metal glove, and nothing more.

It made Durima think, for a moment, that this whole mission was a hoax. That the Ghostly God had sent them here knowing they would be killed by the Spider Goddess. That Master had known that the gauntlet was powerless and so had sent her and Gujak here as the punishment for their earlier failure at North Academy.

That's exactly the sort of thing Master would do to us, Durima thought as despair began to climb up her spine. *Send us on a 'mission,' only for that mission to turn out to be nothing more than our punishment for daring to fail.*

She had no time to dwell on that depressing thought, however, because in the next instant the Spider Goddess launched herself off the wall directly toward them. There was no way to dodge, no way to avoid the Spider Goddess's attack.

Yet despite the despair that was gradually smothering her hope, Durima's instincts kicked in. She shoved Gujak's gauntlet in the direction in the Spider Goddess even as

Gujak cried out in fear and terror. Durima did not expect this to do anything, but as they were going to die anyway, she saw no reason not to do it.

The Spider Goddess was unable to change her trajectory. Just as Durima wondered what it would feel like to be eaten alive by a goddess, the Spider Goddess collided with Gujak's outstretched gauntlet-covered hand, and stopped.

Literally. The Spider Goddess halted in midair like a giant was holding her. She went completely still and rigid, her twelve eyes unfocused and confused. Her smoky, sickening stench washed over Durima like a tidal wave, but the katabans was so taken aback by this sudden, unexpected turn of events that she didn't even notice it.

"What ... is this?" said the Spider Goddess in a trembling tone Durima had never heard in a god's voice before. "Why ... do I feel ... like ... like ..."

The Spider Goddess gave off a huge, shuddering sigh. Her whole body shook like the earthquake from earlier. Her teeth began clicking madly and her eyes suddenly became refocused.

"No!" the Spider Goddess cried. "No! What is this? The pain ... by the Powers, the pain ..."

Before Durima's horrified eyes, the Spider Goddess's legs began disintegrating. Starting from the tips, the Spider Goddess's legs slowly dried up and turned into dust. The disintegrating effect slowly made its way up the Spider Goddess's legs to her body. It was like watching a crumbling stone statue, but far more terrifying because the Spider Goddess was sobbing.

"No," said the Spider Goddess. "No ... I can't ... this isn't possible ... please ... let me live ..."

Her begging and pleading did not appear to touch the disintegrating effect. If anything, it seemed to goad it, because the disintegrating effect sped up. In less than a minute, all eight of her legs were gone and her underbelly was halfway gone. Her behind went next, the dust falling to the webbing below like snow on a winter day.

Although the Spider Goddess's body was almost entirely gone, she managed to fix all twelve of her ugly eyes on Durima and Gujak. The hate and fear in them was completely unlike anything Durima had seen in the eyes of a deity before. Durima had been looked upon with contempt and disappointment by Master and other gods in the past, but the look in the Spider Goddess's twelve eyes—obvious despite their spidery appearance—was so far removed from what other gods had looked like that Durima was actually afraid.

"You ... fools ..." said the Spider Goddess, her voice little more than the echo of a whisper. "What ... have ... you ..."

She did not get to finish her sentence because the disintegrating effect reached her head. In the next second, the last remains of the Spider Goddess fell onto the webbing below, leaving little evidence to show that she had been there at all.

Both Durima and Gujak stared with horror at the spot where the Spider Goddess had been. Neither of them moved or said a word. Durima even forgot to breathe for a moment. Her heartbeat quickened, which was the only sound she heard in the whole chamber.

Then, as automatically one of the automaton children of the Mechanical Goddess, Durima reached for Gujak's gauntlet. Gujak didn't protest or even seem to notice when she grabbed his arm and brought the gauntlet as close to her eyes as possible. She wanted to read what was written on the knuckles, to see now if she would get an explanation of what just happened.

Most of the text was still faded, and the poor lighting did not help, but there was one word on the middle knuckle that was as clear as possible. Durima was surprised she could read it, seeing as the gauntlet was clearly an ancient object, but read it she did.

The single, solitary word written on the middle knuckle in Divina, was this:

God-killer.

Chapter Seventeen

Seeing Uron about to kill him, Darek realized that he had a lot of things that he still wanted to do in life. He wanted to graduate from North Academy and leave the school to see the wider world; wanted to become a more proficient mage; wanted to serve Lord Xocion with all of his heart, soul, and strength; and maybe even get married and have kids someday.

He would never get to do any of that now. Uron's strange black ball, apparently made from his own flesh, would undoubtedly end his life. He didn't know exactly how it would do that, but he doubted it would be painless.

The Magical Superior was still unable to help. At this point, Darek would have been glad even for the Ghostly God's help, but that deity was obviously out for the count, too. And Darek couldn't count on any of the students or teachers from the school to help; no one knew he was even awake, much less that he was in the graveyard, facing down an enemy no one had even known existed until now.

And Darek was still too weak to protect himself. His arms and legs felt like jelly, though they were getting better. Even if he was in his best shape and at full magical power, he doubted he would be able to defeat Uron. While he did not know Uron's full magical power—he couldn't sense it—

he understood that Uron was so far above him in sheer power that he might as well be an annoying insect in Uron's ears than a real threat.

That realization alone sapped him of much of the strength that he had managed to recover, as little as it was. He simply watched as Uron's ball grew larger and larger. It even started to bubble, like boiling water in a pot.

Then Uron hurled the ball at him. It flew through the air straight and true, Uron's aim impeccable, directly toward Darek. The flying ball of death was coming at him at impossible-to-dodge speeds. Not that Darek had felt tempted to try.

Without warning, Darek felt a powerful magical spike nearby. He did not have time to look for the source of the spike, however, because the ball of death exploded in midair, sending black bits and pieces flying everywhere. Darek raised his arm to avoid getting the worst of it, but he couldn't help but stare at the spot in the air where the ball had been earlier.

"What?" said Uron in complete and utter disbelief. "How did it explode? Who did that?"

Uron looked toward the Magical Superior and the Ghostly God, but they were still unconscious and clearly in no position to do anything. An angry frown crossed Uron's lips as he looked around the misty graveyard for whoever had blown up his ball.

"Show yourself!" Uron shouted, his voice echoing eerily. "Or I will tear this entire school to pieces with my bare hands!"

Then a voice spoke from somewhere within the mist. "You sound angry, Uron. Why not take a moment to cool down and think rationally about the fact that you just tried to murder an innocent mortal in cold blood?"

This was followed by the sound of footsteps across the uneven stone path that snaked through the graveyard. It was hard to tell what direction they were coming from, especially with the odd magical spike that had completely messed up Darek's senses. It felt like a hundred gods had appeared in the graveyard all at once, but that did not make any sense to Darek until the source of the magical spike stepped out of the mist and into the general area.

Uron hissed when he saw the being, like he was still a snake. "So the God of Martir decides to show himself after all."

Skimif, the being who had walked out of the mist, did not look bothered by the clear hostility in Uron's voice. He simply looked from the Magical Superior to the Ghostly God, and then looked at Darek.

"You all right, Darek?" said Skimif. "You weren't hurt, were you?"

Darek could not answer. He had never actually met Skimif in person before. Oh, he'd heard much about the God of Martir, of course, particularly from Mom, but actually seeing Skimif in the flesh was a completely different experience from merely hearing about him.

It took Darek a moment to realize that Skimif was the source of that hundred god magical spike he had felt earlier. Again, he had known that Skimif was the strongest being in all of Martir, but feeling Skimif's energy levels personally was like seeing a Great Berg blizzard for the first time.

He's generating so much power, Darek thought. *How does he handle all of that? Anyone else wouldn't even be able to stand with that kind of power flowing through them. He truly is the God of Martir.*

"He's too shocked to speak," said Uron. "Or maybe he's so dumb that he forgot *how* to speak. These mortals haven't shown themselves to be the brightest bunch."

Skimif shook his head. "You must have a very low opinion of mortals, Uron, because I know several whose intellect, creativity, and wit are a match for that of any god or goddess."

"And you assume I think the gods are much smarter," said Uron. "In truth, they are quite easy to manipulate. But it doesn't matter how intelligent mortals or gods are. How did you know I was going to be here?"

Skimif folded his muscular arms over his chest. "You haven't done a very good job of covering your tracks over the years, Uron. I've been paying attention to your presence as your power grew over the last three decades. I knew it was only a matter of time before you decided to show yourself."

"The Ghostly God told you he was not going to do anything wrong ever again," said Uron with a scowl. "Why did you not believe him? I pegged you as a naïve, trusting fool who always looks for the 'best' in even the worst people."

"I do look for the best in others," said Skimif, nodding.

"But I am also realistic enough to know that some people are more prone to lying than others. I was aware that the Ghostly God had been lying when I confronted him on the issue, but I also knew better than to push the subject when he clearly had no respect for me or my authority."

"I understand most gods have no respect for you or your authority," said Uron. "Some leader you turned out to be."

Skimif held out his hand. A gold scepter with a ruby topping it appeared in his hand, looking as dangerous as a sword. He swept the scepter before him like an ax.

"The point is, I knew that the Ghostly God would try to get to the school's graveyard again," said Skimif. "And I allowed him to do so because I didn't want him to know I was watching him. I originally intended to step in at the last possible moment and stop him before he could open the casket, but something came up and I was briefly unable to act."

Darek wondered what had came up that had left Skimif, of all gods, unable to intervene. There wasn't someone else like Uron running around Martir, too, was there?

Skimif looked very tired, even slightly stricken, which might have been a clue as to what had distracted him. Whatever it had been, it must have been serious if it was bad enough to shake the God of Martir himself.

"Luckily, I recovered just in time to save Darek," said Skimif. Then he glanced at the unconscious Ghostly God. "I think I will need to have a long talk with the Ghostly God once this is all over."

Uron cracked his neck again. "You're assuming that you

will live long enough to have that talk with him. Considering how I intend to destroy everything in this world—including you—I think that that is not a safe assumption to make."

"You're the one making unsafe assumptions around here," said Skimif. "You're assuming that you will defeat me. You have no proof that that is even possible."

"The proof is in my power level," said Uron. He gestured at his body. "The power I wield is equal to yours in every way. I may not have authority over the gods, but that does not diminish my own abilities in any way, shape, or form. It just means I do not have to worry about fools who refuse to respect my authority for no good reason."

"That's another unsafe assumption you just made there," said Skimif. "You're assuming that *all* of the gods disrespect my authority. You couldn't be any wronger about that."

It was then that several more magical spikes—each appearing one after the other, almost too fast for Darek to keep track of—erupted inside the graveyard. With each magical spike, Darek's senses were assaulted by all of the magic that was pouring in. It wasn't quite as much energy as Skimif's, but so much at once really took a toll on Darek's senses, forcing him to try to ignore the majority of it in order to avoid overloading his senses.

As each spike faded, beings began appearing out of the mist, dozens of beings, each one completely different from the last. One looked like a scrawny old man, but his glowing body and wise appearance identified him as Nimiko, the God of Light. The one who appeared next to him was little more than a cloud of leaves that took on the form of a lion;

clearly the Leaf Goddess, Goddess of Leaves.

A deep, shuddering roar shook the ground and a second later, the head of a huge baba raga appeared out of the mist from behind the back wall of the graveyard. Its tusked mouth and thick body made the Tusked God, the God of Sea Mammals, look even more terrifying than Uron. His tongue lashed out at Uron, but he dodged it easily.

All together, Darek counted at least twenty-five gods, not counting the Ghostly God or Skimif, but he sensed more of them hiding in the mist. The gods surrounded Uron on every side, effectively cutting off every possible escape route.

Uron looked around at his surroundings like a trapped mouse. "I don't understand. How did you get so many gods together like this?"

"As I said, not every god disrespects my authority," said Skimif. He gestured at the assembled deities. "These are the gods and goddesses who chose to support me, despite my past. They believe in the importance of obeying the dictates of the Powers and the Powers dictated that I am their leader."

Uron's shocked expression quickly turned into a sneer. "Are you expecting me to be impressed? There are maybe fifty gods here out of the hundreds who live in Martir. If this is the best you could gather, then you truly are hurting for help."

"The only one who is going to be hurting around here is you," said Skimif, pointing at his enemy. "You see, Uron, each one of these gods knows what you are planning to do and each one of the gods will do everything in his or her power to crush you like an ant. Because Martir is our world and we all live in it and are responsible for protecting it from threats like you."

Darek didn't see any way that Uron could get out of this situation alive. Skimif and fifty of the gods (who, interestingly enough, appeared to be evenly split between the Northern and Southern Pantheons) versus one ... whatever Uron was. Uron was clearly not a being to be reckoned with, but against so many powerful opponents all working to take him down, Darek didn't see how he could possibly win.

That thought gave Darek the strength to stand up. His knees were still weak, but in the presence of so many gods, he wanted to show that he was strong enough to stand by them and help however he could. He pulled his new wand out of his robe pocket and aimed it at Uron.

"The only reason that my gods haven't attacked you yet is because I haven't ordered them to," said Skimif. "They're waiting for my signal."

Uron's eyes darted around the area, but Darek didn't feel nervous about that. There was no way Uron could escape, nothing he could use to attack the gods, much less defeat them. He was as good as trapped and there was not a thing he could do about it.

Then Uron looked at Skimif ... and grinned. "I guess, then, that your gods will be waiting a very long time for that signal. Because you will never get to use it."

Uron held out his arm to his right. The Magical Superior,

who was still lying on the ground (although he had been stirring like he was waking up), vanished into thin air. The next moment, the Superior appeared in Uron's hands. The fingers of Uron's right hand wrapped around the Superior's windpipe, while his right hand held the Superior's body upright.

Skimif took a step forward, while the other gods made various sounds of disgust and annoyance. "What are you doing with the Magical Superior?"

Uron rolled his eyes. "I see why the Powers made you the God of Martir. You are easily the slowest god of them all."

"Let the Superior go!" Darek shouted, causing the gods to look at him like they had forgotten he was even there. "Don't you dare harm him or I'll—"

Uron burst out into laughter, cutting Darek off. "Ha! You, a pathetic mortal, are threatening *me*? The audacity is humorous and well-appreciated. Please, this is too much."

"I understand what he's trying to do, Skimif," said Nimiko, who stood near Darek. "He's using the Magical Superior as a human shield."

"That's a little bit closer, God of Light, but not quite entirely correct," said Uron. He tightened his grip around the Magical Superior's neck, making the headmaster choke. "I am using him as a human fortress, to allow me to ride out the siege that you gods have put me under."

"What nonsense," said one of the gods, a winged woman with an eagle-like face who Darek thought was the Avian Goddess. "Why are we still standing around here waiting? Skimif, order us to attack and wipe out this fool from the face of Martir."

But Skimif didn't look likely to order any of the gods to do anything. He seemed to be thinking, but whatever he was thinking about must not have been good because he was frowning in frustration.

"Skimif will never order you gods to attack me," said Uron. "Not even if I was one step away from completely destroying this world you call home. Because he knows I will end this mortal's life if he does and innocent blood will be on his hands."

Skimif's silence was all the confirmation anyone needed to know that Uron's claim was accurate.

"What will you do, then?" said Nimiko. "Just because we won't attack you doesn't mean we'll let you get away so you can complete your plans later."

"Nimiko is correct," said the Avian Goddess. "We will stay here until Skimif orders us otherwise. You can't hold the Magical Superior forever."

Uron didn't look disturbed by the presence of so many deities all deciding to wait it out. He simply chuckled. "Interesting. We must be more similar than I thought. My plan, too, is to wait out this stalemate, although unlike you, I know it will end and when it does, I will be the last one standing."

"How arrogant," said the Avian Goddess, brushing her bangs out of her eyes. "What makes you think you will win?"

Uron's eyes flickered up toward the sky. "Why ruin the surprise? You will all learn soon enough ... learn, and tremble."

Chapter Eighteen

"We killed a goddess. We killed a goddess. We killed an *actual* goddess."

"Shut up."

"We killed a goddess."

"What did I say about shutting up?"

"*We killed a goddess.*"

Halfway up the stairs leading to Bleak Rock's exit, Durima stopped and turned to face Gujak. Her partner, who still had some of the Spider Goddess's sticky webbing trailing along behind his feet, was staring at the gauntlet attached to his hand as if it was some kind of terrible infection that had no known cure. For once, Durima agreed with his feelings, as the gauntlet (*God-killer*, as the writing had said) was a dangerous weapon that no one should have.

Even so, Durima grabbed Gujak's face and forced him to look at her. It was much harder to do than she thought. Gujak's eyes were practically glued to the gauntlet, like he thought it was going to stab him in the back if he took his eyes off it for even a second. Granted, that might not have been an entirely unreasonable fear, considering what that evil thing was capable of, but Durima still managed to get him to look her in the eyes.

"Gujak, I know," said Durima, speaking fast and low. "I

know we killed a goddess. I know we did something no one besides the gods themselves is even supposed to be able to do. I know that we committed an unthinkable and unforgivable crime against the gods themselves. I know we have probably invited the wrath of every god from World's End to the Great Berg down upon us. But whining about it won't do us any good. We need action. If we move fast, we might be able to ward off the worst of what is to come."

"How?" said Gujak. His lips trembled like he was about to cry. "I don't even know what the punishment for killing a goddess is supposed to be. I don't think there even is an official punishment, considering no one has ever done this before. Do you think the Council or the gods will make up a gruesome execution method just for us?"

"Not if we act fast," said Durima. "Listen, Master wanted us to get this gauntlet for him. If we bring it to Master, who should be at North Academy at the moment, and explain the accident, maybe he will be able to defend us from the other gods."

"Durima, do you honestly believe that?" said Gujak with a sniffle. "You know how Master feels about us. I don't think he'll hesitate to throw us into the Void if it meant he would avoid getting into trouble."

"Do you have any better ideas?" said Durima. She pointed at the stairs under their feet. "We stay here, the gods find us and kill us. I know Master doesn't really care about or like us much, but he's our only chance at survival here. Unless you want to die, but I don't, obviously."

"I don't want to die, either," said Gujak. "It's just ... I

can't even begin to describe how horrible this makes me feel. All my life, I've always striven to serve and follow the gods as best as I can, but now ... oh, I am a murderer of the gods. *Murderer of the gods, Durima.* Do you understand how serious that is?"

"I understand it perfectly," said Durima. "Probably even better than you, actually."

"Then why aren't you freaking out like I am?" said Gujak. "You're so calm and collected and it just doesn't seem appropriate for an accomplice to a god-killer like me."

Durima shuddered when she thought about how the Spider Goddess had died. But she gave Gujak a hard look directly in the eyes, which was the only way she knew how to calm people who needed it.

"It's a lesson I learned in the War," said Durima. "Panicky soldiers got killed. Calm ones survived. Same principle here. We panic, we die. We keep calm and maybe we'll live."

"*Maybe*?" Gujak repeated in horror. "Durima, we have to turn ourselves in. At least, I should turn myself into the Katabans Council. I deserve whatever punishment they decide to give me."

Durima growled. "The Council? Those pompous idiots aren't worth even turning yourself into. We need to get to Master. He's our only hope at this point."

Gujak slapped Durima's hands off his face and took a step back. "Sorry, Durima, but I ... I disagree."

"You disagree?" said Durima. "Are you even listening to yourself?"

"I'm listening to my conscience," said Gujak with a gulp. He looked so terrified, yet despite that he continue to talk to Durima like he was braver than he looked. "And my conscience says that I should turn myself in and accept the consequences for my actions, like a good servant of the gods would."

Durima sighed in exasperation. Gujak had always been more of a goody-two shoes, by the book kind of katabans than her, but until now she had forgotten just how blindly devoted to the gods that he was.

"Gujak, the Katabans Council is full of pompous crooks who don't give a damn about the law of the gods," said Durima. "You know that. You've met them before. They will execute you without a trial because they want to look like they're good for something, rather than being busybodies who don't have any right bossing the rest of us katabans around."

"I don't care," said Gujak. "That's just your opinion. I'm going to the Council and there's nothing you can do to—"

Durima punched Gujak in the face as hard as she could. The blow sent Gujak falling backwards, but before he could fall down the stairs, Durima caught him and pulled him up. He was completely unconscious, his eyes closed and his breathing shallow. A dent shaped like her fist was on his wooden head, but other than that, he didn't have any other serious injuries.

Good, Durima thought. *I need him in one piece if we're going to go to Master and ask for his help.*

Slinging the unconscious Gujak over her shoulder like a

sack of potatoes, Durima dashed up the stairs as fast as she could, taking them two at a time, heedless of the danger of slipping on a wet step. There was no time to waste worrying about that when there were far worse consequences awaiting both of them if she failed to find Master quickly.

Thankfully, the Spider Goddess apparently lived alone, because Durima did not run into any servants or minions that might have served her while she lived. Of course, they probably would have run away the minute they felt the Spider Goddess's death, which made sense, as there was no way the death of a goddess could be ignored by any katabans for long.

In fact, as Durima reached the top of the staircase and emerged into the narrow hallway from before, she found it odd that the gods had not yet struck her and Gujak down. They had *killed* a goddess, and yet they had lived for longer than five seconds.

Either the gods don't know that she's dead or they're dealing with something else, Durima thought, running down the hallway back toward the slide. *Then again, maybe they're too afraid of Bleak Rock to investigate what happened. Maybe they're waiting for us to leave the island before they'll try anything.*

That thought probably should have sapped her motivation to leave Bleak Rock, but if anything, it gave her greater motivation to leave as soon as possible and find Master. She just hoped that she was fast enough to use the ethereal to get from Bleak Rock to North Academy; not a terribly difficult distance to travel, given the way space/time worked in the ethereal, but hardly a simple five minute stroll through the woods, either.

The last obstacle between her, Gujak, and freedom was the slide they had taken down into Bleak Rock in the first place. It was still very dark, almost pitch-black now that Gujak was not conscious enough to use his light, which forced Durima to use her own luminimancy to allow her to see the entrance at the very top of the slide.

Yet even that wasn't as big of a problem as it could have been. Durima tensed her back legs, gathering all of the strength that she could, and launched herself and Gujak through the air toward the opening. She expected to hit her head against the ceiling, but it must have been much higher than she thought, because despite how high and far she jumped, her head never hit anything.

She landed hard on the top of the slide, almost lost her balance due to Gujak's weight, but soon recovered and dashed outside to the exterior of Bleak Rock.

As soon as she did, a wave of sleet fell into her face. The abruptness of the ice cold sleet was shocking, causing her to try to come to a halt. Unfortunately, the ground was slippery beneath her feet, sending her sliding across the layer of sleet on the ground all the way to the edge of the cliff.

Durima tried to stop, but she was going too fast. In an instant, she went off the side of the cliff and fell toward the ocean waters below. Or she would have, if she hadn't reached out with her free claw and dug it as deeply as she could into the side of the cliff.

Even then, she only succeeded in slowing their descent. Her claw tore through the rock as they descended, sending dust and dirt into her eyes, until it finally caught on something too thick for it to cut through, thus stopping them abruptly about halfway down.

Panting, blinking her eyes to get the dust out of them, Durima looked down below at the crashing waves that beat against the island's base. She then looked at Gujak, who despite the fall wasn't even stirring, which was good because knowing Gujak, he would be freaking out if he was awake at the moment.

Then Durima looked up at the sky. Although it was quite dark due to it being night time, Durima could tell that the sky was completely covered with dark storm clouds that poured sleet. Being so close up against the island, Durima and Gujak managed to avoid the worst of it; nonetheless, Durima could feel her fur getting cold and wet as the sleet fell from the sky by the bucketful.

That's why I lost my footing and slid off the cliff, Durima realized. *It must have been sleeting hard for several minutes before we even got out of Bleak Rock. But why ...?*

The answer came to her immediately: The Spider Goddess had also been the Goddess of Sleet. Without her around to control the sleet, it was no wonder that the weather around Bleak Rock was going insane. This was probably a temporary affair, as Skimif would no doubt take control of the Spider Goddess's domains soon enough. Even so, if the other gods had not sensed their sister's death earlier, then surely they would notice the uncontrollable sleet that was pounding the seas and conclude that something was amiss.

Which just gives me extra motivation to get the hell out of here, Durima thought.

Entering the ethereal from their current position would be difficult, dangerous even, but not impossible. Once, during the Katabans War, Durima had jumped off a tall cliff to evade capture from enemy soldiers and had fallen into the ethereal right before hitting the ground at the base of the cliff. It was not something she had done in years, but she figured she could do it.

I have *to do it again,* Durima thought, glancing at the roaring waves below. *I don't have much of a choice.*

After making sure that Gujak was still hanging safely over her shoulder, Durima focused on a spot just below them. She didn't see why she couldn't open the ethereal here; however, it could be difficult sometimes to predict where a portal to the ethereal, opened in the air, would take you. Sometimes, if you did it wrong, you could end up on the other side of the world, although that kind of mistake was usually only made by young katabans who weren't familiar with ethereal travel.

The hardest part was letting go of the cliff to fall into the portal that would open and catch her. Despite the pressure on her claw, the heavy sleet, and Gujak's own weight, Durima's instincts forced her to hold on as long as possible. That was probably because she couldn't see the portal yet, only the terrifying, violent waves that beat against the base of the island like an army battering down the door of an enemy fortress.

Another reason to hate physical bodies, Durima thought with a scowl. *Dumb instincts that aren't based in reason or evidence or facts. They only care about the appearances of things, not the actual nature of—*

Without warning, the rock that she had hooked her claw around broke. Panic rising in her chest, Durima could not help but scream as she and Gujak fell toward the loud ocean waves below, which continued to bash at the island's base even more violently than before.

But they didn't fall into the ocean. Instead, a portal opened up between them and the sea and it was that portal they fell into. As they passed through, the world around them became dark and silent, the only sounds being Durima's screams as they became lost in the dark void between Martir and the ethereal.

Then everything slowly came back into view and Durima landed hard on the shining white road that was the ethereal. The fall took her breath away, but she recovered quickly enough. She floated back to an upright position and, without taking even a moment to think about it, immediately flew down in the direction that she knew would take her to North Academy.

She flew as fast as she could, past dozens of other katabans traveling along the ethereal. No one tried to stop her, but she got several odd looks from most of the katabans she passed. No doubt they noticed Gujak hanging unconscious over her shoulder, but hopefully they would assume that he was injured and she, as his kind and caring friend, was trying to get him to a doctor or healer as fast as she could.

Of course, the main reason for her speed was because she didn't want the others to know about what she and Gujak had just gotten away with. She didn't sense any fear or unexplainable terror in the other katabans, which maybe meant they didn't even know the Spider Goddess was dead yet.

They'll know soon enough, Durima thought. *And when they do, they'll stop at nothing to tear us apart.*

One of the useful advantages of the ethereal was the way in which space/time worked. Whereas a journey from Bleak Rock to North Academy in Martir would take, depending on your speed and method of travel, anywhere from several weeks to several months, in the ethereal, the same journey would only take perhaps fifteen minutes. And that was if you were an inexperienced ethereal traveler who didn't even know about all of the shortcuts you could take.

Durima was no inexperienced ethereal traveler. She veered to the left, imagining another portal, but rather than a portal that opened up to another part of Martir, it was a portal that would take her to another part of the ethereal, closer to where she could get off at North Academy. It was a tricky move, but not terribly difficult after some practice.

Then that portal appeared before her and she jumped into it. Unlike traveling between Martir and the ethereal, this 'inter-ethereal travel,' as it known among katabans, had no real transitioning sequence.

One moment, she was on the right side of the ethereal; the next, she found herself floating on the left side. It was difficult to tell, of course, due to lack of said transitioning sequence, but certain clues—such as the position of the stars in the sky above, which resembled North Academy—told her that she was indeed close to where she had to be.

So Durima once again flew down the ethereal. There were few katabans here, mostly because it was generally impossible to enter North Academy via the ethereal due to the spell that 'locked' the school's portal.

But Master had told her that he would negate that spell once he got to North Academy so that Durima and Gujak could directly enter the school's graveyard without needing to climb the Walls as they had done on their first trip there. She just hoped that Master had succeeded in doing that, because if he didn't, then she and Gujak were going to be in big trouble.

In less than a minute, Durima found it. The portal to North Academy was open for the first time in ... well, she didn't know how long, seeing as it had been locked for as long as she could remember. Through the portal, she saw mist and darkness, but she didn't stop to observe more closely because her fear of being caught by her fellow katabans drove her ever forward without hesitation.

Durima launched herself and Gujak directly through the portal. As always, everything around her went dark and breathing became difficult, but only for a moment. In the next instance, she landed on the dirt of the graveyard feet first, almost tripping over her own feet before catching herself and regaining her balance. Gujak's arms and legs flopped uselessly against her body, but he still didn't stir even one inch.

It took Durima's eyes a moment to adjust to the darkness and mist, as she had transitioned from the ethereal to Martir far more quickly than she normally did. Thankfully, it only took her a few seconds to adjust ... but when they did, she wished they hadn't.

All around her, everywhere she looked, were gods. Not just a handful of gods, but ten, twenty, thirty, maybe even more than that. Some stood on the ground, like Nimiko, while others flew or floated in the sky above, such as the Avian Goddess. The Tusked God towered over everyone else and even Skimif himself, radiating as much power as all of the other gods combined, was present.

Not only that, but she soon noticed Master, the Ghostly God, lying unconscious on the ground near an open grave. He looked like someone had punched him out. He wasn't even stirring. He could have been dead and Durima wouldn't have been able to tell the difference.

Durima hardly believed what she saw, largely due to the overwhelming, almost primal fear that was overriding her rational thinking skills. She had gotten here as fast as she could, hoping against hope that Master would protect her and Gujak from his siblings, but she had jumped straight into the middle of the largest gathering of gods she had ever seen in one place. And all of them were looking at her and Gujak, as though the two katabans' sudden appearance had taken them by surprise.

That was when Durima heard someone cry out in pain and fall to the ground. She looked toward the grave again and saw the Magical Superior lying on the ground like he had taken a walloping as well. That puzzled her for a moment before she sensed a powerful presence appear right next to her.

Looking to her right, Durima saw, with horror, a being with purplish-black skin, the same color and texture as Uron's. He had a terrifying human/snake face hybrid and he smelled like a rotting corpse, even though he appeared to be as alive as anyone else. Sheer power radiated from his form like light from the sun, a level of power equal to that of Skimif's.

At that same moment, Gujak awoke with a start. He jerked so suddenly in her arms that Durima had to drop him. He landed on his bottom at the feet of the being that Durima had never seen before, blinking rapidly as he returned to consciousness.

"What?" said Gujak, looking around at all of the gathered gods. "Where are we? Why are there so many gods here? And who are you?"

Gujak addressed that last question to the snake-skinned being who stood above him. Why Gujak apparently wasn't afraid of him, Durima didn't know. Perhaps he was still waking up or maybe he was just that dumb and naïve, as Durima had always suspected he was.

The being smiled a smile that reminded Durima of how Uron had looked whenever it was pleased. "You're just in time, Durima, Gujak. I thought for a moment that maybe you two had failed in your mission, considering your general incompetence, but when I felt the Spider Goddess's death, I knew then and there that I had won."

Gujak blinked. "What?"

"What do you mean, the Spider Goddess's death?" said a slightly panicked voice nearby.

Durima glanced in the direction that the voice had come from. One of the school mages was standing there, perhaps one of the students. He had short brown hair, a long face, and a small nose. His robes were ripped in some places and he looked like he hadn't gotten a good night's sleep in years.

What's a mortal man doing here, of all places? Durima thought. *Now that I think about it, what is anyone doing here? Who is this guy who looks like Uron? Why is Master unconscious? Why are there so many gods from both Pantheons present? And why is Skimif himself among them?*

She never got a chance to verbalize her questions, however, because the being who looked like Uron bent down and grabbed Gujak's right arm, the one gloved with the God-killer. Durima recognized the way the being's long fingers wrapped around Gujak's upper arm from her days in the War, as he was using a technique she had once used on an enemy soldier. But it was too late for her to look away or stop him.

The sound of wood being torn apart, mixed with Gujak's screams of terror and pain, split Durima's ears and even made some of the gods flinch. The only being who didn't seem affected was the one who had ripped off Gujak's arm.

Holding Gujak's ripped-off arm over his head like it was a prize he had won in a game, the Uron lookalike grabbed the God-killer and pulled it off Gujak's hand. Much to Durima's surprise, the being succeeded in removing the gauntlet from Gujak's arm, which he then tossed aside like garbage. As for Gujak himself, he lay unconscious on the ground, perhaps having lost consciousness from the pain he had experienced when he lost his arm, although due to his wooden body, he was not bleeding.

In one smooth motion, the Uron lookalike shoved the gauntlet onto his right hand. Flexing his metallic fingers, the Uron lookalike smiled triumphantly at the gods, many of whom were now looking at him like he was a dangerous wild animal. Durima took that moment to grab Gujak and drag him away from Uron, but the strange being didn't seem to notice, or if he did, didn't care enough to try to stop them.

"Uron," said Skimif. His voice was tight. "What is that thing you are wearing?"

It took Durima a moment to realize that Skimif was addressing the Uron lookalike who had just torn Gujak's arm off.

Why does this being have the same name as Master's pet snake? Durima thought. *Wait a minute ... they can't possibly be the same being, can they?*

The Uron lookalike whose name was apparently Uron held up the God-killer for everyone to see. "I am surprised you don't recognize it, Skimif. As the God of Martir, I assumed that you, at least, would know what this is, but I guess even you do not know all of Martir's mysteries. But I will tell you what it is: Your destruction."

"Hold it," said a winged goddess, who Durima recognizcd as the Avian Goddess. "Earlier, you mentioned the death of the Spider Goddess. Did you mean that our sister is dead?"

"Of course I did," said Uron. "Didn't you feel her death a few minutes ago?"

"They didn't," said Skimif, drawing all attention to him. "I sensed it before anyone else due to my status as God of Martir, but I didn't want the other gods to panic or forget about you in their quest to destroy whoever killed their sister. I've been holding back the panic this entire time and hoped I wouldn't have to let it go until you were gone."

"So it's true," said Nimiko, looking as broken as a mortal who had discovered the death of a favorite sibling, rather than a god. "But ... how? The Treaty forbids gods killing other gods. And mortals most certainly can't do it. Even katabans are incapable of killing us. This must be a trick."

"It's no trick," said Uron. "If you won't believe me, then believe Skimif. After all, Skimif is supposed to be honesty incarnate, isn't he? He has no reason to lie to his own servants and thus demoralize them right when victory was in your grasp."

"That still doesn't explain how that happened," said Nimiko. "As I said, gods cannot be killed except by other gods, but even that is prevented by the Treaty."

"It was these two who had done it," said Uron, gesturing at Durima and Gujak. "And it was with this that they achieved it."

He shook the God-killer on his hand. It looked deceptively plain, so much so that Durima might have dismissed it as nothing more than a normal metal gauntlet if she had not known its true nature as a terrifying weapon that, in the wrong hands, could be used to cause untold damage to the world.

And I have a feeling that it just fell into those wrong hands everyone talks about, Durima thought as she watched Uron strike a triumphant pose.

"Many obscure legends exist about this object," said Uron. His voice was growing mad with glee, making him look even scarier than he normally did. "Magical historians call it the Hand of Apocalypse; heathen historians have referred to it as the Liberator. Neither name is quite as fitting, however, as the God-killer."

"God-killer?" This came from the human mage she had seen earlier, who had somehow gotten over his human fears of divinity enough to talk. "Does that mean it ... it ..."

The mage seemed too horrified by the implications to finish his sentence.

But Uron finished it for him, saying, "Yes, Darek Takren, the God-killer does exactly that: Kill gods."

At that moment, an intense fear swept over all of the gods present. Some retreated deeper into the mist, looking troubled, while others vanished completely, like they had run away. Only a handful held their ground, like Skimif and the Tusked God. Even the Ghostly God seemed to have felt it, because he moaned in his unconscious state and muttered, "Not that ..."

"Ridiculous," said the Avian Goddess with a huff, although the way she had moved slightly farther away from Uron made it clear she didn't think it was quite that ridiculous. "There is nothing in Martir that can kill the gods. The Powers designed us to be at the very top of the hierarchy of the world, and even with Skimif now above us, we're still heads and shoulders above everyone else."

"Call it what you will, but that doesn't change the fact that the God-killer exists and is even older than you gods," said Uron. "It was created by the Powers, just like you were, and was designed specifically so that mortals could use it in the event that you gods lost your way and had to be dealt with permanently."

"He's telling the truth," said Skimif, his tone bitter. "When I ascended to godhood, the Powers gave me a lot of information about Martir that few know. The God-killer was among that information, but I didn't think to tell anyone or do anything about it because it was safely hidden within Bleak Rock where no one could reach it. I never thought it would be used against us."

"Correct," said Uron. "The Powers gave the God-killer to the Mysterious One for safekeeping when they realized that it was too dangerous to leave anywhere else. They gave him strict orders not to tell any of the other gods about it, which is partly why he has kept such a mysterious persona for so many years."

"But if you have the God-killer, then does that mean ... you can kill us?" said Nimiko.

"Indeed," said Uron. He flexed the fingers of the God-killer. "That was the whole point of my plan. Without the God-killer, my entire plan would be far more difficult to complete than it is. If I am to destroy Martir, I must first destroy its gods, northern *and* southern. And the God-killer will allow me to do just that."

Durima wanted to hide. Shame filled her when she realized that she and Gujak, far from being obedient servants of the Ghostly God, had instead helped this ... this monster get one step closer to destroying Martir. There was still much about this situation that she didn't understand, but she understood that she and Gujak may have inadvertently helped destroy their world.

No, Durima thought, shaking her head as she glanced at the unconscious Gujak. *Not Gujak.* He *wanted to turn himself into the Council. I was the one who insisted that we take the God-killer to Master. This is all my fault no matter how you cut it.*

The Avian Goddess landed on the ground. She had the face of an eagle, but the body of a human woman, her arms replaced by her massive black and white wings that looked strong enough to break rock.

"Am I the only one not trembling in my boots here right now?" said the Avian Goddess, looking around at her fellow gods with disgust. "He may have the God-killer, but that doesn't mean he's invincible. We're the gods of Martir. We've dealt with far worse than some upstart being from the Prior World. Or am I going to have to tear him limb from limb myself?"

She said that while staring hard at Skimif. Although Skimif was clearly the only god on the same power level as Uron, he looked like he wanted to run away, which Durima thought was a rather pathetic way for the leader of the gods to look.

"You gods have never dealt with me before," said Uron. "But go ahead. Attack me. Show your brothers and sisters that there's nothing to be afraid of. I am getting tired of standing here talking anyway. I want action. I want my world back."

"Very well," said the Avian Goddess. She glanced to the left and right. "Anyone care to join me or will I have to kill him on my own?"

None of the other gods stepped forward to join. This was the strangest thing Durima had ever witnessed in her life. She had always thought of the gods as being superior to katabans in every way, including in sheer confidence, yet most of these gods, both northern and southern, were standing back like frightened little children.

"All right," said the Avian Goddess. She turned her attention to Uron. "How do you want to die? Maybe I could peck out your eyes and watch as you bleed to death. Or maybe I will chew you up and feed you to some poor starving chicks in dire need of a good meal. Then again, I imagine you'd make a poor meal for a growing baby bird. Nothing but skin and bone, that's what you are."

Uron kept flexing the fingers of the God-killer, which was starting to creep Durima out. "I find it surprising you intend to fight me at all. I am much closer to Skimif in power than you. Don't birds usually fly away when faced with a predator they can't defeat?"

"Only cowardly little sparrows would think to do that," said the Avian Goddess. "I am much closer to the eagle hawk, a powerful hunter and predator in its own right. They're known to kill baba raga in battle, which I think is an appropriate comparison to make in this situation."

"Then what are you waiting for?" said Uron. "Peck my eyes out, feed me to your chicks ... do whatever you wish. I can handle it."

"Very well," said the Avian Goddess. She spread her wings wide, a ten foot wingspan at least. "For Martir!"

The Avian Goddess flew at Uron far faster than any normal bird could. She aimed directly for his chest, but despite how terrifying she looked, Uron held his ground. He punched his other fist into the God-killer, but that was the only movement he made as she drew closer and closer.

Uron suddenly thrust the God-killer at her. The Avian Goddess must have seen that coming because she banked upwards at the last possible second, going up and over Uron's head. She landed on the ground behind him and slapped him in the back with one of her wings.

That blow likely would have killed an ordinary mortal and seriously wounded a god, but Uron didn't even flinch. He whirled around, reaching with the God-killer for her wing, but the Avian Goddess jumped back out of his range.

"Flighty bird," said Uron, spitting at the ground. "Did you suddenly become afraid of me? Or are you waiting for your siblings to come in and help?"

Based on the apprehensive looks of the other gods, it didn't seem likely any of them would step in and help the Avian Goddess. Not that it seemed to matter to her. She crouched low to the ground, bringing her wings close to her chest, looking like a hawk about to pounce on a mouse.

"I'm just looking for the perfect opening to attack," said the Avian Goddess. "You act all tough, but everyone has a weak point. All I need to do is find it."

Uron laughed. "Find it? You can't beat me, though I admit it is brave of you to try. You are nothing more than a weak little chick trying to avoid getting killed by a large feline."

"Odd comparison to make, considering you used to be a snake for a while," said the Avian Goddess. "And I don't know if it worked this way in your world, but here in Martir, quite a few species of bird are known to kill snakes and eat them."

Once again, the Avian Goddess flew at Uron. Uron raised the God-killer, probably to grab her, but the Avian Goddess once again flew over him. As she did so, she sank her sharp, deadly-looking claws into his shoulders and lifted him straight off the ground. Her movement was so sudden that Uron appeared too shocked to react.

By the time the realization of what she was doing dawned on his face—which was when he was at least fifty feet in the air—it was too late for Uron to do anything about it. The Avian Goddess flipped in the air and hurled him toward the ground back at the spot where he had been standing previously.

Uron crashed into the ground hard enough to form a small crater and send dust clouds flying into the air. The impact was enough to shake the ground under Durima's feet for a brief moment, a heavy enough impact that Durima was worried that the ground itself would crack open.

Thankfully, her fears proved unfounded. As the dust settled, the Avian Goddess landed on the ground a few feet away from the crater that Uron lay in. As for Uron, he didn't get up or make even the slightest noise to indicate that he was still alive.

There's no way that blow could have killed him, Durima thought. *The Avian Goddess is powerful, but not that powerful. If Uron really is on the same power level as Skimif, then that should have maybe only stunned him at best.*

But the longer she watched, the more likely it seemed that Uron was down for good. She couldn't sense Uron's energy level, but considering that he was not a god, katabans, or mage, perhaps that had something to do with it.

Just then, she heard someone running over to her. She looked to her right and saw that it was that human mage from earlier, the one she had heard Uron call Darek Takren. With the gods' attention on Uron's crater, she wondered why he was coming over to them.

He's going to attack us, Durima realized. *He probably knows that we broke into North Academy last week. He's taking advantage of the Avian Goddess's battle with Uron to take me and Gujak out.*

She readied herself for a fight, but as Darek drew closer, the look on his face was less angry and more concerned. He was looking at Gujak, who lay as unconscious as always at Durima's feet.

Darek stopped only a couple of feet from them. His eyes were bloodshot and his robes were splattered with dirt, but he genuinely didn't seem threatening to Durima. If anything, he looked concerned, perhaps for Gujak's health, based on the way he was looking at her unconscious partner.

"How is he?" said Darek. He spoke in a low voice, like he was afraid of disturbing the gods' attention. "Why isn't he bleeding?"

Durima, taken aback by his questions, nonetheless answered, "He took on a wooden body when he became a physical being, so he doesn't have any blood to spill."

Darek looked at her with an incomprehensible look on his face, which made Durima think he was stupid until she remembered that none of the human mages, except for the Magical Superior, could understand Godly Divina, the language most katabans spoke.

Some education they give their students here, Durima thought.

Before she could figure out how to communicate in a way that Darek would understand, a low groaning sound came from the crater that Uron had made. It sounded like Uron was in terrible pain, causing Durima to flashback to the War, when she had heard some of her fellow soldiers groaning—usually screaming—in pain as they died. She cut the flashback short, however, because she didn't want to be distracted in such a tense situation.

"Oh, you survived?" said the Avian Goddess in a mocking voice. "But I guess that makes sense. You are, after all, the great Uron. Of course a wee little birdie like me couldn't kill you. Still, I hope I crippled you for life, you bastard."

There was no response to that, as Uron had ceased groaning in pain. A hushed silence fell across the graveyard, making Durima feel like they were at a funeral instead of at the battle for Martir itself.

What happened next was so abrupt and sudden that Durima wasn't even sure it had happened. Uron leaped out of the crater as fast as a lightning bolt. His purplish-black form, little more than a fast-moving blur, cut through the air like a tiger.

The Avian Goddess only had enough time to caw in surprise before Uron landed in front of her and grabbed her neck with the God-killer. He whirled around to face the other gods, holding the flailing Avian Goddess before him like a captured bird.

"Behold," said Uron. His skin was cut in several places, allowing a strange blue liquid that might have been blood to bleed out. "This is the fate that befalls all of the gods of Martir, both strong and weak."

Durima knew what was going to happen next, but that didn't stop her from feeling horrified and disgusted as the Avian Goddess's body slowly turned to dust. The Avian Goddess beat her powerful wings against Uron's body as hard as she could, but he didn't even flinch under her ferocious attack. He just stood there, smiling, watching as the disintegrating effect slowly made its way up from the Avian Goddess's feet to her neck.

This time, the disintegrating effect seemed to happen faster than when it had with the Spider Goddess. In a minute, perhaps less, the Avian Goddess's head disintegrated, leaving nothing more than a pile of brown dust in Uron's hand, which he dropped onto the dust at his feet.

As soon as the remains of the Avian Goddess settled, the other gods fled. The Tusked God disappeared deep into the mist, Nimiko vanished in a flash of light, and every other god or goddess who had been present vanished in their particular way. Not a single one stopped to explain where they were going or if they were going to return. They just ran like a nest of frightened mice from a hungry cat.

In even less time than it took for the Avian Goddess to die, almost all of the fifty or so deities who had been present to save Martir were gone. Only Skimif and the Ghostly God remained, and the Ghostly God was still unconscious and so in no condition to help.

Uron licked some of the Avian Goddess's dust off his hand and grimaced. "Tastes like dirt. I thought it would taste like chicken."

"Where did the other gods go?" said Darek, looking around wildly. "Lord Skimif, is this part of your plan?"

Skimif sighed. "No, it's not. They ran away because they were afraid of Uron, or perhaps more accurately, they were afraid of the God-killer."

Darek's shoulders slumped. "So they're not coming back?"

"Unlikely," said Skimif. He put a hand on his heart. "It took all of my willpower not to join them. The God-killer frightens me as much as it does them. I can only guess where they all might have run off to in order to escape it."

"It doesn't matter where they run or where they hide," said Uron as he dusted off the God-killer. "I will find and kill every one of them personally. It is the only way to pave the way for the return of my home."

Durima considered their current situation. It was her, one human mage who was still in school, the Magical Superior (who, based on the way he was lying, was clearly too weak to even stand), Skimif, Gujak, and the Ghostly God.

Six, Durima thought. *Actually, the Superior, Gujak, and Master are down for the count. So that's three: The most powerful god in the world, a student mage, and me. Against the only being in the world who can kill a god and isn't afraid of us in the slightest. And technically, the only one of us who is even capable of harming Uron is Skimif, so that brings down our total number of fighters to one.*

"Granted," Uron continued, "it will be tough to track down every last one, but in the end, it will be worth it. All I need to do first is kill you, Skimif, and then go and hunt down the rest of your fellow deities."

Skimif took a step forward. "Why do you think you'll be able to defeat me?"

"Are you really that dense?" said Uron. He held up the God-killer. "This is why I *know* I will defeat you, Skimif, but not just defeat you. I will kill you, annihilate you from this world. Without your governing presence, the gods will become even more fractured than they are now, which will make it easier to pick them off one by one."

"You won't win," said Skimif, who sounded far more confident than the situation warranted, in Durima's opinion. "I won't let you. I saved this world from one apocalypse. I will not let it be destroyed by another."

"Brave words, coming from someone who will crumple to dust as soon as I touch them," said Uron. "But why do we wast time talking? Let us fight. And once the dust settles, only one of us shall be left standing."

Chapter Nineteen

Seeing all of those gods run away had shaken Darek more than he'd like to admit. He had had hope earlier that Skimif, along with his cohort of fifty gods and goddesses, would be able to defeat Uron and that their world might survive after all.

Now, however, Darek was beginning to think that maybe their chances of survival were lower than zero. He was glad Skimif was willing to fight (despite not being sure where Skimif's confidence came from, considering that Uron had just killed a goddess right in front of their eyes), but he only had one concern now: Getting the heck out of the graveyard before Uron killed them all.

Skimif and Uron had taken their battle into the mist. Darek saw flashes of explosive energy in the mist, heard both of them yelling and screaming at each other, and felt huge spikes of energy every time one of them attacked the other. Granted, most of the energy spikes belonged to Skimif, but Darek could still sense Uron, although it was much harder to do because of Uron's otherworldly nature.

Of course, this was exactly why Darek was going to get himself and the Magical Superior out of here. He hoped to get the Superior back to the Arcanium, where they could wake all of the teachers and students and evacuate the whole school. It was a sad thought, abandoning North Academy, but with no guarantee that Skimif would win this fight, Darek felt it was a necessary measure that the Magical Superior would no doubt agree with if he were conscious.

As for the two katabans, Durima and Gujak, Darek tried to communicate to them that he was going to leave the graveyard, but his inability to speak Godly Divina made it nearly impossible to let them know. He wanted to heal Gujak, whose bloodless stump concerned him greatly, but he wasn't sure that Durima would let him.

I'm not a very good panamancer anyway, Darek thought as he ran to the Magical Superior, who lay on the ground nearby. *The katabans probably know how to heal themselves better than I do.*

The Magical Superior looked awful. His robes' rich auburn hue was obscured almost completely by the dirt covering them. Uron's finger marks were visible in his neck thanks to the light that Darek conjured from the tip of his wand.

Despite all of that, the Magical Superior was alive. His chest heaved up and down, which meant he was breathing. Darek was surprised that the Superior was still alive, considering how he had taken a blast that had knocked out a god, but he supposed the headmaster wouldn't be the Magical Superior if he couldn't handle something like that.

The challenge, then, was in waking the Magical Superior and getting him out of the graveyard while avoiding Skimif and Uron's fight. Behind him, it sounded like two hurricanes were fighting each other or, based on the sounds of tombstones being blasted to bits, perhaps it was two earthquakes instead.

The mental imagery is ridiculous either way, Darek thought as he squatted over the Magical Superior. *Even so, I still need to get us out of here. The school depends on us.*

He shook the Magical Superior, but the Superior barely even stirred. Darek considered picking up the Magical Superior and just hauling him out of the graveyard like that, but even the thought of picking up the lightweight Superior was enough to make his bones ache. He himself was still recovering from Uron constricting around his body, not to mention all of the stress that was taking a toll on him.

Then I'll just lift him using telekinesis, Darek thought, glancing at his wand as he did so. *Should be pretty simple. I'll levitate him out of here easy.*

Just as Darek aimed his wand at the Magical Superior, he heard someone running nearby. Looking up, he saw Durima, with Gujak slung over her shoulder like a rolled up carpet, running over to the Ghostly God. She stopped before him, carefully deposited Gujak on the ground, and then began shaking the Ghostly God in an obvious attempt to awaken him.

Why would she do that? Darek thought in alarm. *Doesn't she know how evil he is? He's the only god I wouldn't mind Uron killing, to be honest.*

Much to his surprise, however, the Ghostly God began to stir. He made a loud, strange groaning sound that reminded Darek of a blizzard. Then he slowly sat up, putting one hand on his forehead as he used his other hand for support.

He recovered rather quickly, because he soon lowered his hand from his head and looked around in confusion. Durima then began rapidly speaking in Godly Divina. The Ghostly God listened, but he didn't move, not even when a particularly big blast of energy from within the mist lit up the whole area like the sun for a brief moment before the light faded.

By the time Durima finished, the Ghostly God looked incredibly angry. He rose to his full height, his face contorted into a snarl, and he looked directly at Darek.

Darek immediately aimed his wand at the Ghostly God, despite knowing that there was not a spell in the world he could cast to defeat a god. Still, it was better than doing nothing, in his opinion, because it at least showed he was serious.

"You," said the Ghostly God, pointing at Darek. "How is Skimif's battle against Uron going?"

Darek gulped. "I don't know. They're in the mist and I can't see them."

The Ghostly God shook his head. He glanced into the mist as a loud *bang* noise rattled Darek's jaw. "I must leave. There is no way I can defeat Uron if he has the God-killer, as Durima here just told me. Even though I'd like to take that snake and skin him."

Darek was surprised to hear bitterness in the Ghostly God's voice, as if he was angry that he had been betrayed by Uron. Of course, that made sense. The gods certainly weren't above desiring or carrying out revenge, as many of the stories about them attested.

That was when multiple things suddenly came together in Darek's mind, like the pieces of a puzzle falling perfectly into place. He looked over his shoulder at the mist, which flashed with a different color every time Skimif or Uron attacked each other, and then looked back at the Ghostly God.

"Ghostly God," said Darek. "I have a request I'd like to make of you that I hope you will see fit to honor."

The Ghostly God looked at Darek in disbelief. "You do remember that I am a *southern* god, yes? Which means that I would never even think of honoring any request that a mortal made of me, no matter how small or large?"

"I know," said Darek. "And I hate having to ask you, but you're the only god around here, so I had to take a chance."

The Ghostly God tapped his chin, almost like he was interested. "I will admit that I admire the fact that you mortals tend to be brave enough to ask even us southern gods for favors. Or perhaps it's stupidity on your part. You mortals aren't exactly known for your intelligence or cleverness among us gods."

"It doesn't matter if I'm smart or clever," said Darek. He jerked a thumb over his shoulder. "I am going to go help Skimif defeat Uron, but in order to do so, I need your help."

The Ghostly God frowned. "Durima told me that Uron can kill gods. I hardly think he will have any trouble killing a mortal like yourself, even if you fight alongside Skimif."

"I know," said Darek, nodding. "But right now Skimif and Uron are evenly matched. If I can distract Uron for even just a moment, I might be able to give Skimif the opportunity he needs to land the killing blow."

"Definitely stupid," said the Ghostly God. "Nonetheless, you have piqued my interest. What is your request?"

Darek put a hand on his chest. "It's simple. As a god, you can grant mortals your protection. The protection is supposed to protect us mortals from other gods and even grant us some of your strength; however, I think it could possibly make me strong enough to take on Uron. I am asking for you to grant me your divine protection as I go into battle."

"It's true that even we southern gods can grant mortals protection if we want," said the Ghostly God. "But in all of my centuries of existence, I have never saw fit to grant any mortal my protection before. You know how we southern gods feel about mortals."

"My request isn't finished yet," said Darek. He pointed at the Magical Superior. "I want your servant, Durima, to take the Magical Superior to the Arcanium and to tell the school faculty and students that they have to get out of here now."

Durima looked like she wanted to argue that point, but the Ghostly God held up a hand to silence her even before she spoke. He didn't look pleased by Darek's requests.

"So you want two things from us," said the Ghostly God. "My protection and the lives of your fellow students and teachers, essentially. Yet you forget the one rule about asking a god for help: You must offer me something valuable in return."

Darek bit his lower lip. What he was about to offer the Ghostly God was something he didn't want to offer him, but considering how serious and urgent the situation was (which he was reminded of every time he heard Skimif roar in pain), he didn't hesitate to speak.

"In exchange for those two things, I will swear my life to you just as I've sworn my life to Xocion," said Darek. "Not only that, but I will be your servant for ten years or until you choose to dismiss my service."

He knew that that would get the Ghostly God's attention. The God of Ghosts and Mist began stroking his chin. He had a skeptical look on his face, as if he was looking at the offer from every angle in order to spot any deceit in it. There was none to be found. Darek's offer was genuine, but that didn't mean the Ghostly God would actually take it.

"That is very interesting," said the Ghostly God. "But I have already had negative experiences with human servants, particularly human mages. The female who called herself Aorja worked for me and look how well that turned out."

Darek shook his head. "Aorja ... she was a liar and a deceiver. You couldn't trust her. I'm more honest than she. I'll serve you better than she. I promise."

"I admit that it is a tempting offer," said the Ghostly God. "And I am in dire need of more servants. With Uron's betrayal, Aorja's imprisonment, Gujak being out of commission, and Durima being criminally incompetent, I could use a servant who I could actually trust and rely upon to do my bidding."

"But not anything bad," said Darek. "I won't do a repeat of what you were trying to do here at North Academy if you accept my offer."

"Why would I ever repeat this mess?" said the Ghostly God, gesturing at the crater Uron had made earlier during his fight with the Avian Goddess. "Besides, this plan was never really mine in the first place. I now realize Uron was manipulating me the entire time, the bastard, so I doubt I'll ever even consider doing something this ridiculous again."

"Good," said Darek. "So what do you say? Do you accept my offer or not?"

The Ghostly God was quiet for longer than Darek liked. The sounds of battle between Skimif and Uron were as loud as ever, although that didn't stop Darek from worrying about what would happen if Uron managed to get one blow in on Skimif with the God-killer.

Finally, the Ghostly God nodded. "Your deal is reasonable. In exchange for ten years of service to me, I will grant you my protection and have Durima here take the Magical Superior back to the Arcanium. She will also alert the rest of the teachers and students about what is going on here so they may have time to evacuate in the event that Skimif is killed by Uron, although I have no idea where in the world they could evacuate to if *that* happened."

Durima didn't look happy about the arrangement for some reason. Maybe she didn't relish the thought of having to carry the Magical Superior around, even though he really wasn't all that heavy or large.

Not that it mattered to Darek. As he stood up, he shuddered, feeling a cold aura cover his body. It was only for a moment, however, and soon the cold aura vanished, making Darek feel like he always did, although he was no longer quite as tired as he once was.

"There," said the Ghostly God. "What you just felt was my protection falling over you. It will last only as long as I choose to let it last. Or until Uron inevitably kills you."

Darek rolled his shoulders. "That's an encouraging thought."

"No one has ever accused me of being an optimist," said the Ghostly God. "But I do try to honor my end of the deal. Durima?"

Durima had a bland expression on her face as she walked over to the Magical Superior. Darek stepped back as Durima gently picked up the headmaster and tossed him over her shoulder. She even picked up his staff and then, without looking at Darek, dashed back to the Ghostly God. She hauled Gujak over her other shoulder and in the next moment was gone, jumping over the walls and running into the mist that covered the graveyard like a veil.

The Ghostly God watched them go, a look of severe distaste on his features. "I will have to punish both of them later if we all survive this."

"Why?" said Darek.

"That is none of your business," said the Ghostly God. "Now, are you going to go help Skimif or not?"

"I am," said Darek. "I just wanted to know where you are going to be while Skimif and I are risking our lives for all of Martir."

"Back on Zamis, of course," said the Ghostly God. "And if you fail ... well, you had better not, or it is the Mind

Chamber for you."

Darek had no idea what the Mind Chamber was and he didn't get a chance to ask. With a final wave, the Ghostly God disintegrated into mist like an illusion.

Deciding that he could live without knowing what the Mind Chamber was, Darek turned and dashed into the mist in the direction of Skimif and Uron's fight. He just hoped that the Ghostly God's power had granted him enough strength to help.

Chapter Twenty

As Durima ran across the area between the Arcanium and the graveyard, which was far less misty than the graveyard had been, making sure not to drop either Gujak or the Magical Superior, Durima could not believe what that human mage Darek had just done.

He bargained with Master, Durima thought. *Bargained with him. When was the last time Master made a deal with anyone who* wasn't *a god?*

Granted, it wasn't like the deal was in Darek's favor. The Ghostly God was the one who clearly benefited from it, seeing as he would get a new servant for a full decade if it all worked out. Still, Durima hadn't thought any mortal could bargain with one of the southern gods, but Darek had done just that.

Has nothing to do with his negotiation skills, Durima decided. *It was just that the current situation is so serious that it requires this kind of drastic action. He's an opportunist, and no more.*

Then again, Darek had clearly offered to heal Gujak, an action she could not see benefiting him in any way. Perhaps Darek was simply an honest human being who wanted to do the right thing and help whoever he could.

A tight smile crossed Durima's lips at that thought. *Just like Jakuuth Grinfborn during the Katabans War.*

She glanced over her shoulder as best as she could while carrying both the Superior and Gujak. A thick cloud of mist covered the graveyard, obscuring her view of it, but the sounds of battle raging in it and the occasional flashes of power from within told her all she needed to know about what was going on.

Whether Darek is a saint or a liar, I hope his help is enough to aid Skimif in defeating Uron, Durima thought. *And while I would normally pray to the gods to grant Darek and Skimif victory, after seeing them run from Uron, I am not sure what good it would be.*

Darek was glad he had been smart enough to get the Ghostly God's protection before he had run headfirst into the battle between Skimif and Uron. Otherwise, he would have been incinerated when he stepped into a huge, fiery inferno that burned the air around him.

Who had caused the inferno, Darek couldn't tell. His lungs burned for air and his skin boiled. His robes somehow managed to avoid catching flame, but they felt like burning oven mitts due to their thickness, turning what was normally an advantage in the Great Berg into a liability right off the bat.

The flames obscured his vision and their roar filled his ears. Nonetheless, Darek raised his wand and summoned a wave of water to put out the flame. The inferno went out in an instant, but the collusion between water and fire created a heavy steam that made breathing difficult and caused sweat to drench his body.

But it also allowed him to see the battle between Skimif and Uron for the first time since it had started. He saw them standing not far from him, maybe two or three dozen yards from his current position, both panting, energy swirling in their hands as they circled each other like squabbling tiger lions.

Both looked like they had been through a war. Skimif's majestic white robes were torn or burned in several places and his scepter was nowhere to be seen. A large gash stood out on Skimif's chest, although oddly enough it was not bleeding.

Uron didn't even have any clothes anymore. He seemed to have discarded Braim's funeral robes or maybe had lost them in his fight with Skimif. His naked body was covered in thick, bleeding gashes, looking almost like poorly done tattoos, but Uron was clearly strong enough to go a few more rounds with Skimif. The God-killer was the only part of him that seemed unaffected by the battle, but the reason for that was obvious.

Darek also got a good look at their battlefield. Most of the tombstones were either crushed into pieces or broken in half. A few graves had even been blown open entirely, revealing old wooden caskets that had been buried hundreds of years ago. It pained Darek to see the graves of so many respectable mages destroyed, but there were more important things for him to worry about at the moment than desecrated graves.

He pointed his wand at Uron and focused on freezing his legs. He knew the ice wouldn't defeat Uron, but it might throw him off balance long enough for Skimif to get in a few good blows.

Thankfully, Uron was so distracted by Skimif that he didn't even notice Darek was there until his legs suddenly became frozen in a block of ice. Caught off-guard by this sudden event, Uron fell onto his side, a shocked expression on his face like he couldn't believe he hadn't seen that coming.

Skimif looked over his shoulder and saw Darek standing there, still aiming his wand at Uron. "Darek? What are you —"

A shattering of ice cut Skimif off. Uron flew at him, holding the God-killer in front of him, but Skimif vanished and Uron ended up slamming the God-killer into the ground where the God of Martir had been standing moments before.

Then Skimif reappeared next to Darek, a look of intense disapproval and worry upon his aquarian features. "What do you think you're doing here? Uron will kill you. You should get out of here now while you have the chance."

"I'm going to be fine," said Darek, although he found it hard to meet Skimif's eyes. "I made a deal with the Ghostly God. I have his protection. As long as I don't do anything stupid—"

"Like attack Uron?" said Skimif. "Who, I might remind you, is on the same power level as me?"

"Why discourage the mortal from trying to kill me?" said

Uron, a smirk on his face. He stood up and dusted off the God-killer. "He will die anyway. Why put his death off any longer than it needs to be?"

Uron launched himself across the misty graveyard directly toward Skimif and Darek. Darek raised his wand to attack, but then Skimif shoved him out of the way with enough force to send Darek stumbling several feet away.

Darek stopped stumbling as soon as he got control of his senses, however, and looked up just in time to see the God-killer only a handful of inches from Skimif's face. He almost cried out, "Skimif, look out!" but that turned out to be unnecessary because Skimif vanished into thin air.

As Uron landed, Skimif reappeared behind the nigh-godly being and grabbed him by the shoulders. He lifted Uron over his head and hurled him into the ground, causing Uron to plow through the earth, destroying even more headstones and sending dust and dirt everywhere

Skimif didn't hesitate for even a moment. He began hurling energy blasts at Uron, even before his opponent had slowed to a stop. Sometimes he would throw in a lightning bolt as well, or a fire ball, but he relied mostly on bright blasts of energy that looked powerful enough to blow up a city.

Darek got to his feet, watching in awe as Skimif blasted Uron into oblivion. At least, until Uron leaped out of the cloud of dust and mist that had covered him and, while still in the air, hurled a dozen blasts of some kind of reddish-black energy that Darek had never seen before in his life.

That didn't scare Skimif, however. He slapped the

energy blasts away as they came at him, doing it so fast that it looked like he wasn't moving at all. He grabbed the last energy blast, however, and hurled it directly back at Uron.

Uron spun out of the way of the blast in midair and then came to a crash landing on the graveyard floor. His crash caused the ground to shake under Darek's feet and almost throw him off balance, but he managed to avoid falling over, though just barely.

Then Uron, without missing a beat, slammed his fists together, creating a massive sound wave strong enough to crack the earth where it went. Skimif, on the other hand, held up his hand and unleashed a sound wave of his own that collided with Uron's.

Darek only knew that the two sound waves had collided because of the racket it made. It was like listening to a hundred active volcanoes going off all at once, with a dozen huge thunderstorms creating thunder for good measure, and for the long moment in which the racket happened, Darek went completely deaf.

Then the sound faded and Darek's hearing returned, but now his ears hurt. His knees were getting weak again and he was finding it harder and harder to stand.

Damn it, Darek thought. *I didn't give myself time to recover. I'm only standing because the Ghostly God's power is giving me the strength to stand.*

He forced himself to stay upright and aimed his wand at Uron again. This time, he was going to skip the ice and go straight to pyromancy. It wasn't his specialty, perhaps, but he knew enough pyromancy to make his next attack the most ferocious yet.

A huge burst of flame, like a bomb going off, shot out of the tip of his wand. The burst was strong enough to send Darek stumbling backward from the recoil, although he felt confident that it would hurt Uron, maybe even distract him long enough for Skimif to defeat him.

But to Darek's shock, Uron jumped straight through the fire blast. He landed with a roll on the other side and was back standing upright immediately. His skin wasn't even singed, although the top of his head was smoking slightly.

"How cute," said Uron, casting an amused glance in Darek's direction. "The mortal thinks he can hurt me just because he has the protection of a god. What a fool."

Uron dashed toward Darek, a look of murderous intent in his eyes, but before he could reach Darek, a pillar of stone erupted from the ground and struck Uron in the stomach. The blow hit him so hard that he went flying into the air.

The next instant, Skimif was in the air in Uron's direction. He slammed both of his fists down onto Uron's head, sending Uron crashing to the ground below.

This time, Darek was ready for the inevitable tremor that would occur when Uron hit, but as it turned out, that was unnecessary. Uron vanished well before he hit the ground, almost like he had melted into shadow, causing Darek to gulp in fear.

"Where did he go?" said Darek, looking in every direction. "Where did he—"

The scent of a corpse mixed with an unwashed snake body made Darek whirl around. Uron stood right behind

Darek, towering over the mage like the titanic being he was. Darek aimed his wand directly at Uron's heart, but Uron grabbed Darek's wand arm and twisted.

A seemingly loud *snap* echoed through the graveyard as terrible pain shot through Darek's body. He let out a scream of anguish as he dropped his wand and fell to his knees. His arm was broken and it felt like someone had stabbed a thousand of the world's sharpest knives into his joints.

Then Darek felt Uron's hand grab the back of his head and lift him up by it. Darek lashed out weakly at Uron's grip, but he was too weak to do much more than annoy the pseudo-deity, who chuckled at his attempts to harm him.

"Try as much as you'd like, mortal, but you can't even touch me," said Uron. "Even with the blessing of a god, you are nothing more than a weak mortal who is destined to perish."

"Put him down!" Skimif yelled. "Or I'll—"

"Or you'll what?" said Uron. "So long as I hold Darek, I know you won't try to touch me. You risk killing him if you attack me. Trust me, I know how much you hate putting the lives of mortals in danger, Skimif."

Uron twisted Darek around in his hand until Darek was now facing Skimif. It was hard to focus on the God of Martir, however, when his broken arm continued to send waves of pain into his body, especially now that it was hanging limply at his side in the air.

"Now, then," said Uron. His breathing was harder than usual, like he was getting tired. "We can end this battle very easily, Skimif, if you would but let me touch you once with the God-killer. In exchange, I will let Darek go free."

"That's a deceptive deal and you know it," said Skimif, shaking his head. "You will kill Darek no matter what I do as part of your plan to destroy Martir. I wasn't born yesterday, Uron."

"I didn't think you were," said Uron. "But that doesn't mean I can't use your own fondness for your former kind against you."

Then Uron brought Darek's ear closer to his mouth, allowing Darek to smell his breath, which smelled like a decaying corpse in the sun.

"Tell me, Darek, who do you think will kill you?" said Uron in a whisper that was probably loud enough for Skimif to hear. "Will it be Skimif, who finally understands the importance of making small sacrifices for the greater good, or will it be me, who understands that in order to build something great, you must first destroy something terrible, like yourself?"

Darek was in too much pain to respond. He just grabbed his broken arm, but that didn't do much to get rid of the pain. He wanted to spit in Uron's face, but unfortunately he wasn't facing the pseudo-deity.

"I guess he'd rather wait and see than make a wrong prediction," said Uron as he thrust Darek out before him, away from his terrible breath. "That makes him wiser than you, Skimif, and he isn't even a god."

Skimif, like Uron, was panting, which Darek did not take to be a very good sign. Yet for some reason he didn't look as worried as he should and his eyes kept flicking up toward the sky, as if he expected it to start raining any minute now.

"I am still waiting for your answer," said Uron. His fingers dug deeper into Darek's head, applying more pressure to his skull. "Will you kill Darek or will I? Those are your only two options."

Then, unbelievably, Skimif smiled. "False dichotomy, Uron. There is one more choice you forgot about. Or, rather, a choice you didn't even know I had."

Darek felt Uron's fingers tense around his head. Uron said, "What are you babbling about? What other choice do you have that I do not know about?"

Skimif's eyes met Darek's for a brief moment, but in that brief moment, Darek understood exactly what Skimif wanted him to do. He didn't understand exactly why Skimif wanted him to do it, but he figured that Skimif had to have a plan behind it, so he decided to ignore his broken arm and act.

Darek reached behind himself as far as he could with his one good arm and unleashed a burst of ice at Uron's face. It worked. Uron dropped Darek like a rock as he yelled in surprise, but before Darek even fell to the ground, Skimif's disembodied hand appeared out of nowhere and grabbed his collar, stopping his fall with a jerk and sending even more pain up his shoulder.

When Darek blinked, he found himself sitting on the ground next to Skimif. Ahead of them, Uron was tearing at the ice that Darek had splattered over his body, which was more than Darek had expected to be able to summon in this situation.

"Darek, get down," said Skimif, without looking at him. "We win."

Darek didn't understand what Skimif meant and didn't get a chance to ask, because Skimif raised one hand and snapped his fingers.

From the sky above Uron, a loud roaring noise, like the engine of an airship, tore through the air. Darek only had enough time to see two massive pillars of orange energy blasts descend from the mist before Skimif shoved him to the ground and covered him with his body.

Before Darek could protest that this position hurt his arm, a massive *bang* echoed through the graveyard. Then flames and hot energy covered them, but Darek didn't actually get hurt because Skimif's body acted as a shield. Still, Darek heard and saw the flames and even heard what might have been Uron shouting in pure agony, but it was hard to tell because the roar of the flames drowned out every other sound, even the sound of Darek's own thoughts.

Just as the lights and sound were beginning to wind down, there was another *bang* and another round of massive flames and energy swept over them like a tidal wave. This time, Darek closed his eyes and covered his face with his other arm, trying to keep his calm and succeeding just barely.

The *bang* came again and again, each time louder than the last. The *bang* happened so much that Darek was certain that Skimif was somehow using his power to destroy not just Uron, but the whole school, and maybe the whole world as well.

But then, as quickly as the *bang*s came, they were gone. The flames and energy passed away and night returned, although due to the heat radiating from the ground, it wasn't as cold as it had been a moment ago.

Then Skimif stood upright and looked over his shoulder in the direction where Uron had been standing. "Looks like he's gone."

Darek sat upright, again ignoring his broken arm so he could focus on what the graveyard looked like now that the energy pillars were no longer destroying the world.

The last of the mist was totally gone now, likely evaporated by the flames and heat. Without the mist obscuring the graveyard, Darek saw that the spot where Uron had been standing was a large, deep crater that looked like something you'd find on the Volcanic Isles rather than on a graveyard in the Great Berg. The air smelled like flame and ash, an awful smell that made Darek's stomach churn. There was not even a hint of Uron's existence anywhere, like he had simply vanished—or was blasted—into nothingness.

That didn't mean Darek let his guard down, though. For all he knew, Uron was hiding somewhere and would strike as soon as he or Skimif relaxed. That seemed like the sort of thing Uron would do.

"He's not here anymore," said Skimif.

Darek looked up at Skimif. "How did you know what I was—"

"I guessed," said Skimif. "After all, I was once a mortal myself, so I know how you mortals tend to think."

"But how do you know he's gone?" said Darek. "I mean, I

can't sense him anywhere, but that could mean he's just hiding."

"Unlikely," said Skimif, shaking his head. "If Uron was still here, I'd still be fighting him. He's gone, likely slithered back into whatever hole he crawled out from in the first place."

The pain in Darek's broken arm spiked, but he was so interested in what had happened to Uron that he managed to ignore it for the moment. "So Uron is still alive?"

"Unfortunately, yes," said Skimif. "I intended those blasts to turn him into dust, but I think all it did was convince him that he needed to retreat for now and rethink his plans. I don't know where he is, but I'm sure he's still out there somewhere."

Darek tried to stand, but the pain in his broken arm forced him to remain where he was. "Then we have to stop him, we have to look for him, we—"

Skimif bent over and grabbed Darek's broken arm. He squeezed it gently and Darek felt some kind of warmth pass through his arm. In a second, it no longer hurt, and when Skimif let go of it, Darek experimentally moved his arm. Though it was slightly stiff, it didn't hurt at all.

"Darek," said Skimif in an unusually authoritative tone. "You need to rest. I know the Ghostly God's protection offered you some of his strength, but you're still mortal and you still have all of the same limitations as any other mortal."

Darek rolled his shoulders. "I know, but—"

"I am going to have another word with the Ghostly God

about recklessly putting the lives of mortals in danger like this," said Skimif with a scowl.

"Doesn't matter," said Darek. "I don't know if you know, but I've already pledged my life to him for ten years. And I don't intend to go back on my word, even after this."

Skimif looked at Darek uncomprehendingly. "A mortal serving a southern god? I know Aorja served the Ghostly God, but I thought it was because she was crazy. Yet you seem perfectly sane to me."

"I'm not so sure about that," said Darek, as he began to realize just how reckless his offer to the Ghostly God had been. "But anyway, what caused those massive energy pillars from earlier? Did you summon them?"

"Sort of," said Skimif. "But I had a little help."

He pointed at the sky, causing Darek to look up to see what he was pointing at.

Hovering in the air over the crater where Uron stood was a large airship, one much bigger than the *Soaring Sea* had been. Two gigantic cannons hung from its underside, smoke trailing from their barrels. The airship itself was as blue as the ocean sea on a summer day, with aquarian words written on it in white paint.

Darek blinked. "Is that an airship?"

"From the Undersea Institute, yes," said Skimif. "It's more like a warship, which doesn't make sense for a school to have, but it's a good thing they had it."

"The Undersea Institute?" said Darek in surprise. "Is there anyone on board I would know?"

"Yorak, for one," said Skimif, nodding. "She's piloting

the ship herself, actually. She's a pretty amazing woman despite her old age."

"But I don't understand," said Darek, scratching the back of his head. "I thought the Undersea Institute didn't want anything to do with the Academy anymore. Why did they come here?"

"It's not because Yorak wants to apologize to the Magical Superior or anything like that," said Skimif. "She came because I went to the Institute and told her that I might require her aid in defeating Uron. Actually, that was before I knew about Uron, but I knew that there was a powerful threat, equal to my own, just waiting to show up. So I recruited Yorak to help me prepare for it."

"But ... what was that stuff she shot from the cannons of her ship earlier?" said Darek. "That kind of power is far too much for your average mage to hold. Even Yorak couldn't control that much energy."

"I gave them some of my own," said Skimif. He gestured at the large cannons. "Those cannons on their ship are designed specifically to hold and fire magical energy. I had to redesign them so they could withstand my own energy— it's too much for the average mortal machine to hold—but it wasn't a problem."

"Let me get this straight," said Darek. "You put some of your energy into those cannons so that the Institute mages could blow Uron to bits?"

"More or less," said Skimif. "I had called them in earlier today so they could be here by tonight, but they were supposed to be a last resort. I thought the other gods and I would be enough to take him down on my own, but when those cowards ran, I had to bring in the big guns."

He spoke fairly neutrally about the other gods, which surprised Darek, as he would have been incredibly angry if the same had happened to him. The only indication that Skimif was displeased with the other gods was the word he used to describe them: 'cowards.' Even then, Darek didn't hear any disapproval in the god's tone. It seemed like Skimif was trying to hide his true feelings about the other gods for some reason.

That made Darek feel eerie, so in order to ignore those eerie feelings, he said, "Well, I'm glad you did. That seemed to have done the trick."

"For now," said Skimif. "There's no telling where or when Uron will show up again. I will have to make sure that the other gods are ready to take him down at a moment's notice."

"We can help," said Darek. "The other mages and I here. I bet if you asked, every one of us would do whatever we could to help you find Uron."

Skimif shook his head. "Thank you for the offer, but I am afraid I must reject it. Uron is too dangerous for you mortals to fight or even help fight. Even the Magical Superior and Yorak are no match for him in a straight fight. This is a job for the gods and the gods alone."

Darek knew he shouldn't argue with the God of Martir, but he was so determined to help that he felt it was justified. "But Uron has the God-killer. He can kill gods now. You saw what he did to the Avian Goddess."

Skimif winced, like Darek had punched him in the gut. "Yes, but we're still the only ones who can deal with him. I will simply let all of the gods know to remain out of arm's reach of him and not to engage him if they find themselves alone with him."

"Are you sure there isn't anything we can do to help?" said Darek. "I mean, we mages dedicated ourselves to the gods, after all. We are your servants and followers. There's a reason we're known as the People of the Gods, after all."

Skimif scratched the back of his head. "I don't want any of you hurt. You mages have your own role to play in this world, and that role doesn't involve hunting down genocidal ex-scientists hellbent on shattering the foundations of this world in order to bring back theirs."

"But—"

Skimif glared at Darek. That look alone was enough to shut up Darek, who suddenly realized just how angry Skimif was. He had been so caught up in coming up with objections to Skimif's orders that he had never noticed the way Skimif was scowling.

"Don't question me," said Skimif, the gentleness in his voice gone, replaced by an authority that did not tolerate dissent. "If you truly are dedicated to the gods, you will listen to my orders, which are to stay out of the Uron situation, and not question them."

Even with Skimif's glare and angry tone, Darek still managed to sputter, "But I—"

"Uron almost killed you back there," said Skimif. Then he turned away. "I have to go. Uron is probably going to lay

327

low only for a little while. I have a lot of important things to get in order so that we will be ready for when he reappears."

Darek opened his mouth to ask what Skimif was going to do, but when he blinked, Skimif was gone, like he had never been there in the first place.

Chapter Twenty-One

By the time Darek returned to the Arcanium, he discovered that practically the entire school was present in the courtyard. Thanks to the torches that had been set up on the perimeters, he saw every single student and teacher in the school gathered together. All of them were talking loudly and, while their voices were too mixed for him to tell exactly what they were talking about, he knew they were all speculating about what happened in the graveyard that night.

Guess Durima didn't tell them to evacuate after all, Darek thought. *Or maybe they somehow know that it's safe to stay here, at least for now.*

No one seemed to notice Darek yet (although many of the students were looking up at the blue airship, which was heading toward the sports field to land) as he stood outside of the circle of torches that illuminated the courtyard. And he was so exhausted and worn out from the events of the night that he just wanted to sneak by and get back to his bed at the Third Dorm, although with so many students out, he doubted he would succeed, even if he had been a master of the Thief's Way. He didn't want to talk to anyone right now, not even to his friends.

Before he could figure out a good way to get past

everyone without being noticed, the voice of the Magical Superior rang out: "Students and teachers of North Academy, listen to the urgent news regarding the events of the night that I have received from Skimif."

All of the students and teachers looked toward the steps of the Arcanium. Darek also looked in that direction and saw the Magical Superior standing at the top of the steps. He was leaning on Mom for support, looking weaker than Darek had ever seen him before. He clearly needed rest and maybe a visit from Eyurna to make sure he wasn't suffering from any long term injuries, but whatever Skimif had told him was apparently important enough for him to forgo that, at least for now.

"I am glad I have your attention," said the Magical Superior. Although his voice was made louder and clearer by magic, it mostly succeeded in emphasizing just how tired the Superior was. "While I was resting earlier, after being brought here by the katabans known as Durima, I received a vision from Skimif. I know I should be resting still, but I also know that many of you, including me, have questions about what happened in the graveyard tonight, urgent questions that demand an immediate answer."

Darek's shoulders slumped. He wondered why this couldn't wait until morning, but he didn't say anything in order to avoid drawing attention to himself. Instead, he took advantage of the crowd's distraction to make his way around the perimeter of the circle of torchlight, his eyes on the rebuilt Third Dorm.

Yet even as he tiptoed as silently as he could, he found

himself listening to the Magical Superior's speech.

"Tonight in the school graveyard, a new threat to Martir arose," said the Magical Superior. He sounded close to fainting, he was so weak, which made the fact that he could still talk at all impressive to Darek. "A threat powerful enough to challenge the gods ... a threat named Uron, the Great Snake."

Darek paused. Where did 'the Great Snake' come from? Uron was not a snake anymore. Did Skimif make up that name or did he know something Darek didn't?

The crowd of students and teachers, meanwhile, erupted with gasps and questions, which were quickly silenced when the Magical Superior raised his hand.

"I know you have many questions about Uron, but much of his history and purpose are a mystery even to me," said the Magical Superior. "Know only this: Uron's ultimate goal is to destroy all of Martir and replace it with the world he came from. And to do so, he is going to kill the gods."

"Aren't a couple of gods already dead?" one of the students shouted from somewhere in the middle of the crowd. "Didn't we all feel it when they died? What happened? And are we still going to be evacuated from the school?"

The crowd began shouting more questions at the Magical Superior, questions about the status of those two gods and the exact circumstances under which they died, but then he raised his hand again and the crowd went silent again.

"I don't know all of the details behind the deaths of those

two gods," said the Magical Superior. "But I do know that there is nothing we mages can do about Uron. Skimif has given me strict orders to inform you that the gods will be handling Uron and that we are not to worry about it. And to answer your last question, no, we will not be evacuating the school tonight."

"But how can we not worry about a being who can kill gods?" said another student. "It's not right!"

"When Skimif speaks, we listen," said the Magical Superior. Then he sighed. "You may also be wondering about the blue airship that has landed in the sports field. I can tell you that that is another Institute airship, but for now, I order all of you to return to your dormitories and to rest until tomorrow morning. The teachers will make sure that every student returns to his or her dorm and gets some much needed rest, so don't think you can get away with staying up tonight or sneaking out."

"But we still have so many questions!" another student shouted from the crowd. "Why are the Institute mages back when they said they weren't going to return?"

"You may ask the Institute mages whatever you like in the morning," said the Magical Superior in a firm voice. "It has been a long, stressful night for everyone and the best cure for a long, stressful night is a long, restful sleep. To your dormitories. Now."

With that, the Magical Superior turned and walked back into the Arcanium, Mom at his side helping him. As soon as he began heading back into the Arcanium, the teachers began herding the students back to the dormitories. The students complied as peacefully as they usually did, but Darek heard many of them whispering among each other, no doubt trading theories as to who Uron was and what really happened in the graveyard.

There will be a million rumors in the morning about what 'really' happened tonight and not one of them will involve me, Darek thought. *Thankfully.*

Nonetheless, Darek managed to slip into the crowd unnoticed. Coincidentally, he found himself walking next to Jiku, who was wearing his school robes over his pajamas and was walking barefoot along the stone path, perhaps because he had had no time to get his shoes on.

"Darek?" said Jiku as they walked with the crowd. "Where were you tonight? When Noharf sent out dreams to everyone summoning us to the courtyard, I saw your bed was empty. Thought maybe you had already gotten up, but why are you robes so muddy and dirty?"

Darek leaned in closer to Jiku and whispered, "I was in the graveyard when Uron attacked. Saw it all with my own eyes."

Jiku put a hand over his mouth to stifle his gasp. "You were? You have to tell me all about it."

Darek yawned. "Tomorrow. Tonight, I just need to rest, like the Magical Superior said."

Thankfully, Jiku seemed to understand, because he did not argue the point.

The stressful events of the night before had cured Darek's insomnia; in fact, he slept so soundly that it seemed like only a minute after his head hit the pillow that he awoke with a start. Through the open window, the first rays of the rising sun were beginning to sneak in, signaling that the morning had already come.

Not that he wanted to get up. Although he had managed to make it back to his and Jiku's shared room last night without much trouble, right now, he was so tired that he could barely even move his body. No doubt it was the excitement and stress of the night before that had left him this way. He was surprised that he hadn't just slept through the whole day.

Then again, maybe this is the morning of the day after the next, Darek thought. *Though I'd probably feel better rested than I am now if that was the case.*

But he wasn't alone in his room this morning, despite how much he wanted some time to think about and consider what he had done and seen last night. Jiku was sitting on his own bed opposite Darek's, a mug of warm hyper juice in his hands. The middle-aged mage looked like he must have just gotten up himself, because even as he sipped from his mug, his eyes had bags underneath them and he seemed sluggish.

"Good morning," said Jiku with a yawn. "I thought you were never going to wake up."

Darek rubbed his eyes, but he didn't get up from under his soft, warm blankets. "Were you awake this whole time waiting for me to wake up?"

"More or less," said Jiku. He leaned forward a little. "You said you'd tell me about what happened in the

334

graveyard last night in the morning. It's the morning, so I'm waiting."

Darek wanted to hide his face under his pillow and tell Jiku to bother him later, but Darek had a feeling that that wouldn't work. Besides, he had told Jiku that, so he decided to go ahead and do it.

So, as briefly as he could, Darek explained all of the events of the night before. It was hard because he was very tired and he didn't remember everything, but he remembered enough to deliver a faithful explanation of the events to Jiku, who sipped from his mug every now and then but otherwise didn't say much.

When Darek finished, Jiku looked so distraught and confused that Darek actually worried for his health.

"By the gods," said Jiku, staring down at his mug of hyper juice, which was steaming slightly. "I can't even begin to imagine everything you experienced back there. You witnessed the death of a goddess."

Darek nodded. "Yes. And based on what those two katabans said, they had killed another goddess earlier."

"Two goddesses dead in one day," said Jiku. He shuddered. "If Uron is still out there, like you said, I have a feeling that that record might be broken again sometime soon."

"I hope not," said Darek. "I don't even want him to kill another southern god."

"Speaking of the southern gods," said Jiku, "*what* were you thinking, becoming a servant of the Ghostly God? The southern gods, in case you forgot all of your Deity 101 lessons, *eat* humans. What's to stop the Ghostly God from summoning you to wherever he lives and then having you for lunch?"

"I know," said Darek. "It was a stupid decision for me to make, but I was desperate. I don't think there's any way out of the deal I made with him, so I'll have to live with the consequences of my decision."

"Or *die* with the consequences of your decision," said Jiku, shaking his head. "The Ghostly God doesn't sound like a very good master anyway, if he's the reason Uron managed to get a new body and the God-killer."

"Not much I can do about it," said Darek. "But you know, Aorja served the Ghostly God and she wasn't eaten."

"Who's to say he wasn't planning to eat her at some point?" said Jiku. He sighed. "But I guess there's no getting out of that deal. When you choose to serve a god, you usually can't back out of whatever deal you made with them unless they choose to terminate it themselves."

"Got that right," said Darek. "And maybe I never will have to serve him. He hasn't summoned me to his island or contacted me yet."

"He will," said Jiku. "When, I don't know, but the gods don't hire servants only to ignore them. Once the Ghostly God has something he needs you to do, or maybe if he wants a light snack, he'll summon you without hesitation. Guaranteed."

Darek groaned. "You're right. Anyway, what happened to those two katabans? The ones who brought the Magical Superior back to the Arcanium?"

Jiku blinked. "I didn't see them myself because by the time I got to the courtyard, they were gone. But I spoke to Junaz and he told me that they had left through that ethereal thing that katabans use to get around. He said he doesn't know where they went."

Darek considered that. He had been hoping to thank Durima for getting the Magical Superior out of there, but if they were indeed missing, then it seemed unlikely he would see them again.

Then again, Durima and Gujak both served the Ghostly God, didn't they? Darek thought. *Maybe I will serve alongside them someday and will be able to thank her then.*

"What do you think is going to happen from now on?" said Jiku, breaking Darek out of his thoughts. "Now that this Uron fellow is around, do you think anything will ever be the same?"

Darek shook his head. "Of course not. I don't know where Uron is or what he's doing right now, but he was very serious about destroying Martir and everything in it. He'll lay low for a while, but now that he has the God-killer, I don't think he's going to just give up and go home."

"He doesn't even have a home to go back to, if your story is true," said Jiku with a snort. "But I worry for the gods. Normally, I wouldn't, but if Uron does indeed have a weapon like that, then the future of the gods—and Martir in general—isn't as certain as I'd like it to be."

"On that, I agree," said Darek. He yawned. "Jiku, I really need to go back to sleep. I can barely move as is. Maybe we can talk some more later."

"All right," said Jiku, nodding. He glanced at his hyper juice. "Need to refill my cup anyway, and then go and tell your mother you're okay. She was extremely worried about your absence last night."

Darek smiled. "Tell her I'll be all right and I'll give her a hug next time I see her."

Jiku chuckled, but didn't say anything else. He stood up and walked out of their room, closing the door gently behind him as he did so.

As Darek closed his eyes, trying to relax his mind and body enough to go back to sleep, he found that he couldn't. He kept thinking about Uron, who was still out there in the world somewhere, and the Ghostly God, who no doubt planned to give Darek a call to remind him about their deal later. He also thought about Durima, who he still wanted to thank for her help, and Aorja, who he found he missed, despite the fact that she tried to murder him.

Whatever the future holds from now on, it's outside of my control, Darek thought. *Unfortunately.*

With that, he forced himself not to think about any of it anymore. It was difficult, but he remembered what Noharf had taught him about emptying his mind before going to bed, and in just a few minutes, he had soundly returned to the world of dreams.

Continued in:

The Mage's Limits

A year after the disappearance of the dangerous god-killer called Uron, Darek Takren is torn between his desire to follow the teachings of his headmaster and his desire to achieve the limitless yet forbidden power he needs to help the gods protect the world.

To make matters worse, a powerful and charismatic mage claiming to be the son of a god has escaped from prison, seeking revenge for wrongs committed against him long ago. His targets: North Academy, the school that Darek calls home, and World's End, the island of the gods.

To save his home and his friends, Darek must infiltrate the deranged demigod's army of criminals and kill him before it is too late. Yet when this mage offers Darek the unlimited power he desires, killing the mage no longer seems quite as simple the task as it once appeared.

Available in ebook and trade paperback formats wherever books are sold!

Bonus short story:

What Sharks Hide From

Archmage Yorak, headmistress of the mage school known as the Undersea Institute, swam through the Trenches of the Crystal Sea, her powerful legs propelling her through the water not nearly as silently as she'd like. Her tiny, whale-like eyes darted back and forth across the muddy, dark trench she was in, searching for any sign of the monster that she and her pupil, Auratus, had come here to slay. She sniffed several times, but did not pick up any unusual scents; water, mud, black fish, some seaweed, a few cobra eels here and there ... but nothing she hadn't smelled before.

Then Yorak heard something hurtling through the water toward her. She glanced upwards, reaching for her magic stone strapped to her arm, when she saw that it was only Auratus. She would recognize that goldfish-like head and those long legs anywhere.

"Auratus," said Yorak as her pupil stopped in front of her. "What did you find?"

Auratus shrugged. *Nothing, ma'am. Just the carcass of a headless shark.*

Yorak scowled upon hearing Auratus's voice in her head, which was the only reliable form of communication that her mute pupil could use when talking with her. "How close by?"

Half a mile or so to the west, Auratus said. *Blood everywhere. Looks like it went down fighting.*

"That means the monster must be nearby," said Yorak. "How fresh was it?"

Very fresh, said Auratus. *I didn't see any other clues to the monster's identity. Like I said, blood everywhere.*

"That's not good," said Yorak, shaking her whale-like head. "Not good at all."

Do you want me to keep looking, ma'am? Auratus asked.

Yorak sighed. "I suppose. But be careful. Remember, this is the thing that sharks hide from. I trust your magical ability, but stronger mages than you have been killed by much weaker creatures than this by underestimating their foe."

Auratus put her hands together. *Yes, ma'am. Don't worry about me. If I find anything, I will let you know right away.*

Yorak nodded. "Fine. Go, then."

Without hesitation, Auratus swam back up to the top of the Trenches. Yorak watched her go before resuming her own journey through the deep sea Trenches, although she could not help but worry about her pupil anyway. While

Auratus was easily the most magically gifted student at the Undersea Institute, neither she nor Yorak had a clue as to what they were looking for. There was a very good reason Yorak had given that warning to Auratus.

It was for the same reason Yorak had chosen to take only Auratus with her on this dangerous mission. Over the last week, students from her school had reported seeing unusual activity among the great gray sharks that lived in the Trenches near the Institute. Great gray sharks were well-known for their bravery even in the face of overwhelming odds, which was why it was considered alarming that so many of them were going into hiding all at once. It was even worse when several students discovered the corpses of great gray sharks ripped to pieces in isolated places, as great grays were considered the alpha predators of this part of the ocean floor.

Something big is out here, something that isn't supposed to be here, Yorak thought. *If it can kill great gray sharks, then it is easily a threat to the lives of my students. And anyone or anything that threatens my students' lives must be dealt with swiftly.*

Like most things in life, however, that was easier said than done. Yorak and Auratus had been out here for two or three hours now. Yorak had entered the Trenches knowing it would probably take them a while to find the monster, as the Trenches were large and deep, home to many different species of fish. She didn't even know if the monster was down here or if she would recognize it when she saw it.

Of course, the lack of any wildlife down here is a good indication that something is around, Yorak thought. *The only question is, what?*

One possible creature that could do that was a kraken. But krakens did not live in this area of the Undersea. Most lived far, far to the south, beyond aquarian civilization, and few ever journeyed this far north. Besides, krakens were too huge to hide for long. That meant something else was out here chopping up great gray sharks like salmon.

That frustrated her more than anything. Before becoming the head of the Undersea Institute, Yorak had been an expert in marine life. She knew—or thought she knew, anyway—every single creature put in the Undersea by the Powers at the beginning of creation. Even now, she could still name and list the habits and habitats of almost any sea creature known to aquarian kind.

Except for this one, which meant that Yorak had discovered a new predator species, or she had forgotten one. The first possibility was exciting, although dangerous, because discovering a new species of fish would add to the prestige that being headmistress of the Undersea Institute already gave her. The second possibility was far less exciting but equally dangerous, seeing as it was an indictment on her memory and would make it hard for her to deal with whatever she was looking for down here if she ran into it.

A sudden, unexpected smell forced Yorak to come to a stop. It smelled like leather and soap, but it also had the scent of a great gray shark, a slimy, dank scent that could not be mistaken for anything else. She didn't recognize the

343

first scent at all, as it didn't smell like any sea creature she had smelled before.

Instinctively, Yorak reached for the magic stone on her arm and patted it. She felt the magical power stored within it, which reassured her somewhat; even so, she still couldn't actually see the creature that the great gray sharks were afraid of. That leathery, soapy smell had to belong to it.

Something moving through the water above caused Yorak to look upwards. Much to her relief, it was only a great gray shark, apparently by itself, swimming in the murky waters above her. It didn't seem to notice her, but that was fine because Yorak knew how territorial great gray sharks could be. She wondered, though, why it wasn't hiding like its cousins. After all, with a monster lurking around here that could kill great gray sharks, this particular shark was taking a huge risk being out in the open like this.

It's even stranger because it can't be out hunting, Yorak thought. *Great gray sharks do most of their hunting early in the morning and late at night. They usually sleep during the day. Why is it out now?*

That was when Yorak's sharp eyes noticed some kind of strange, black webbing wrapped around the shark's body. Yorak's first impulse was to dismiss the web-like contraption as netting from a human fishing ship above, perhaps lost by its owners. It wasn't unusual to see various sea creatures stuck inside human netting, so at first she wasn't alarmed by the netting around the great gray shark.

Then the webbing glowed bright purple for a moment before the light faded.

That's not netting, Yorak thought. *That's something worse. Far, far worse.*

She watched the shark carefully as it swam peacefully by. Then she heard more swishing through the waters and saw another great gray shark swooping down from above. Its massive jaw, lined with three dozen rows of sharp teeth, opened as it shot toward the webbed shark like an arrow, using a common attack-from-above trick that many great gray sharks used when hunting prey.

But the webbed shark swam out of the way, causing the other shark to shoot past. The webbed shark did a loop-de-loop in the water and then darted down after the other shark, which was going at an uncontrollably fast speed. The webbed shark sank its teeth into the back of its enemy and pushed the other shark down toward the bottom of the Trenches as fast as it could.

Yorak swam backwards out of the way as the webbed shark and its enemy slammed into the dirt floor of the Trenches. The sudden collision sent clouds of mud and dirt into the waters, briefly obscuring Yorak's vision, but she could hear the two sharks wrestling on the seafloor, tearing and slapping at each other with their teeth and tails, and causing even more dirt clouds to rise from the Trench floor.

Why are these two sharks fighting each other? Yorak thought in horror. *Great gray sharks* never *fight each other except when they both want the same prey. What on Martir is going on here?*

Then blood began to mix with the dirt cloud and the sounds of battle from within became quieter. Chunks of flesh flew out of the dirt cloud as the noise of teeth tearing through flesh told Yorak that one of the sharks had emerged victorious, but she didn't know which one did until she saw a strange purple glow within the cloud that faded quickly.

Looks like the webbed shark won this one, Yorak thought. *And, most likely, every other battle it has been forced to fight since last week.*

Because Yorak now knew exactly what the great gray sharks in the Trenches were hiding from. It wasn't some foreign monster or undiscovered species of giant fish that was killing them. It was a fellow great gray shark, driven mad by the parasite that clung to its body like a tangled net.

Yorak recognized that parasite, although it had been many years since she had last studied them. They were known as pseudo-nets by humans and deceitful webbing by aquarians. In appearance, they resembled the fish nets used by human fishermen or the webbing of a spider; in truth, they were actually a parasite that clung to the skin of other sea creatures and took control of their mind and body. These parasites would then force their host to go crazy, attacking and killing anything that they deemed a threat to their existence. Even aquarians were not immune to being controlled by these parasites, though it was rare for that to happen, seeing as most aquarians were smart enough to fight back against its mind control powers.

Deceitful webbings were very rare and usually only found among the sunken wreckage of human fishing ships, where they pretended to be inanimate netting. Due to the fact that they couldn't move very far or effectively on their own, webbings usually waited until a suitable host swam by, which they would then attach themselves to and force to take them wherever they wanted to go.

This was the first time in decades that Yorak had seen a deceitful webbing so close to the Institute. It was also the very first time she had ever seen a deceitful webbing take control of a great gray shark. Not only that, but this particular webbing was bigger than most, which meant it was smarter and stronger than most webbings were.

I have no choice, Yorak thought as she rested her hand on her magical stone. *I'll have to kill the shark. It's been like this for at least a week, maybe longer. When a webbing has been attached to its victim for that long, there's literally no way to remove it without killing the host.*

Yorak had a great respect for great grays, as they were powerful, resourceful creatures of the sea that played an important role in the Undersea's ecosystem. But that was exactly why she had to put this one out of its misery. Deceitful webbings always caused intense pain in their hosts and this great gray was more of a threat than a help to the environment at the moment. Not to mention it could kill or harm her students if it came near the school.

With the dust cloud settling, Yorak saw the webbed shark tearing apart the corpse of its attacker. It was a disgusting sight, watching as its teeth shredded through the corpse's skin, with blood staining the webbed shark's mouth, but Yorak got over it quickly. She had seen worse in her days; besides, the webbed shark didn't seem to notice her yet, so this was the perfect opportunity to attack.

Yorak tightened her grip on her magical stone. A simple ice spell, freezing the creature in a block of ice, would likely do the trick.

She raised her hands and focused on freezing the shark where it was tearing into its defeated foe. The magical energy flowed through her body and out her hands, but before she could freeze the shark, it stopped ripping its enemy into shreds and looked up at Yorak suddenly, as if it had just noticed her.

Then the great gray shark hurtled toward her through the water. Without thinking, Yorak snapped her fingers and ice began forming on the great gray shark's body, rapidly encasing it in a block of ice that was thicker than the icebergs of the Great Berg to the far north.

As soon as the ice began forming on the great gray shark, however, the webbing that had controlled it launched itself off the shark's body toward Yorak. This took her by surprise. She had never heard of a deceitful webbing voluntarily leaving its host like that. She had always heard that deceitful webbing stayed with their chosen host to the end, especially if they had been attached to that host for a long time.

As a result, Yorak was too surprised to dodge the webbing. It slammed into her, as heavy as a weighted net, and quickly wrapped its net-like body around her like a blanket. That soapy, leathery smell was right in her nostrils now, but added to it was the metallic scent of blood from the deceased great gray, a stench so overwhelming that it made Yorak's stomach churn.

She tried to fight against the webbing, but it had ensnared her so thickly that she couldn't even move her limbs. She tried to concentrate long enough to perform some kind of spell, but her concentration was broken when she felt the suction cups of the webbing stick onto many parts of her body. She had been captured by an octopus once before, but the webbing's suction cups felt like slimy knives digging into her skin, causing her to cry out in pain.

But that wasn't even the worst of it. Yorak was rapidly losing control of her muscles. Her brain began to ache, like she was having a bad headache, getting worse with every passing second. She recognized it as the webbing trying to overwhelm her mind, and it was hardly a joke, either. The mental assault on her brain was relentless, like a great gray tearing apart its prey, making it almost impossible for Yorak to think straight.

This webbing is more powerful than normal webbing, Yorak thought. *Must fight it somehow.*

Unfortunately, Yorak had let her guard down too long. Now she couldn't control her body at all and was beginning to give into the webbing's mental assault. The pain was almost completely overwhelming. Yorak had always heard about how painful the mental assault of a webbing was, but she now thought that all of the stories she'd been told had greatly underestimated how painful it was.

Blacking out, Yorak thought. *Can't do that. Black out, and the webbing wins. No telling what it will do with my power at its command.*

By now, Yorak was almost ready to give in. Her control

over her own body and mind were rapidly slipping. She didn't even feel like she was in her own body anymore. She was like an outsider looking in, and she didn't like what she saw.

Just before the webbing completely dominated her mind and body, a terrible ripple of pain tore through her whole self. She screamed because the pain was so overwhelming, even more so than the pain that the webbing inflicted on her. It felt like someone had stabbed a hot, burning sword straight through her chest. Her vision blurred. She almost lost consciousness, but then the pain faded, and in a few seconds, her vision returned.

Floating in the water before her was the deceitful webbing. It took Yorak's pain-filled mind a moment to realize that, if the webbing was floating in the water in front of her, then it was no longer wrapped around her body. She looked down at her body to confirm that and saw various suction-cup-shaped sores on her arms and legs, the only visible signs of the webbing's grip on her.

Why did it let go? Yorak thought. *Deceitful webbings rarely voluntarily release their hosts.*

Then the corpse of the deceitful webbing was pushed out of the way by someone, and Yorak found herself floating face-to-face with Auratus. Her pupil's eyes were even bigger than normal as she looked over Yorak's body with obvious concern.

Archmage, how do you feel? Auratus asked. *Do you need my help? I can cast a few healing spells on those sores on your skin.*

Yorak blinked. "Auratus? When did you get here?"

A few minutes ago, Auratus replied. *I had forgotten to tell you that the corpse of the great gray I found earlier showed signs of having been torn apart by another great gray. I returned to tell you just in time to see that deceitful webbing attack you. Killed it by stabbing it with a sharp rock I found on the sea floor.*

Yorak rubbed the sores on her arms to soothe the pain a little. "Thank you, Auratus. I thought I was going to die."

You're welcome, said Auratus. She glanced at the frozen great gray behind her and then at the dead deceitful webbing still floating in the water. *Do you think that this deceitful webbing was the thing that scared the sharks?*

Yorak nodded. "I suspect as much. We will need to keep a close eye on the behavior of the great grays over the next week or so to see if they return to their normal hunting patterns, but I think they will."

And if they do not? Auratus asked.

"Then we go hunting again," said Yorak. She sighed. "Now, Auratus, could you be a dear and help me swim back to the Institute? The deceitful webbing's attack left me too weak to make the journey back on my own."

Yes, ma'am, Auratus said. *But I think I will bring the deceitful webbing back with us as well. I think Kokar will be interested in studying its corpse for research purposes.*

Yorak grimaced when she saw Auratus grab the webbing's corpse and stuff it into her bag. "You are certain it is dead."

One hundred percent, ma'am, said Auratus, patting her

bag closed. *Now come on. You need medical attention immediately, which you can't get if you're out here. I am sure the other students are worried about us, so let's not leave them in suspense for any longer, okay?*

Yorak nodded as Auratus swam under her left arm and began leading Yorak back the way they'd came. Yorak took this moment to think about how horrible the deceitful webbing had been and how she pitied its last host, the great gray shark that she had frozen, for it had not been lucky enough to have a loyal pupil like Auratus to save it from the webbing's grasp.

About the Author

Timothy L. Cerepaka writes fantasy and science-fiction stories as an indie author. He is the author of the Prince Malock World series of fantasy novels and the science-fantasy standalone *The Last Legend: Glitch Apocalypse*. He lives in Texas.

Find out more about Timothy L. Cerepaka at his website, http://www.timothylcerepaka.com.